Also By Edward Lemond

The Baptism of Alden Oakes

Birds of Appetite

September Blow Soft

Equal Affection

This Close To Me (Stories)

Overheard (Poetry)

Verticals of Frye (Editor)

The Breach House Anthology (Editor)

The Breach House Anthology Volume II (Editor)

The Breach House Anthology Volume III (Editor)

Journey in Bardo

Journey in Bardo

A Novel by

Edward Lemond

ATTIC OWL BOOKS

Lemond, Edward

Journey in Bardo

ISBN: 978-0-9780510-3-7

First paperback edition 2007
Second paperback edition 2011
Third paperback edition 2013

Attic Owl Books
379 Beausejour Street
Dieppe, NB E1A 1Y5
Canada

E-mail : elemond@bellaliant.net

Printed in the United States of America
By www.lulu.com

For my sister Judy,
for my brothers,
and in memory of Bill

Bardo

**The time between death
and entry into rebirth.
The realm of ghosts.**

PART ONE

One

The walk from the gate to the baggage claim seems long, nearly a mile, through hordes of people who are mostly absent, talking on cell phones, checking schedules, writing notes to themselves, or just thinking their own private thoughts. It takes you half an hour to collect your bag and see it through customs.

When it is your turn the security officer wants to see what is inside your bag. He leads you into a room that is empty except for a sturdy table with a hard yellow surface. He opens the bag wide, spreads it flat.

Not everyone is subject to such scrutiny, you remark to yourself. You feel the tension in the muscles of your neck. Your eyes feel scratchy. You look at him without seeing him. You give short, clipped answers to his questions. You have trouble catching your breath. You feel the ground moving under your feet. You close your eyes. You find yourself alone in the room.

There is not enough time now to call Anne, you have to hurry ahead to catch your plane. It is bigger than the plane that brought you to Montreal but just as packed.

Your seat is by the aisle, about a third of the way back. It is raining outside and the take-off, into dark clouds, is bumpy. Once above the clouds everyone breathes more easily. The seat belt sign is turned off and lunch is served.

You are hungry when you see the food being set out on trays, the chicken breast breaded to keep it moist, the green beans cut neatly at both ends, the mashed potato shaped to resemble a scoop of ice cream, the tossed salad crisp in its black plastic container, the coffee scalding hot.

You recall the strange tone in Anne's voice when you said good-bye at the airport, and you wonder why it seems even stranger, the farther away you get. It was the way she said, *Don't worry about me, I'll give Sally a call* that caused a chill to run up your spine. She had made up her mind that she was not going to be bothered by your going.

Of course, you had made up your own mind, even before this. Something new is happening between you, after so many years of marriage. You do not know if it is driving you apart or drawing you closer. You have a feeling that whatever it is, it is out of your hands.

In the seat next to you is a man who looks to be about ten

years your senior, with white hair and white beard, in a yellow sleeveless sweater over a white dress shirt. For the first part of the flight he makes himself inaccessible, listening to a tape on a set of sculpted earphones. He continues listening during the meal, which he picks at without very much interest.

When the trays are removed he continues listening to his tape. You pick up the novel you are reading, Timothy Findley's *The Piano Man's Daughter.* This seems to be the cue for him to remove his earphones, clear his throat, and speak.

He asks if the book you are reading is a novel. He slurs his words. He does not look at you directly, but sneaks a look, and you wonder if he was drinking before boarding the plane.

When you admit that it is a novel, he is happy to be able to tell you that he does not read fiction, ever. He has better things to do in the time he has left, he says.

You do not know where this conversation is going, so you say nothing. There is an awkward silence, while he nervously drums his fingers on his knee. He wants to say something and even mutters the word 'Chicago' but then stops.

He holds up the tape player for you to see, as if it were a piece of evidence to be considered. In a voice pitched slightly higher than before he asks if the music bothers you.

Not at all, you reply. It does not sound like music but more like static, or the ocean.

At the breakfast table, before the drive to the airport, Anne kept talking about Sally and could not seem to talk about anything else. Sally is her best friend, and they have been neglecting each other, Anne thinks. They are going to have lunch together more often and talk about things that never seem to get talked about. Girl things.

But you have nothing to worry about, according to Anne. Sally is likes you and has only good things to say. She speaks her mind, but she's not mean-spirited.

It just so happens that I can't live without you, Anne insists. I don't mind telling you because it's true. But if you are wise you won't let it go to your head.

But you know very well that she could live alone, even if this is not what she claims. She lived alone before you met. She did quite well. The way she explains it goes something like this: she was living alone and doing quite well, but she knew that there was something missing in her life. No one else knew it but she knew. If you had not happened to come along, she would have continued to live this life of outward contentment, inward unease.

The bell sounds, the seat belt sign comes on again. The captain warns that there is a pocket of turbulence ahead. He asks flight attendants to find seats and get strapped in. You tap your white-haired neighbor on the shoulder and point to the sign. He puts both of his hands over his earphones. It's to block out any sound, any signal but his music, you think.

Almost immediately you feel the first bump as the plane hits the pocket of turbulence. In the window the sky is blue. Suddenly, the plane seems to fall straight down, for about two seconds. Your book flies upward. You make a feeble grab for it.

Everyone around you falls silent, as they hold on and try to anticipate the worst. Your neighbor's face is as white as his beard. His eyes are closed. The only thing you can think is *He's having a heart attack.*

Only when the plane comes out the other side into the calm do you begin to relax. Nothing in the sky has changed. You marvel that a force that's invisible can be this powerful.

You hear the captain's voice again, apologizing because the turbulence was stronger than expected. You look at your neighbor, relieved to see that he is still breathing. He sits with his back pressed against his seat, his two hands still holding tight to his earphones. The tape player itself is tucked safely under one thigh.

Like several others you turn and look back toward where there seemed to be the loudest concentration of cries when the plane first lost altitude so suddenly. Several people are looking closely at a passenger in a seat six rows behind you. A woman wearing a black velvet jacket over a short black skirt that shows the beginning of her backside as she bends forward blocks your view of the injured person. The jacket is so tight around her shoulders as she bends forward that you can see the curve of the spine in her upper back.

A stewardess approaches from the rear of the plane and leans in to have a look. The stewardess and the woman in black are so close that their heads almost touch.

You think the injured person must be a young girl because she takes up so little space.

The plane banks sharply to the left, which sends everyone scurrying back to his seat. Only the stewardess remains in place, to attend the injured person. Again you hear the captain's voice, warning that there is more turbulence just ahead.

I'm going to take the plane a bit higher and see if we can avoid it, the voice says.

With everyone seated you can see the injured person clearly. It's not a child but a very old man who has a trickle of blood running down from the corner of one eye. The stewardess is dabbing at the cut and in her calm, composed way she's asking him one question after another.

He nods to everything but you doubt if he understands very much of what is being said. The injured eye seems to be swollen shut. He has a head shaped like an egg, with a small, nicely rounded chin and a huge, oblong top of the head. If he was wearing a hat, he's removed it. The head is completely bald.

The stewardess is holding very tightly onto the back of the old man's seat with her free hand. You doubt if this would do very much good if the plane were to hit another similar pocket of turbulence.

Everyone stays in his seat, buckled up, for the rest of the flight into Chicago. No one says much of anything. The experience leaves everyone feeling deflated, there is nothing to talk about, nothing to celebrate at the end of this flight.

The most that can be said is that you've reached your destination. You know there will be lawsuits and the rest, and you know that you will have nothing to do with that.

Two

In the window you can see the lake, the shoreline of the city, and the urban sprawl that extends as far as you can see. You plan to spend a few days in Chicago, exploring and gathering material for the book you are writing.

You have arranged to meet Ellen, your sister, whom you have not seen in six years. You are to meet her in the lobby of the Palmer House Hilton, where she is staying. She is in town on business. There is a special exhibition at the Art Institute that she has told you she wants to see, and you have agreed to come along.

Ellen is seeing a therapist and much of what she is working on, so she tells you, has to do with Father. Her memories are different from yours, more consistently dark. Some of yours are dark, some are not so dark. Some are happy, some are not so happy. Most are beyond reach, lacking precision, like a long tangle of words that seems never to end and never to add up to anything.

She feels that Father did not care much about her when she was growing up. He did not follow her progress in school the way he did that of his sons. He was not interested in what career she might want to follow. She remembers the house in which she grew up to be an unhappy house, Father's brooding silences and flashes of anger coloring everything.

You have a few memories, though only a few, compared to the wealth of memories that your sister has retained or been able to recover. Some persist year after year, like black flies around the windows of a car that has stalled while crossing a field of corn stubble in late summer. You remember the summer your family moved to your new home in Lafayette and your father asked you to help put up new storm windows. You climbed separate ladders, one on each side of the window. Something happened, something went wrong. You're trying to get the screw to go in, but the hole is blocked with an old screw that broke off long ago.

Through no fault of your own, the screwdriver slips from your grasp and falls to the ground. With one hand Father is holding the window in place, with the other he is holding on tightly to a rung of the ladder. He is running out of patience.

Try another hole, he says. You may be smart in school, but when it comes to something practical like putting in a screw, you're useless.

Useless, how often you feel useless, when you're working with him. Useless, hopeless, clueless, whatever goes with less, you're it. What good does it do you, working with him, learning from him, absorbing his energy, taking in his teaching.

In the dark basement his torch glows. In the dark basement, in the damp basement he pours molten lead into the places where the pipes join. The torch glows.

You work with him, you listen to him, you do his bidding.

You're in the belly of the beast.

He sends you to the truck for a bolt, a nut, a washer, a wrench, whatever. You cannot find what he wants, more often than not.

The truck is old, ten years old, unwashed, dirty and grimy, as ugly as it can be. It has side panels that open from the top, inside which he keeps his tools and his supplies, everything he needs and everything you cannot find.

You search inside, outside, all around, knowing you will never find what you were sent for. And to know that you must repeat the same act over and over and never find a way to answer him.

Does he not have any idea what this is doing to you.

You return to the basement, to the dark basement where he's waiting, where he's counting on you. Or if he's upstairs in the bathroom, where the toilet is plugged and overflowing and the water gushing over the floor, you look for him there.

You have to tell him that you have not been able to find what he wants. You have not, could not, did not find what he wants. And you never will.

He says nothing, but his look of disdain says it all.

These sorts of memories that you have held onto like you would hold onto a lifeline are few and far between. Traveling back will stir up other memories buried deep in you, that's the idea.

You won't worry too much at this point if they turn out to be pleasant or unpleasant. You won't worry if they are true or false. The main thing is that they are vivid and rich in detail.

Buried memories, dreams, basic facts like dates and names and places, family stories and legends, these are the ingredients that you will need before you can write the book that you want to write.

When the plane lands you are asked to stay in your seat while medics come to remove the old man. He exits in a wheelchair, to light, scattered applause.

As he goes by, you see that he has a patch over the injured eye. He grips the arms of the wheelchair with his two hands, as if he were about to lift himself to his feet.

He has large, bony hands, with a skin that is so thin and so dry that it is translucent, the color of very lightly tanned leather.

As soon as the wheelchair is past, you stand up to get your briefcase and jacket out of the overhead compartment. You hand your neighbor his coat.

You move on without any further exchange of pleasantries.

Everyone is quiet, glad to be safely on the ground, glad that no one was more seriously hurt.

As you move out of the plane and into the terminal you can see a few passengers splitting away.

Though they are fewer in number, all the talk and excitement is in their camp.

Three

Along the corridor on the way to the baggage claim I stop and give Anne a call. She can't talk because someone is at the door, a workman who has come to look at a problem that we've been having with the roof. When it rains hard, water runs down inside the chimney and stains the wall in the bathroom.

Our conversation is short and sweet. My words feel rushed. I'll give you a call when I get settled someplace.

I'd better go. He'll think I'm not home.

Talk to you later.

I hang up the phone, proceed to the baggage area, gather my belongings, and make my way along another corridor and down a flight of stairs to the Avis rent-a-car counter.

After I have given her my name, the young black woman at the counter, without looking at me, locates my reservation on her screen.

She gives me a print-out together with a heavy sigh which seems to say that she is overworked and underpaid and if she could find something better to do with her life she would. She refrains from looking at me as she says, Have a nice day.

I hand the print-out to an attendant at the door, who takes me across to a parking lot where a car is waiting for me. It is a mid-size car, a Saturn, metallic green, brand-new looking, though the odometer shows 2,547 miles.

And just as quickly as that, I am behind the wheel and on my way, heading toward downtown Chicago on Highway 90.

It's a Wednesday, and the late afternoon traffic is not particularly heavy leaving the city. In the direction I'm going it is light. The car is roomy and handles well. I feel relaxed and comfortable.

It feels good being on my own. I'm going to spend a few days in Chicago, exploring parts of the city that my grandfather knew when he lived here in the 1920s. I know very little about my grandfather because no one ever talked about him.

Everything I know about him can be summed up in a couple of lines. One day in November, 1927, he left his family. The date, as it is written down in a family Bible, was November 20, 1927. No one heard from him again. Stories and legends get woven around facts as bare as these.

He had been working for the Chicago-Indianapolis-Louisville

Railway Line – the CIL. The Monon everyone called it – the Hoosier Line. He often traveled to Chicago on business. There came a time, in the early 20s, when he acquired an office in Chicago and spent his weekdays there, coming home only on weekends. The family saw him less and less often. He began to seem like a stranger visiting.

One weekend he simply did not return. The family hired a private detective, but every lead proved false. Two years after the disappearance, in December, 1929, the family decided to move to California and stay with relatives.

No one in the family ever talked to me about my grandfather. Not my father, not my mother, not my grandmother, no one. Not a word.

And I did not ask.

Father, nineteen at the time, remained behind. The disappearance of his father must have been like a blow to the body, like a hard fist to the chest, one that hurt him and bothered him all his life.

To write the book I have in mind I will have to know more about the Chicago of the 1920s. This was a bustling, roaring time. This was the city of gangs and gangland killings, the city of Al Capone.

There should be plenty of room for comedy, tragedy, romance, and endless speculation.

I get off Highway 90 at Division and drive through downtown Chicago along Michigan Boulevard. Palmer House, on Monroe Street, where I'm to meet my sister, is still standing, still in business, still thriving, after seventy years or more. Parking proves to be a problem, as I circle the block without success.

It seems pure accident that I discover the entrance to a mammoth garage behind the Art Institute – so mammoth I have trouble finding my way out on foot. It is a warm spring day and I enjoy the walk of several blocks.

In the lobby I wait for my sister Ellen. The desk has no record of her being registered but I'm sure this must be a mistake. We talked by phone just a few days before I left, and agreed as to the time and the place of our meeting.

I sit in a comfortable chair facing the front desk, and I wait.

I take out the envelope of photographs I've brought with me and look at the only one I have of Ellen. She and Mother are standing together in front of our old house in Battle Ground.

Ellen is maybe nine or ten. Both are dressed in their Sunday best, including hats and gloves. They have the same happy smile. Mother has her left hand gently and nicely on Ellen's left shoulder. She's leaning forward just slightly, to be closer.

From the evidence of this picture Ellen likes the Mother she has, though now she believes that this, like so much else, was never really the case. The picture gives a false impression, according to Ellen's present way of thinking. But I do not see it.

Ellen is holding something in her left hand. A figure hangs on a string that is wound about her hand. It looks like a finger puppet. Maybe a gingerbread man. In any case, a figure of some kind.

She stands so straight and tall. She seems so happy. Is it Mother who makes her happy. Or the little friend she holds in her hand.

Four

I have waited an hour for Ellen, to no avail. Has there been a misunderstanding. Has she had a change in plans. Her job often calls her away at the last moment. She works for a brokerage company, where she specializes in mergers and acquisitions. She works behind the scenes, on the technical details that make or break a deal. Therefore, she is key to the company's success, but she's not always recognized as such.

There is a commotion at the front desk. Voices are being raised in anger. A man is arguing with one of the clerks. As he argues, he gets more and more agitated. He waves his arms. He spits his words. He is enjoying this, I think.

He is the kind that will find something to fight about, anywhere, anytime. The bright blue sweater makes him look heavier above the belt than below. With the blue sweater, and the unruly white hair, and the white goatee, and the face red with anger, I mistake him for the man who sat next to me on the airplane from Montreal.

But when he turns and looks at me, I see his face, and it is nothing like the man on the plane. It is long and narrow.

The clerk, a woman, is trying to explain that all rooms have been booked. It's not possible to move to a different room.

I specifically asked for a room with two beds, the man says. Look here, I made a note of it. I was given a number.

She assures him that the piece of paper he is holding out to her means nothing to her.

Am I supposed to sleep in the same bed with my son then.

She could arrange to have a cot set up for his son.

Is that how you treat people in Chicago. You charge an arm and a leg and then you ask them to sleep on a cot.

For a brief, unprofessional moment she is at a loss for words. He asks if there is someone higher up he can talk to. She opens a door behind the counter and waits there silently, framed in a yellow-gold light, for that someone 'higher up' to come to her aid.

She closes her eyes wearily and waits, and for the first time I can see the lines of tension in her face. She has a young face, and already she is world-weary. She wears false eyelashes, long, black eyelashes that curl like faded tulips. She has a small nose, a small mouth, and a round chin. She is not pretty at all, when she is not smiling and being her bright self.

I am on my feet now, ready to leave and get away. At the same time I'm fascinated by the scene unfolding before my eyes, the same way I sometimes find myself glued to the television screen when I know I'd be a whole lot better off doing something else. There is a game being played out, maybe not for my benefit, maybe not even for my edification.

The man in the blue sweater drums his fingers on the counter as he waits for satisfaction. In the doorway behind the counter the woman listens to instructions from her superior. I glimpse a shadowy figure, someone very tall, thinner than would seem the norm for the Chicago of today, dressed impeccably in black, with dark hair combed straight back, and slicked down.

She nods her head. The man in black disappears. She comes forward, smiling again, her confidence restored. Behind her the door is quietly shut. I take a step forward, to hear how it's going to be played out.

Addressing him as 'Mr. Walker,' she offers him an executive suite for the night, where they have had a cancellation. And then tomorrow we can move you into a room with two beds.

Walker has a fit of coughing, as if choking on his own snot. He wants to know what it would cost extra. She assures him that there will be no extra charge.

He looks around him, as if looking for someone suspicious hiding in the shadows. I suppose that will do, he finally concedes.

He receives a new set of keys and instructions as to how to make the transfer from his old room to his new room. There is an exchange of pleasantries that echoes softly, unconvincingly through the lobby. This is my cue to leave but just as I start for the front door, Walker turns and sees me.

He holds up an index finger telling me to wait while he completes negotiations with the desk. Something in his manner keeps me rooted to the spot.

When he comes across the lobby to where I am standing, the first thing he says is, You've been watching, or should I say spying. I suppose you found it amusing.

It looked like you were going to come to blows there for a moment.

Sometimes you have to stand up for your rights. Isn't that the American way.

I don't know about that. Seems to have worked out for you though.

Are you staying at the Palmer.

Actually, no. I was supposed to meet my sister here, but she couldn't make it.

I'm just at the point of naming the place where I am staying, but some instinct says not to.

His son is not getting in till later, and in the meantime he wants to spend a few hours at the Art Institute. He asks me to come along. He could use the company.

The Art Institute was on my agenda, but for tomorrow, not today. I feel I'm being corralled into something I don't want, but I can't think of anything else to say except, All right, I'm game.

Five

While Walker goes upstairs to change rooms, I wander into the bar and sit at the counter. I ask for a beer. The TV that hangs from the ceiling is tuned to an all-news channel. There's something about a bombing raid over the mountains of northeast Afghanistan, in search of an enemy that is once again on the run, but just as dangerous as ever.

I sip my beer and tune out the news. At the end of the bar the bartender is washing and drying tall glasses and arranging them neatly on a shelf behind him. A young man with a briefcase sits alone at the bar. In a booth in back a man and a woman lean toward each other across the narrow table, talking so softly you cannot even hear the hum of their voices. No one is paying attention to what is happening on the TV.

So many years have gone by, it seems strange to be sitting in a bar in the Palmer Hilton in downtown Chicago, alone in this new America. I've held on to my passport, made any number of trips south over the years, followed American politics closely, but it is just now that I am beginning to see how drastically the country has changed.

I no longer know my country. I am like a traveler coming into a strange land and feeling disoriented and ignorant. But also feeling excited because I am encountering the exotic. Chicago, I suppose, can only seem exotic if you come from very far away, in time and in space.

As we approach the Art Institute the traffic and the crowds of people get my blood racing again. Standing at the bottom of the stairs and looking up at the two lions guarding the entrance to the building, I remember the time I lived in Chicago, in the fall of 1964. Father had died the previous summer, and I had lost my direction. I had no idea what I wanted to do with my life, other than 'turn on and drop out.'

When my father died it was like a stone had been rolled back from the mouth of the cave where I had been hiding, chained up. I could step outside and see real trees, animals, people. I could hear a woman's voice, the sound of a dog barking. I could breathe!

I stayed with a friend in an apartment on 55th Street, near the university. Two or three times a week we'd go downtown to roam the streets, drink beer and sneak into the cinema on Clark Street to watch movies that lasted all night long.

We loved the walk home in the hours just before dawn, when the city was at its most peaceful and most natural. We would stop and have a smoke on the steps of the Art Institute. We were penniless, we had no prospects, but we felt the future belonged to us. The fierce lions were standing guard over us, giving us their approval.

After a smoke we'd go for a swim in Lake Michigan, in the first light of dawn. We'd plunge into the chilly waters off Jackson Park and feel that we were plunging into a scene from one of the Ingmar Bergman films we had just seen.

Some of these films we watched again and again, feeling that in them was the secret that would open the door into the room where we would be able to turn and see ourselves for the first time. In *The Seven Seals* we entered into a barren landscape that just for this reason promised a kind of enlightenment. We became conscious that there was more to life than fun and games, as we looked at scenes of death and destruction.

When my friend, after much prying, found out that I was still a virgin, he vowed to put an end to this sad state of affairs. Until I got fucked I couldn't call myself a man, he drummed into me until I came to believe it too.

One night, on our way home from the movies, we got into a taxi and asked the driver to drive us someplace where we could 'have a little fun.' He drove us deep into the south side of Chicago, and it did not look like much fun the way the houses were laid out and the way the streets got narrower and narrower and the way the occasional pedestrian glared at us.

All the houses were the same, little brick houses two stories high, with steps in front. We came to a house that was the only one on the block with a light in the window. It was four o'clock in the morning. No hint of dawn.

You boys want me to hang around, or you be okay, the driver winked at us.

He was a big, powerful man who could have been an ex-football player for the Bears, and whose face was just as black as it could be. We told him to come back in an hour.

They had the whole thing down to a science. The woman who answered the door didn't say a word, just nodded, maybe because it was so late, maybe because she knew everything she needed to know about us, just by looking. She had the body of a twenty-year-old but her face was much older.

She led us up the stairs, like leading lambs to the slaughter. Somehow, on the way up, the price was negotiated and the money handed over. It seemed like a lot but I had no way of knowing if it was too much since this was my first time and I didn't know what it was I was buying, exactly.

There were six separate rooms on the second floor, each about the size of a walk-in closet. We could hear voices inside the first couple of rooms. My friend went into a room on the right, at the end of the hall. Just before closing the door, he looked back at me and gave me the thumbs up.

I entered the last room on the left. I don't think the girl who was waiting for me there was more than sixteen years old. Even more surprising was the fact that she was Mexican, not African, and spoke not a word of English, or pretended not to. She did everything by gestures and a little grunt that meant 'okay' but came out sounding like 'key.'

She was gentle and sweet but it was clear that she had done this a thousand times. She didn't ask me to wear a condom and I was too shy to ask her if I should. She didn't have to do anything to coax my erection into being, other than smile at me.

She told me to lie on top of her and when I did she raised her legs and put them around me. I could feel the bones of her ankles where she had placed them in the small of my back, ever so lightly.

She seemed to be in a state of permanent readiness for whatever was going to happen, because even though she was clearly bored out of her mind, not the least bit excited, I could hardly feel a thing when I put it in though it was just as big as it could get.

Just to be there was so new and so beyond anything I had imagined that in a matter of seconds it was all over.

Six

At the end of a long hallway there is a cafeteria where we can grab a bite to eat before seeing the exhibitions. Walker sits across from me at a small, square, dark-green table, and picks at his food. For just under ten dollars you can get a soup and a sandwich, with a glass of beer.

Walker crumbles a handful of crackers into his soup. A room divider hides the cafeteria line from our view. I cut my sandwich into half, and eat one half. The soup, a lentil soup with carrots, is hot. The carrots are sweet tasting, from Mexico.

He's waiting for me to say something, so I ask him what brings him to Chicago. He's meeting his son for a long-delayed vacation together. His son lives on the west coast, so they don't see each other that often.

He says they have a deal that his son will come with him to places he likes to haunt and he will go with his son to a nightclub he has heard about but never visited. He says, It sounded like a fair deal to me.

I ask him what kind of places he likes to haunt.

Bookstores, mostly. Out of the way, authentic restaurants. I'm not so keen on art but there's an outstanding collection of armor at the Art Institute that I'd like to see. The main reason I'm here is to attend an opera. I've become an opera enthusiast in my old age. Wagner is my particular obsession.

He talks about the opera he is in town to see - Wagner's *Parsifal*. When I confess that I have only a vague recollection of the Parsifal story, he offers to give me a detailed exposition. I order a second beer and let him talk. I'm not really listening, I'm drifting in and out of his story.

He mentions a character called Kundry, which wakes me up because for a split second I thought he had said cunt. There's a scene where Kundry washes the feet of Parsifal but when I suggest that this sounds like Mary Magdalen in the Bible washing the feet of Jesus, Walker gives me a sour look and says nothing.

I know next to nothing about opera, I confess.

Very few people do, which may be just as well. I'm sure my son knows even less than you. But he's agreed to come along. On top of that there's a lecture that I haven't told him about, in conjunction with the opera. He's going to have opera coming out his rear end. It won't do him any harm. He might learn something.

All the young want to know about these days is computers and rock music and videos and junk like that. Anything else is too taxing.

That seems a little harsh.

Do you think so. Then your experience must be very different from mine. He appears ready to launch into a history of his experience of the young, but I'm able to ward this off by moving my chair back and turning and looking toward a table near the wall, where a woman suddenly laughs a very loud, uninhibited laugh.

Walker has nothing more to say, for now. He makes a lot of noise with his knife and fork but he has yet to take the first bite. I notice he is not wearing his blue sweater but has changed into a cream colored jacket that is too big across the shoulders - some Chinese designer's misconception of North American body shape and style.

He has put the sandwich aside as inedible and begun to sip at his beer, which has lost its head. I'm just about to say something about the time I lived in Chicago and about the way I'd like to weave several of these incidents into the book I'm planning to write when he stands up and mumbles something about 'my waterworks.'

He disappears down the hallway toward the men's room. It's clear he's not interested in my story. Then again, why should he be. I'm thinking about getting up and leaving, but before I can budge he's back.

We sit for a minute in silence. Apparently he's willing to sit here forever, rather than listen to another word of my soul searching. Finally I ask what I hope is a general and harmless question: When, uh, is your son supposed to arrive.

He arrives when he arrives. He takes a deep breath, as if the words just spoken had sucked the oxygen right out of him. That's the way he is.

I'm reminded of Ellen because that is the way she is, the way she has always been. She arrives when she arrives, or she doesn't arrive. Walker seems to be able to read my mind because when he looks at me he quiets right down. What he sees seems to assure him that I will listen to him without interruption and without censure.

When it comes to this father and son business, he continues, we are not exactly on the same wavelength. He thinks his main goal is to put as much distance between himself and his father as possible. I think that a son owes a father a little respect, at a minimum. How this chasm has come into being is in fact a fairly complicated story. If you're interested, I'll try to make it as simple as I know how.

He does not wait for me to nod agreement but launches into the simplified version, assuming, until the evidence suggests otherwise, that I am on a level with all the other dolts that people his world and that need things reduced to the bare bones.

We haven't seen much of each other the last ten years, he begins, ever since his mother and I separated. He dropped out of college after his freshman year and moved west, to get as far away as possible from his bickering parents. I don't know much about his life during these years. I heard that he was working on a fishing boat. He sent me a postcard from a place called Bella-Bella. There was something about building a house on a piece of land he'd bought.

A year or two went by with no communication whatsoever. Then I heard that he was in Vancouver, attending university. He needed money. He won't talk to me, so the money has to go by way of his mother. What kind of a grudge is he holding. She doesn't know or if she knows she's not saying. My role is to feed money into the account and to ask no questions. Needless to say, I'm not thrilled with this arrangement. Would you be.

Not for very long.

I talked to a lawyer. According to our agreement she has full custody and I'm obligated to shell out so much a month for support, even though she's working full-time. There was no legal obligation to support the kid on top of that. If he wants to go to university, let him come to me. He never did. So be it.

The years go by. He lives in Vancouver, selling skateboards. Then he hears that his mother has cancer. She has only a few months to live. He flies east to be with her. We run into each other one day on the street. What do you say to your only son after you haven't seen him for seven years. What are you doing with your life. What kind of a job do you have. Are you married. Any kids. Did you ever think about getting a job.

We end up sitting in a coffee shop talking for three hours and discovering that we like each other after all. Maybe like is too strong a word. The point is we talked and we agreed to keep in touch. His mother seemed to get better. She had leukemia. Then she caught pneumonia and died very suddenly. I was not made to feel welcome at the funeral but I put in an appearance. We met afterwards and talked about getting together.

I was already planning a trip to Chicago so I suggested he meet me there. Meet me in Chicago, isn't that the title of an old song. He went along with the idea but I'm not really sure why. It's one of the things I hope to find out, when he turns up. I suppose I should add *if* he turns up.

The way you talk, it sounds less and less likely.

All I can say is, I plan to keep my side of the bargain.

My beer is finished, and there is nothing more to say. I push my seat back and turn to one side, as if to study the flow of traffic in that direction.

I'm ready to leave. I've had enough.

If you're free tomorrow, we could continue this conversation, Walker suggests.

I'm not thrilled with the idea, to say the least. It doesn't feel much like a conversation to me, more like a monologue, and I don't want any more of it. I'm heading, uh, south tomorrow. Leaving bright and early.

Until this moment, I had no such plan.

What about a cup of coffee in the morning.

All right, why not. Where shall we meet. I am confident, at this point, that this is one appointment I'm not going to keep. I'm playing along, but I don't know why. I could just say I have other plans, it's none of his business, but I don't.

What's the matter with me.

Ever heard of Water Tower Place. They say the Pump Station is worth a look.

All right, fine.

Nine o'clock then. In front of the main entrance.

Can't wait. We both get up at the same time and start for the exit. Down the long corridor as we approach the main desk, Walker sees a sign directing him toward the George F. Harding Collection of Arms and Armor and he veers off in that direction.

He gives me a bright smile, the brightest yet, and mutters something that I do not quite get. The only thing I can guess is *cheers*.

I continue toward the main lobby and the stairs leading to the Impressionists. The farther I am away from Walker, with each step I take, the easier I breathe.

Seven

At the top of the stairs the first painting I see, in the middle distance, is Seurat's *Sunday Afternoon on the Island of La Grande Jatte*. In books this painting has always left me cold, so as I approach I am anxious to see if the real thing might surprise me.

It is a very large canvas, over ten feet across. This in itself is a jolt, and to get close is to go into this altogether too calm, too balanced, too harmonious scene. I feel sick, the way everyone is lost in his or her own world, even the children.

Maybe lost is too strong a word, or not strong enough.

Alone. Everyone is alone in the world, this is the message that comes across loud and clear.

There is one couple, near the center. The woman has her arms up and around the man's neck and that's nice. Is he looking at her. I don't think so. His head is bent, turned to the side. He is looking at me, the viewer who happened by.

All the energy in the picture is sucked right out of it, where those eyes of his betray his apathy.

There is nothing alive in this painting, with the exception of the seven tree trunks in the upper right-hand corner, which glow with a fire that captures the eye.

This, perhaps, is nothing but an accident of science.

It helps, I think, that we get away from the human element and move into something dark and unformed.

In the dark there is a light glowing. This alone brings tears to the eye.

The owl hoots, and the madman awakes.

Around the corner I catch a glimpse of the madman I come to see. Of the eighty or so self-portraits Van Gogh left behind the one that's here is from Paris, from the spring of 1887.

The head is turned, so that we have a three quarter view of the left side of the face. Dominating everything is the left eye, with its haunted, defiant look. The face is bony. The beard is red. In the ear are five red brush strokes, repeating in color and texture the strokes of the beard.

It is this ear, and the five brush strokes in the ear that bring the work to life for me. I've found what I was looking for, and I don't want to leave.

But it's almost closing time, so as much as I'd like to, I can't stay here forever. How much time has elapsed. Ten minutes.

Twenty minutes. For a moment I've forgot about time.

A woman steps back from a painting she has been examining, and I do a two-step to avoid a collision.

This places me so that I am looking into the next room of paintings, that is, the room I have just come from. And there in the crowd, his head of white hair above everyone and everything else, is Walker.

Here is a madman, in the flesh, I have come to believe. He is much too close for comfort.

I'd rather get out of here before he sees me.

I duck down and hurry off in the opposite direction. There's no time now to look at works of art, be they masterpieces or not.

I turn one corner, then another, then another, until it seems I am caught in a labyrinth. I approach a guard, standing at the opening between rooms, silent and imposing. Without saying a word he points to a sign, set up on a kind of tripod, which in turn points the way out of the building.

Goodbye Walker. I will come back another day, when you are gone and the memory of you has faded.

If someone speaks your name I will wonder what it means.

Eight

I'm staying at the Quality Inn on Madison, at I-94. This is a Quality Inn unlike any I have seen, seventeen stories high, swimming in a sea of traffic.

I'm on the sixth floor, looking north. The traffic is heavy, the flow smooth and steady. It's after eight. The sun is down.

I'm thinking about going out into that traffic. In a brochure on my desk I've taken note of several possible night spots. There's one in particular I like the sound of – The Jazz Oasis.

Maybe I'll go there.

It's on West Erie, at Sedgewick. On the map it doesn't look far. Maps can be deceiving, I know.

I stand at the window watching the traffic go by. The more I think about it, the less I want to go out.

The truth is, since Anne and I have been together, I no longer like going out alone. When I was alone I went out alone, and I felt more lonely when I did. It took me years to get used to being alone. It was only when I had learned to live with my loneliness that I stopped feeling so lonely.

By far the loneliest time of my life was the summer Father died. It was between my junior and senior years at college. I had a job at a General Motors parts plant in Anderson, Indiana. My job was to measure noise pollution at various locations in the plant. I took these measurements and made beautiful colored charts showing where it was safe to work, and where it was dangerous.

Everywhere I went I listened to the noise and I did not hear the voices speaking to me. Father was dying of cancer, but I knew nothing of his pain. I did not want to know. I was not listening.

I had my own life to live and screw everyone else. I ate alone at a restaurant downtown, feasting on something I had never tried before. Sweetbreads they were called – heart, kidney, brain.

I saw a raw, black and white movie version of *Lady Chatterley's Lover*, made in France, with English sub-titles. The words, the images struck so deep I saw myself splitting into two parts – my everyday, lackluster self and my hidden, lonely self.

I sang to myself as I walked to work, loud enough to startle the occasional passer-by. Nobody knows the sorrow I've seen.

One day Mother called me at work, and she said, You'd better come home. Father's not well.

I did not hear the urgency in her voice, because I did not

want to hear the urgency. I waited a day before hitchhiking home.

Maybe it was a hundred miles home, maybe a hundred and fifty. But it was afternoon when I got there and Father had died during the night and he was gone.

The body was gone, and my chance to say good-bye was gone. No chance to say my good-byes, no closure, for years.

The next summer too was lonely. After graduation from college I made my way to the west coast, to see what all the fuss was about. I was supposed to begin graduate work in the fall but my heart was not in it.

I was living in Oakland, within walking distance of Berkeley. The few times I ventured onto the campus I felt out of place. I was more interested in the bars just off campus. Even more interested in the hot, crowded streets of downtown Oakland at night, where hustlers, pimps, toughs, young people, townspeople, tourists, and cops swarmed like bees in a beehive.

I was feeling lonely and ripe for the picking. I had very little money. Everything I had brought west with me I had dragged to the pawnshop.

I spent my mornings at the public library. Afternoons I'd lounge by the side of a lake in a different part of town. There were couples in rowboats and families walking among the trees across the way and people lying on the grass next to me reading or sunbathing.

They seemed curiously detached from one another, and from me.

One day on my way out of the park a man stopped his car next to me and asked me if I wanted a ride. Maybe it was the first time anyone had spoken to me in days. Maybe there was something very sweet in his voice.

I said yes.

He lived in a nice neighborhood in Oakland, with his parents. His parents were out of town. I remember a lush backyard, with shrubs all around, and flowers. There was a deck with a covering of grape vines.

I remember him on the phone, to friends in the world of theatre. He was telling them about me. He was very pleased with his catch.

Maybe he was forty years old. He reminded me of Charles Laughton, the actor. I felt safe with him.

We had a drink together, a gin and tonic with a sprig of mint, in large, wide-mouthed glasses. We ate outside on the deck, and then I stayed the night.

He wanted sex and then more sex. He wanted to suck me, and he said he had to do that to get really excited.

He wanted me to come into him from behind. You're the man, he said. I didn't quite know what he was talking about.

He was gentle and non-threatening. It's okay if you ejaculate, he said. He wanted me to ejaculate.

He told me to squeeze his balls. He'd do the rest.

After living on nothing for so many weeks, and speaking to no one, I was glad to be in a clean, quiet, well-furnished place, in a safe neighborhood.

The next day we took a bus to San Francisco, and then another bus across town to the beach. I went in swimming, while he watched our things.

Then he took a long walk along the beach, while I stayed behind. I watched the waves come in, one after the other. There was no way to stop them, and there was no way to stop my life unfolding in a manner that was very different from what I thought I wanted.

I felt sadder and lonelier than I had ever felt in my life.

He walked so far down the beach that I lost sight of him. I looked in his billfold and took enough to pay for bus fare back to Oakland. I felt bad about leaving all his things there unguarded.

I think he was giving me this chance to get away if I wanted to. I was to decide whether I wanted what he was offering me.

Nine

The sky is getting dark. I decide to give Anne a call and let her know where I am.

The phone rings three times and then I hear the familiar message. It's a bilingual message, with my voice first in English, then Anne's in French. I like the way she says 'Beep' at the end of her text.

I guess she's in the studio working the night shift. I'll try again later.

I dig in my bag for the spiral notebook. I sit for a while at the desk and jot down notes to help me remember the day's events.

I put down what comes into my head, without trying to pull things together. I don't want to make connections where there are as yet no clear connections.

When I get home and start writing the novel that I want to write, I will see what I can use and what I cannot use. I'll look for the connections that are not so obvious right now because they are at a different level from the level I am living.

I am like a man living out of his suitcase who forgets that there might be something more to life than figuring out where to get his next meal and where to find a decent place to lay his head.

These notes, which seem random as I jot them down, I'll turn into something that holds together, like a weaver at her loom.

I call Anne again but get the same message. Maybe she has decided to meet Sally at a bar downtown and enjoy a night out.

We've been married more than ten years now and very seldom have we gone anywhere except in each other's company. It is good to change old habits now and again, I tell myself.

I would too, if I were in her shoes.

In the darkness the buildings downtown have come alive. Looking out from this window, I see a clean, well-run, friendly city, a lot different from the Chicago I experienced in the 1960s.

Tomorrow I'll go exploring and see how long that impression holds up.

I've brought along a pair of running shoes for days like tomorrow. When I take them out of the bag and set them on the floor under the bed, I see something blue inside the left shoe that was not there before. When I explore further I discover a small blue box that Anne has hidden away.

It is the sort of blue box that a broach or a pair of earrings might come in. I lift off the top and look inside. Wrapped in soft tissue paper is the medal that I gave Anne ten years ago when I first met her. It belonged to my uncle who was killed in the war.

A better word would be *loaned*. She had asked me for something 'dear to my heart' and this was the only thing I could think of. She's had it for ten years, sometimes wearing it for long periods, sometimes storing it away for months and months.

It's about the size of a silver dollar, the edges and the raised decorations shiny and bright, the rest a darker brown. On the front, across the top, are the words 'American Defense.' Below is the figure of a woman, standing tall and proud, with legs apart, a sword in her upraised right hand, a shield in her lowered left hand, bare-breasted, the two breasts like small apples, the shiniest and most prominent feature on this side of the medal.

On the reverse, contained within a shiny thin circle of rubbed brass, are the words: *For service during the limited emergency proclaimed by the President on September 8, 1939 or during the unlimited emergency proclaimed by the President on May 27, 1941.*

My uncle (after whom I was named) must have received this medal sometime during the summer or fall of 1941. There is no mention of Pearl Harbor. Other documents state that he was killed in the Pacific in April, 1942. He left no children, and his sister and his brothers have all died. The medal passed from hand to hand until it came into my possession.

She's written a note and folded it to fit inside the little blue box. It's on a piece of paper torn out of one of her sketchbooks, the sort of thick rag paper that will stand the test of time. I want you to wear this medal on your journey, the note says, wherever it takes you. I'd like to have it back sometime but that's up to you. You're going to be traveling among ghosts, some of them friendly and some of them not so friendly, and I want you to wear this medal around your neck as a charm to keep you from coming to harm. (Sorry about the silly rhyme.)

This is a quotation from a book I've been reading and which made me think about sending the medal along as a surprise. The book is by a man named Wes Nisker and it's a book about what he calls Buddha Nature. He says 'therapy is a way to turn ghosts into ancestors.'

So what I'm wishing for you is that your journey will be a sort of therapy, and that the ghosts that are haunting you will turn into the ancestors that will give you a sense of being rooted.

Love, Anne.

The medal is tied on a rawhide string with a fancy knot that I believe is called a double slip. I like the feel of the cool metal against the skin of my chest.

I take the Findley novel to bed with me. Ede and the piano man have walked several miles out of town, into the quiet of the corn fields. In a hollow in a corner of a field, where Ede has led them to a place she knows, they make love.

No words are spoken, except one: *Here*. She remembers many things, sounds, smells, and the way his hands made wings as he lifted his suspenders wide of his shoulders, but not a single memory of words.

Far away a pack of wolves begins to yip and sing.

The book is arranged in seven chapters, with a prelude and a coda. The first chapter encompasses the years 1889-1890. Subsequent chapters take us through the years, right up to 1939.

So here we have the three generations – Ede the grandmother, Lily the daughter, Charlie the son, who is the storyteller. Charlie looks back at his mother and his grandmother, the lives they led, the men they loved.

Findley brings this all to life, masterfully. I don't know what's stopping me.

Through the open window I hear the steady hum of cars and trucks on the highway below. Downtown, no doubt, things are just beginning to happen, but I am dead to all that.

I touch the medal and press it to the soft spot just below the sternum. There is an energy here that is yet to be tapped.

It is dark out ... The night is young ...

Ten

There's a light coming through the slit in the curtains of your sixth floor room. You don't know where you are, or where the light is coming from.

You swing your legs out of bed and stand up. For a moment you have the mistaken belief that you are home in Canada imagining you are in Chicago. But you realize that this can't be Canada. It's some quality in the noise.

Below, on I-91, you hear cars and trucks honking impatiently in the slow-moving traffic. It's Chicago all right, but not the Chicago of your dreams.

In the Chicago of your dreams everything was waiting to happen. Now everything that's going to happen has happened.

Your grandfather left his family and was never heard from again.

Your grandmother moved to Long Beach, California, where she had friends.

Your father died young, at age fifty-four, having failed in his attempt to set up his own business.

Your mother survived several suicide attempts and lived long enough to see five grandchildren born into the world.

Your brother was fifty-three when he died, two years after triple bypass surgery on a heart weakened by diabetes.

You are the oldest, and it's up to you to piece their stories together. Because after you are gone there will be no one to remember.

The room comes equipped with a coffeemaker and a package of coffee for brewing. While the coffee brews, you arrange a few stones that you have brought with you on a round table near the door to the balcony.

You sit at the table a few moments and listen to the noise of the traffic below. And after a while you get used to the noise and you begin to hear the silence that is inside the noise, in the earth, and in the stones.

There are five stones.

A small red stone, an agate, which you found on a beach near the town of Percé, on the Gaspé Peninsula.

A gray, heart-shaped stone from Herring Cove, in Fundy National Park, New Brunswick.

A round, smooth, gray, almost flat stone that you pocketed

while exploring Indiana Dunes State Park on a previous trip.

An almost perfectly spherical, whitish stone from Parrsboro, Nova Scotia.

A smooth, black, flat stone with a hole in the middle that has a whitish glow when you look at it from a certain angle.

You do not remember where you found this one. It is your favorite.

Five stories, one for every stone...

At Herring Cove by the Bay of Fundy the day before Anne and you were married you did not go looking for a special stone, or for anything special. On that day you had everything you wanted – the earth beneath your feet, the sky that had a more intense blue than you had ever seen, family and friends coming from far and near to celebrate with you.

You sat cross-legged on the beach in a hat that was one size too small, watching the tide go out. You walked barefoot on the smooth pebbles to the water's edge where your brother was standing, watching and listening to a bird just offshore – a loon.

An inland boy like yourself, he was the one who had stayed behind, and because of this he had never seen a loon. You talked of old times growing up together and wished that your father and your mother could be here now, to see both of you happy, after many years that were not very happy.

You talked of the women in your lives, and you marveled at the luck of the draw, and you wondered what you had done to deserve such happiness.

The tide had begun to come in again. You walked back up the beach. When you pointed out to David the place at the top of the beach near the bottom of the hill where the water would touch at high tide he was amazed.

The difference between low tide and high tide is 45 feet, you explained. He shook his head.

You stopped a moment to pick up a stone that for some reason had caught your eye. It was a small stone, less than an inch around, the same gray as countless others on the beach. But this one was in the shape of a heart and it felt good when you closed your hand on it.

David had moved farther up the beach and was standing alone. When you looked at him, with the bare hillside behind him and a few trees above, you realized that you were free of the old jealousies that had plagued you all your life and that had colored your feelings for him for as long as you could remember.

You felt closer to him than you had ever felt, and you knew that you were more like him than unlike him and that this was not a reason to be ashamed, but a reason to be proud.

If you walked like him and looked like him and had the same build and profile, this was not a bad thing.

You both came from the same earth.

Eleven

You decide to skip the free breakfast downstairs and treat yourself to one of the power bars you noticed in a basket on the table by the coffeemaker. This one contains real chocolate plus 'more than twenty vitamins and minerals.'

It's two days past due, but it can't hurt you, nothing can hurt you the way you feel. You have no reason to feel this good but you do.

You shower, brush your teeth, dress, and then turn your attention to packing and checking out. There is a bookstore in town you want to visit.

You're hoping to find some information, even old photographs, about the Monon Railway Company where your grandfather, Edward Avon, worked until the day he disappeared. Or about Dearborn Station, where he had his office.

Until you were six you lived in West Lafayette, Indiana, on a hill above the Wabash River, at the edge of the university campus, It was the river, not the railroad tracks, that dominated your early childhood. The river was the source of adventure and mystery. Ice jams and mud flats.

When you were six you moved a few miles outside Lafayette, to the little town of Battle Ground. Your new house was within two blocks of the train tracks, whereas the river was a mile away.

It was here that you came to know the Monon and its ways. It traveled to far places and gave you the idea that you might do the same one day.

Every day on the way to school and back you crossed the tracks. You listened for the train and when it arrived you waved at the conductor, who did not wave back.

In springtime you roamed the countryside, sometimes with friends, sometimes alone, as far as the bridge across the Wabash.

In summer, on the hottest days, you picked strawberries by the side of the tracks.

In fall you stood by the side of the road and counted the cars as the train roared through town on the way to Chicago and you pictured the girl you had decided, just because she had once spoken to you, was the one for you.

An even number of cars meant that Donna (or Jane or Linda or Martha or whatever her name happened to be) liked you; an odd number meant she did not.

Maybe you were eight at this time.

Twelve

The bookstore – Powell's Downtown – is located at 828 South Wabash, near the Chicago Hilton in the South Loop. I park in a garage on Harrison near Clarke and start walking toward the store.

It is warm for April and after just a few paces I know that I'm going to be too hot in my jacket. I turn back toward the garage.

I go down a set of stairs into a dark cavernous basement. There is a feeling that something dangerous could happen. As I approach the car, I see someone ahead of me, ten or twelve cars away, walking with a hurried step toward a door that opens to a stairway that leads toward a back exit.

I hear voices outside on the sidewalk, or on the floor above me. There is no one in sight.

Still nervous, I fold my jacket and place it in the trunk with my suitcase and my briefcase. My reading glasses, which I will need at the bookstore, I will carry by hand, in their black soft leather case.

I know Powell's a little from browsing their web site. The store, when I go in, is just as attractive and friendly as the website suggested.

There's a stairwell leading down into a basement where it looks like most of the interesting titles will be found. If there are 200,000 titles at this location, it does not feel like it, because the shelves are tidy and easy to search.

I look around for customer service. Toward the back of the store, on the main level, at a desk behind the stairwell, a woman sits facing a computer screen.

She's turned sideways to the flow of people entering the store, in her own space. She's casually dressed, in a yellow pullover, jeans, and dark brown Birkenstocks.

On a piece of scrap paper I have a title I've copied from the website. My handwriting is bad enough I think I'd better read it out. I wonder if you could help me. Do you have a section for trains and railroads. The book I'm looking for is called *A History of the Monon*.

She looks at me strangely.

The Monon, in case you don't know, was a railway line that ran from Chicago south through Indiana, which I believe is now defunct.

She stops what she's doing and stares at me, until I feel that my words must be as garbled as my writing. The railway, or the state, she finally says.

It takes me a second to get the joke. She has a round, pleasant face, and when I laugh she laughs, though she's clearly annoyed at being interrupted.

It's not her job to answer questions, to entertain dense customers with dumb questions.

She asks if I have the name of an author.

It's something like Dole. Maybe Dollair. I'm afraid I can't remember.

I must be the sort of customer she hates.

The title should be enough, she says. She types in the letters, using the middle finger of her right hand only, then clicks on her mouse and waits.

I watch with her for a moment, then turn and look back toward the front of the store. At the front counter, just to the right of the entrance, there is a line-up eight deep, waiting to make purchases. I look more closely.

There are two clerks at two cash registers. There is a young man at one, a young woman at the other. The young man is tall and thin – very tall, maybe six feet eight. He nods and grimaces and gestures, but never says a word.

Perhaps he's deaf.

Or perhaps he's shy, keeping his thoughts to himself, storing up images and anecdotes about some of the strange customers who come his way.

Like the man, the young woman performs her task with a minimum of chit-chat. She's wearing tight black spandex shorts and a white crewneck shirt that touches mid-thigh, just above the shorts.

No dress code here.

The line-up splits into two as it nears the counter. The counter is three feet high and has an antique look – heavy, solid, rough, dark wood.

At the end of the counter, to the right, under a wall of collectable illustrated books that reaches eight feet high, is a display of back issues of various magazines related to book collecting. Seeing that the woman who's helping me is still busy at the computer, I approach the magazine rack.

I pick out a magazine called *Biblio,* with its glossy cover announcing a story about the comedian Jackie Gleason. 'Toward the Light: Jackie Gleason's Spirited Literary Journey,' it's called.

I'm intrigued, because I do not associate Jackie Gleason with books. Mystery novels, yes, science fiction, maybe, but not a collection of rare and valuable books on the supernatural, which is what this article documents.

I associate Jackie Gleason with bare walls, empty bookcases, poor neighborhoods, angry, mindless conversation, screaming matches between husband and wife. Gleason created a number of characters while starring in his own TV show in the 50s, but his most memorable is Ralph Kramden in the sketch called *The Honeymooners*.

He portrays the Brooklyn tenement world he grew up in, with its inevitable tensions and frustrations. Ralph is angry with the world and he doesn't mind letting the world know it.

As befits the era, it is the wife Alice, played by the combative Audrey Meadows, who bears the brunt of it.

The Honeymooners was one of the three or four shows my father would not have missed for the world, in the early 50s. He must have seen something of himself in the figure of Jackie Gleason.

He had the same body build and the same constant concern with his weight. He wore the same kind of hat when he went out. He had the same round face and hurt look.

Gleason, of course, was a great storyteller and a great comic and my father was none of this. Gleason got angry easily and found a thousand ways to show his anger, while my father kept his feelings bottled up inside.

Gleason was a dancer and loved movement and my father, though a good athlete in his youth, was slow and heavy as lead in his movements as he got older.

Gleason had eyes that were alive and popped out to great comic effect. Gleason was everything my father might have wanted to be, if he could have found a way to turn the bitterness in his heart into gold the way bees make honey out of old failures.

The article, mostly about Gleason's outstanding collection of books on the occult, also gives a sprinkling of facts and stories from his life. Born in 1916 to Irish Catholic parents, he grew up in the Bushwick section of Brooklyn. His parents, Herb and Mae, were poor and they fought a lot, usually about money.

But here's the shocker. One day just before Christmas when Jackie was nine, his father failed to come home from his job at an insurance company. Jackie and Mae never saw or heard from him again.

So, there it is. No wonder my father loved Jackie Gleason. He recognized something in Gleason's make-up that the rest of us did not.

A fear of rejection that would never give him a moment's peace.

The feeling of being alone and vulnerable.

But my father took this feeling and turned it in on himself and made himself into a figure more to be feared than loved, whereas Gleason turned it into dance and laughter, into drink and dependency.

Why is it that I do not remember the laughter of my father.

Does anyone remember the laughter of his father.

I think some do. Women, if they are lucky, do.

Father must have laughed, must have been able to laugh. Why else watch Jackie Gleason, Jack Benny, Ed Sullivan, Lucille Ball.

Did he laugh.

I would like to think that he did, on occasion.

There were sides of him, the laughing side, the crying side, the grieving side, that he did not show to us children, maybe did not show to anyone.

How can I not feel pity for a man who does not, and who cannot show his feelings.

Maybe having a father is like having a dream. You keep hoping you will wake up, but after a while it seems unlikely.

Thirteen

I return to the woman behind the stairwell. She's found two copies of the book I'm looking for, one without a dust jacket for fifteen dollars, one with for twenty-five.

The author's name is Gary Dolzall.

I want the one with the dust jacket, I tell her. Just for the looks.

She gives me a print-out with all necessary information and points me to a desk in the far back of the store.

The man who takes my order tells me to wait while he searches the stock of books in the basement.

On his desk there's a photograph that shows him sitting at a table, with two young children by his side. The girl has her hand up, touching the side of his face. On the table is a birthday cake, with many lit candles.

An image from a dream (it feels like one of last night's dreams) comes back to me. My father, returning home after working 'up north' for a few days or weeks, enters the house wearing my winter coat, with the fur-lined hood drawn up.

I cannot see his face.

Mother greets him at the door. Everyone in the house is glad he is home. Glad he is well after being away doing work that we suspect was more dangerous than he is willing to let on.

He doesn't say anything but walks to the counter between the living room and the kitchen and begins looking through a folder of papers. This is the sort of thing that I might do.

I like my father more than ever. He is a little like me. I admire him and want to be like him.

It is often the case that dreams improve on real life.

Finally, I have my book, and I'm about to leave when I decide I had better pick up something about Chicago in the 1920s while I'm here. There is a section on Chicago near the order desk.

The big 'official' history of Chicago is too expensive, so I choose one of the more interesting looking books on Al Capone and his times. I pay for my two books at the front desk and step outside.

I tuck the books, wrapped nicely in brown paper and tied with a string, under my arm. Where do I want to go next, I ask myself.

I want to see something of Chicago, before I head south to

meet my brother. When my father was alive, he was only barely alive.

Say that again. When my father was alive, he would treat us once or twice a year to a trip into the big city, to see a baseball game or a football game.

As well, there were regular trips to Midway Airport, when his mother came to visit.

During the late 40s and early 50s my grandmother stayed with us every summer, for two, sometimes three months. I always wanted her to stay longer.

Her name was Nellie, which was also the name of a baseball player I especially admired in those days - Nellie Fox. From her I gained my love of card games, canasta in particular, my habit of putting ketchup on my eggs, which has annoyed just about every woman I've known, not that the number runs into the hundreds, or even into the tens.

I remember birthday cards with five dollar bills stuck inside, the whirl of an airplane propeller and the noise and the dust. Only much later did Mother tell me how much she hated these visits, because as nice as Grandma was to us children she was also a sort of demon woman who always had to have her own way.

She was a large woman of Swiss-German stock, with a stern look that I see now in some of the photographs. I have no trouble believing that Mother did suffer in silence for many years, though I would not have believed it at the time, when I was under the spell of this visitor from far away.

From there, it takes no big leap of the imagination to understand why my grandfather might have decided to leave one ordinary day in the fall of 1927 and vanish without a trace.

To get to the airport in those days we entered the city by way of the suburb of Calumet, riding the Chicago Skyline, crossing Calumet River and getting off on Stony Island. Somewhere along the way we passed a chemical plant that belched the foulest smelling gas I've ever smelled – the overpowering, unmistakable smell of rotten eggs.

But it was 1957. You didn't ask questions.

The congested highways, the rotten smells, the poor neighborhoods on the south side, Stony Island, Comiskey Park, Midway Airport – this was the Chicago I knew.

Standing outside the wire fence and waving good-bye to my grandmother as she climbed the steps into the plane that would

take her back to her home, in California.
  Not knowing if we would ever see her again.

Fourteen

I wonder what's left of Midway Airport. I'd like to go there and stand at the fence where I waved good-bye to my grandmother, so many years ago.

Let's do it, a voice whispers.

The Orange Line Train from the Loop would get me there and back, my pocket transit map tells me.

I'm standing at the corner of Wabash and Jackson, after dropping my package of books at the car. The train I want runs along Wabash, the east side of the loop. The nearest station is at Adams.

I continue north on Wabash, under the elevated. There is a run-down feeling to these couple of blocks, though not as extreme as I remember from the 60s.

At Adams I stop and look west, into the loop. I don't remember any of these buildings.

To get to the elevated I have to buy a token and then open a gate that leads up a flight of stairs. It is like opening a cage door.

When you're inside, can you get out again. You are in a cage. You're one of the caged.

But I'm not worried. It's still morning. Is this the way it really is. Or have I been away too long.

The train arrives as I come up the stairs to the platform. The car I enter is nearly empty.

I take a seat opposite a window with a view looking west, toward downtown. Along Jackson, behind some moderately tall buildings, looms the gigantic steel and glass Sears Tower.

Across from me, half a car down, two women sit looking at a map together. The map is spread out across both their laps. They are wearing jeans and yellow, nylon raincoats.

On the floor at their feet are two new-looking nylon backpacks.

They sit with their backs to the Sears Tower, oblivious.

They are hikers, explorers, adventurers, travelers, recently arrived in the city, getting their bearings.

The map is folded once, and shows the south side of town, from about Roosevelt south.

One of the women has her hair cut short and dyed purple. It is a cool shade of purple, with a large measure of brown.

Dark, attractive.

She wears wire framed glasses, gold tinted, and a small gold ring in one nostril. Her head is rounded in back, an impressive egg shape.

She could be a lawyer for women's causes – bright, articulate, confident.

The other woman is tiny, under five feet, and with her small, wizened face and dark curly hair could be anywhere from 40 to 70 years old.

When she sees me devouring her map, she looks my way with a friendly twinkle in her eye. She wants to say something and bring me into the discussion but decides not to.

The train stops at Roosevelt. The women whisper in the same low tones, but there is a crispness to their words now, a suggestion of some kind of disagreement that was not there before.

I can make out a word or two, just enough to guess what the argument is about. One of them wants to stop and have lunch in Chinatown, the other wants to wait until later, after they have visited a certain site on the south side.

The small woman, with a half laugh, not wanting to offend, pardons herself and says that she will throw up if she eats another bite after the breakfast they had.

The woman with the ring in her nose does not agree that it was a big breakfast, but with a sigh gives in to her friend's wishes.

The black man sitting opposite them has not heard a word of this, if you could judge by his look, nor has he so much as noticed their existence.

We fall silent for the run-up to Halsted. When the doors open and the women see the sign for Halsted, not Cermak-Chinatown, they return in some confusion to the map, necks bent, faces down, almost to the map, the rush of the hot blood of bewilderment turning their cheeks red.

I finally click on to what has happened. I sit up a little straighter, clear my throat, and point out in the softest voice that I can muster that they are on the wrong train.

This is the Orange Line, I explain, not the Red Line. We're on our way to Midway Airport.

The small woman looks at me with the same twinkle in her eye. She does not say anything.

But when I stare back she says, Shoot me dead.

I like the way she says it, drawing it out. She is good-humored, enjoys life, and likes meeting people.

The train is moving out again, toward Midway.

They are doing a tour of the States, they tell me. Their theme is the blues. The idea is to visit all the major blues centers. They've already been to New Orleans and Kansas City.

When the train stops at Ashland, they make no move to get off. They are coming with me to Midway, and whatever awaits us at Midway. They are the kind of travelers who welcome the chance encounter, who remain open to the accidental, who hear the music in the wind of fate, who embrace the unplanned, who seize the moment.

I like them already. So tell me, is the Blues still alive and well in the windy city.

It is the taller of the two women who answers, she being the more given to analysis. There's a place we really liked, she says, called the Maxwell Street market. Sunday mornings you can hear all the blues you want. Raw street blues.

We met some white guys there who were really into it. Of course, it's not the same as when the black man plays. The black man has got soul. The white man, with a few exceptions, is just on the look out for soul.

Fifteen

The next stop is Archer, halfway to where we are going. The black man gets up and moves to the front of the car, where he sits down again and arranges his long legs the same as before, taking up half the aisle.

But there's no one wanting to pass through, therefore no one that's pissed with him and ready to pick a fight.

Him and his long legs.

Not me, for sure. I'm good.

He has heard enough, no doubt, about the blues, about the black man, and about soul.

When he gets up and moves, this causes the rest of us to shut up, and to blush at the direction the conversation has taken.

It has been forty years since my grandmother died, fifty since I stood at the fence watching her plane taxi for a take-off, more than sixty since her son, my uncle Charlie, was killed in the war.

She was big, in the way German and Swiss women are big. Big arms, big bosoms, big hips. Not tall, but imposing.

In the only picture I have of her she is even shorter than I remember her. My brother and I tower over her, in jeans and white T-shirts and black and white shoes.

She is turned with her back to me, her left arm out, the elbow tucked into my midsection. The forearm and the hand are as big and strong as a man's.

I see my father's eyes in her eyes, and his nose, a big, slightly bulbous nose.

She has the frank, open, straight ahead look of a woman used to having her way. Her mouth is set and firm. No smile, no hint of a smile.

When she says something, you listen. You do what she says, or you get out of her way.

Still today, many years later, I go into the cupboard for the memory of her advice. Nine swallows of water to get rid of the hiccups.

One after the other, slowly, methodically, without breathing.

Count nine, no more, no less.

It works, not every time, as I have found over the years, but more often than not.

The thing to remember is, don't breathe.

My grandfather, the grandfather I never met, never heard

mentioned, thought he would die if he stayed another week in the same house.

His wife kept getting bigger, year after year, and he, the man of the house, kept getting smaller.

Already he was smaller than his oldest son.

He was a small, round man who made no great impact. He would walk into his own house and look around, and it was as if he were not there. The woman's voice was heard, the man's ignored.

His name was Edward Avon.

And so it happened that he began to distance himself from his wife and his children. He felt an aversion to the home and everything the home represented.

To run away, to disappear, to vanish in the morning, seemed like the easiest thing in the world to do, when it finally came down to it.

Sixteen

Through the window workmen in sheepskins and soft leather boots can be seen crossing the gleaming rails. The whistle of the locomotive tells us that we are close to the station.

The frost drives the steam down, under the windows, and between the cars. The platform comes into view, and we slow to a stop.

With the doors open wide, we sit there for a minute, then another, without moving. No one says a word.

We are not sure where we are. We are waiting for something, but we do not know what it is.

The whistle sounds again, but it is the same as before. It is possible that we might not ever leave this station.

Finally a man and a woman come aboard. They have been running, and they are out of breath.

The doors close.

This is what we have been waiting for, all along.

They find seats in the row just in front of me. Close up, through the space between the two seats, the woman seems very young, not even twenty. Her face and lips are painted to make her look older.

She's wearing a hat made of a white embroidered material that fits down tightly over her forehead and covers most of her ears. The jacket is a light yellow that makes the white of her hat even whiter and the black of her handbag even blacker.

They talk in hushed tones. I only hear part of what they say. Don't you worry now … I've got money ... When we get there ...

All the while he is talking the man is stroking the back of her hand with his elegant fingers.

And just where ....

Don't you worry now ... Leave it to me ...

She's young enough to be his daughter. They are running away together, to New Mexico, Arizona, California, Seattle. She's had to leave everything – friends, parents, belongings.

She's worried, she's scared, but it's too late. The man is calling the shots. She can't go back, because she knows she's angered too many people.

He's wearing a dark suit, with a vest and a bow tie. His thick, dark hair is parted in the middle and slicked down.

The girl takes her arm back, puts her fingers together as if she were about to pray, but instead twirls her thumbs.

With her head bent, she watches the movement of her thumbs as if she herself had no part in what her body was doing.

The man lights a pipe and sits back in the cushioned seat, content as he can be.

And what about the wife you're leaving behind, I want to ask him. What about the children. What do you think is going to happen to them, penniless, without any source of income.

So this girl is young, just thinking about her gives you a thrill.

She comes on to you like there's no tomorrow. Just how long do you think that will last.

She'll get tired of you, she'll find someone else, sooner than you imagine.

Think about your children, think how they will hate you. And your grandchildren, think about them, think about them.

I can smell the perfume the girl is wearing. It is a spicy smell, and mixed in is the faint smell of something familiar, like mint.

The neck is long and shapely. There is a brown fuzz so fine it turns the skin to gold.

I could like this girl too, given half a chance. I could run away with her too, no problem.

She can sense that I am thinking about her, falling for her, and she turns and asks me, Do you know how much longer till we get to St. Louis.

She gives the name of the town a French accent. Maybe she is French. That would explain a thing or two.

Her name, I suppose, could be Simone.

I don't think we're going to St. Louis, I explain.

Honey, didn't you tell me we were going to St. Louis, she asks her boyfriend.

He looks at me and doesn't crack a smile. I'm sure this gentleman just forgot, he says.

I think I'm on the wrong train, I say, confused. I get up and walk to the front of the car. The windows are black. It is dark out.

Where did the time go.

Where would I go, if I left home. If I walked out. What would Anne think if I were to disappear just like that.

I would say, the devil made me do it.

The devil says, Cut your ties and be free.

The devil says, I'm real too, try me if I'm not.

The devil says, So you say you love her, whatever her name is, but I tell you, love ends, the spark dies, the curtain falls.

The devil says, Forget love, forget honor, forget what's her name. Be free.

Seventeen

I am oblivious to every stop along the way until we get to Midway.

The doors open. Everyone stands up and moves out.

I find myself close behind the two women travelers. If I am disoriented, they do not seem to be.

They take me in tow. The thrill of it.

The first thing I want to see is the fence where I stood as a boy so many years ago to wave good-bye to my Grandmother.

We look and look, but sadly the fence is no more. Instead there's a row of trees – sweet gum, or sycamore.

The small woman, whose name I do not yet know, leads the way across the parking lot and into the terminal building.

Midway is a monstrously big glass box with every convenience, including, at the foot of an escalator, a Pizza Hut outlet. We find a table near the door, by a window through which we can see waves of humanity passing by.

We order three beers and a pizza big enough for four.

So come on now, the small woman says, reading my mind, you haven't told us your name. We're curious yellow.

I have no intention of lying. There's no need to lie.

It's Charles, but people who know me call me Chuck.

The three beers arrive, and we touch glasses. So tell me, Chuck. What brings you to Chicago.

I'm writing a novel about my father. Chicago is where it sort of all begins.

A novel, eh. Connie, listen to this, Chuck here is writing a novel.

Connie is lost in thought, and doesn't immediately respond.

My name is Jenn, by the way, the small woman says.

Pleased to meet you.

Connie! Are you there!

Connie frowns, leans across the table, right in my face, and almost screams at me.

So, you're writing a novel! Congratulations! Half the people I know, back in good old Canada, are writing a novel. It's the national pastime.

Connie's jealous because she's been wanting to write a novel but can't find the time, Jenn says.

It's not time I lack, alack, it's finding something worth

saying.

There she goes again, putting herself down.

I am not. Connie sits back, closes her eyes, bounces her head to the left and right, hums to the music in her head, and disappears again into her own space.

The little woman is sitting right next to me, on the same bench. She leans a little closer, folds her hands, and looks at me with that twinkle I like so much.

I can feel another question coming on. How does Chicago figure into it.

My father's father worked for a railroad company and had an office in Chicago. He would come home on weekends. This was in the 20s. One day he just disappeared. No one ever found out what happened.

Order number sixty-four, a loud voice calls out.

That's the number of cards in the I Ching, Connie says, making a noise with her chair as she gets up.

They're not cards, Jenn says.

You know, Jenn, sometimes I just hate you.

Let me pay for this, I volunteer, reaching for my billfold.

This is on me, Connie says, moving off.

Jenn takes a sip of beer and wipes the foam from her tight, wrinkled upper lip with the back of her thumb. What about your father. How did he take it.

I don't remember him ever saying much to me when I was growing up. He never took me aside and talked with me. He never showed his feelings. Maybe he didn't have any feelings. My sister remembers him getting angry. Maybe anger was the only thing he felt.

Maybe you've just forgotten. Maybe you need to sit down some day and go deep into your own feelings and memories.

You could be right.

Connie returns with the order of pizza and we dig in.

The more I eat, the better I feel. I must have been starving.

As long as I'm telling lies, I might as well tell a big one. He turns ninety this year. I figure this may be the last time I see him.

Are you planning anything special. If my father were still alive and ninety, I'd take him on a big trip somewhere.

I was thinking about a trip to Hawaii. He's never been to Hawaii.

We went to Hawaii once, a long time ago. Connie stuffs an

extra-large bite into her mouth, mumbling a follow-up that I can't decipher.

The conversation flags, and when we have finished the pizza, I'm ready to disappear. I think I'll see if I can find a men's room.

I slide out from behind the table, give a sort of half-hearted wave, and walk out of the restaurant, to lose myself in the crowd that's passing by.

Eighteen

You catch a train downtown and get off at Lasalle. You walk south to Harrison, where you have left your car.

You are thinking about something else – the blues and the way the blues can lift you up when you're down – and you walk past the parking garage, all the way to South Wabash, before you realize where you are.

You go down the steps to the basement of the garage. The floor is dirty and slippery with grease. There's a feeling of unease that you remember from a few hours ago, and from long ago.

What brings you to this strange, dark, damp place where you have such a strange feeling of déjà vu.

You hear a thumping in your chest, and you know that someone, somewhere, is dying, at this moment.

Someone you know.

You get in the car and exit the garage.

You drive south on Clark. The clock tower at the Dearborn Station looms large.

You turn left on Polk, caught in the flow of traffic.

You stop less than half a block from the Dearborn Station clock tower. There's something here you want to see. To remember.

You've been here before.

The tower is ten stories high, or eleven. It dominates an area of several square blocks.

Like the building below, the tower is made of a dark red brick, almost brown, and has the feeling of something heavy and unyielding.

Looking up through the front windshield of the car you can see the top of the tower and the old-fashioned, Victorian design framing the modern clock.

The clock says five minutes before two.

You sit here a few minutes, near the building where your grandfather had his office, and where he was last seen by his family, eighty years ago.

Is it the same building it was then. Is it a different building.

In 1922 a fire destroyed much of the tower, according to what you've read in various travel guides and history books. Before the fire the tower was Romanesque, with the bottom sections made of pink granite. The top was steeply slanting.

1922 is two years before your grandfather first came to Chicago to work.

You try to imagine what it was like, in those years.

You follow the movement of sunlight across the face of the granite. In the light it is pink. Where it is in shadow it is a deeper color, dark red, and dull.

Traffic rushes by your open window. People are leaving town. You too will be leaving, soon.

This knowledge brings with it a sweet feeling, like drums playing softly in the distance.

What is it about leaving that you like so much.

You start something, you live with it awhile, and you take your leave. There's a beginning, a middle, and an end.

There's an inevitability to things and you can say in good conscience, That's the way it is.

When you were young it was always home you were leaving and coming back to.

Later, it was school, job, marriage.

You leave everything and you start over again. There is a joy in that.

At the age of four you ran away from home for the first time, with a boy a year or two older whose main purpose, it turned out, was to get inside the dime store and fill his pockets with as many goodies as time and daring allowed.

Candy bars, baseball cards, bags of marbles, whatever he could get his hands on.

You could not see anything you wanted, even when prodded by your friend.

This was not your idea of an adventure. You did not like the feel of it. Something in you turned against him.

You made your way up a set of stairs to a mezzanine where you found a man sitting at a desk in a little room.

It was very late when you got home. Maybe ten thirty. The radio was playing music you had never heard before.

You sat at the table with a glass of hot chocolate. People came and went, speaking in whispers. If your parents were angry with you, you do not remember it.

You are good at not remembering.

Everything you need to know about yourself happens before the age of six, someone once said.

In your case it was not talking until you were three and

running away from home when you were four.

One way to write the story of your life would be to talk about the times you have left and gone away.

Another way would be to write about everything you have forgotten over the years and only now, dimly, begin to remember.

Still another way would be to acknowledge everything you have done wrong and imagine doing it over again, differently.

Father dies, you lose interest in school and drop out.

Mother dies, you leave your wife of eighteen years and start a new life, in reduced circumstances, and you elevate it by calling it your hard-won freedom.

Your brother dies, you leave your girl friend of five years, you move to another town, where you know no one.

You meet Anne, you fall in love, you have no intention of leaving her, she is the love of your life, there's no need to say anything else.

There's a pattern to this.

Something happens, something grand, like a death. It has to be grand, a sorrow too deep for words. She will die, you will die, one of your children, God forbid, will die.

Oh, to walk in the cemetery, the rain falling lightly on your head, and to feel that you have lost everything. Can there be a moment more to be desired.

Tears fall like rain, something in you breaks, you are washed clean, you are new again.

It is 1924. Your father is sixteen years old. He waits under the awning, while his own father, Edward Avon, speaks to a man in a taxi.

He admires his father's confident manner. There is a liveliness to his voice, an edge, that he does not have at home.

He is a different man in Chicago.

At home he is quiet. He keeps his thoughts to himself. You never know what he's thinking.

Here, when he talks, people listen. His words have weight.

The man in the taxi accepts his right to speak as long as he wants.

His son, your father, feels proud of him for one of the few times in his life. The feeling runs so deep that tears come to his eyes.

He could stand under the awning, in front of the newly rebuilt Dearborn Station, without moving, forever.

The taxi moves away, around a corner.

A black woman in a flowery dress steps back up onto the curb, to avoid being hit by the taxi.

Her face does not show anger or pain, but indifference.

Nineteen

You want to get moving, you want to get out of Chicago, you want to leave this city, you want to beat the rush hour, you want to find the shortest, fastest way home.

You drive east to Lake Shore Drive, then south to 55th Street. You take Stony Island to the Skyway. You avoid the Dan Ryan like the plague.

The Skyway gets you across the border into Indiana with little delay.

You breathe differently, once you cross the border.

You relax your grip on the wheel. You feel you are in familiar territory.

Images wash over you – faces long forgot, names of those you once knew so well, and loved.

You ask yourself, where are they now.

The traffic thins.

You are driving through farmland. Corn stubble dots the land. Farmhouses with trees in front – oak, maple, or chestnut – and a row of junipers to one side.

Aluminum sided barns.

You feel the open road under your feet. You see the trees on the banks of the Wabash flying by. You smell the dark earth:

You stop the car and get out and walk into a field of hay that is newly cut and fresh.

You stretch out on the ground and cover yourself in the hay. You listen to the silence of the field. You sleep and dream and when you wake you do not know where you are.

The leaves on the trees surprise you. It's April, but already everything is green.

Spring comes late where you live.

In the car you search the radio for some music to listen to. You look for classical music and find instead a jazz station.

Someone is playing an extended bass solo. The fingering is so clean, powerful, and melodious that you marvel at it.

You melt into the wheel. The rhythm drives right down through you to where you are sitting, right down through the hole in your ass.

You have not felt this good in weeks. You are at one with the car. There is no danger. Nothing can go wrong.

You are moving along at sixty miles an hour, it's so easy,

sixty-five, it's a breeze, seventy, it's the right speed.

It's no speed at all. It's standing still.

You could go on like this for hours. You have lost track of time. What does time matter.

Mt. Ayr, Rensselaer, Remington, Monon – these names grow ever more familiar. You are on track for re-entry. You are more than halfway there.

At Remington, where Highway 24 intersects, you pull into a truck stop. You find a self-service pump. You fill the tank with gas and go inside to pay.

The line-up is five deep at both registers. You drift away, into another part of the store, looking for nothing in particular.

Everywhere you go you bump into people, in the aisles with bags of potato chips in their arms, at the rack of magazines flipping the pages to catch a glimpse of a favorite celebrity, by the entrance into the dining room, in the hallway in the back waiting for a telephone.

Everyone seems larger than life, taller and heavier than any people you've seen in years.

Your head swims. You feel faint.

Two men in overalls are talking about the local basketball tournament. One of them raves on about 'them Fowler boys.'

You stand idly by a coffee machine, listening to the men talk, remembering the tone of voice and the accent.

Showed that Jeff a thing or two, the second man says.

You push a button for something called French vanilla, which turns out to taste like hot chocolate, with foam on top.

The line-up is now six deep. There's nothing to do except wait your turn.

You yawn, close your eyes, and wait. It takes forever.

When it is time you leave behind a dollar in change and hurry back to the car.

You circle around the island of pumps, down a hill toward the secondary road that will take you back onto the main highway.

On the other side of the parking area, away from the pumps and the restaurant, you drive close to a newly landscaped area, where the grass is cut close to the ground.

Rust-colored rocks are placed carefully on a bed of mulch. Nasturtiums grow among the rocks.

The approach of your car disturbs a cat that's been hiding among the rocks. It is a large cat, and has an unusual color – a light blue, almost white. The blue is so hard to see it could be a trick of the eyes.

You stop the car and get out.

The cat does not like being looked at. It begins to move away, down the hill toward the road.

It seems more afraid of you than the approaching car. Before you can do anything it crosses into the pathway of the car.

It's not moving fast but fast enough to hit the cat before it can jump away. If the cat is hurt, it does not show it.

The impact knocks it off balance, even lifts it into the air. It lands on its feet, jumps once more, as if to try out its legs, and goes on across the paved road, up a dirt road that cuts through farmland on the opposite side.

Above, on the side of a hill, are a few houses that suggest the suburb of a nearby city. After a moment's hesitation, the car that hit the cat continues on its way.

You cross the street and go looking for the cat. If it is hurt, it will need looking after.

Ahead of you, a hundred yards up the hill, maybe two hundred, the cat is digging its way under a fence, into an adjacent field.

You go round the end of the fence, an old-fashioned wooden fence, into a field that is freshly ploughed and ready for planting.

When you look up you see a dog coming down the hill toward you – a large black dog, sleek and hungry looking.

You have no idea if it is friendly or not. You could be trespassing. You could be in danger.

You scramble back through the fence to the dirt road.

Coming down the road toward you are two girls, on their way home from school, each with a nylon backpack on her back. Tall, athletic girls, with broad, square shoulders.

Middle distance runners, high jumpers, or basketball players.

You're not shy. Your mission is a legitimate one. There can be no mistaking your intentions. There is little chance you will call down this one's scorn or that one's wrath upon your head, just because you want to stop them and talk with them.

You wait for them as they approach. You focus all your attention on the tall dark-haired girl. All your longing.

You're amazed when she returns your look without blinking or turning away.

She gets taller and taller as she approaches. In fact she comes within an inch or two of your own height, at six feet two.

Her dark brown hair, cut short so that it doesn't quite touch her shoulders, has a hint of red in it.

You have the sense, fleeting though it is, that the other girl is just as attractive, but you cannot take your eyes off this one.

This one you could fall for.

There's a moment's awkwardness, while the two girls wait for you to explain yourself.

When you tell them you're looking for a cat that lives around here, which you believe may have been injured in a car accident, your words come out sounding false, made up, fishy.

The tall girl shakes her head. There's a twinkle of amusement in her eyes.

What's this you're trying to pull, her eyes say.

They are not the piercing blue that you might have expected, but a sort of blue-green like the sea when you are standing on a high cliff, the pupils wider and blacker than normal at mid-day.

Is there anything we can do for you, she asks.

If you could tell me where the cat lives, I could go round and talk with the owner. It was a blue cat, a most unusual blue. Maybe you know the one I'm talking about.

The two girls confer with each other. They giggle. They laugh.

One girl whispers into the other's ear. They're making fun of the man, any man who would come lumbering up the hill looking for a blue cat. It's such a pathetic story.

But you wait. You're in no hurry. You're not going anywhere.

You're glad to be on the same road as the two girls. In the same scene. In the same conversation.

The one who talks now, though, is the smaller one, the darker one. Her lips are colored a dark red, so dark it is almost black. Her skin is clear, smooth, and very light, without a blemish. Her eyes are so clear and so penetrating that you cannot look at her.

She is the one with the blue eyes. You don't know this until the moment she begins to speak.

You go up the hill another quarter mile, she says, then take a left on Henry Street. The address is 125 Henry. It's a blue house with a lilac bush in front. The man lives there with his wife and his son who's older than we are and we really don't know why he's still living there.

A blue man lives in a blue house with a blue cat. The next

thing she'll tell you is that he owns a blue guitar.

You'll believe it when you hear it.

You say thanks, and the two girls move on down the hill.

You want to call after them and keep them awhile longer. But you are struck dumb, and you realize that the problem is that the tall girl reminds you of your daughter.

You never know what to say to your daughter.

They skip along, and in a moment they're both gone down the hill and out of sight.

You know you can't follow them. You know nothing good could come of that.

Twenty

The house at 125 Henry Street is small, one story with a steep roof to keep off the snow. Indeed, as the girls said, it is blue.

But small, too small to be impressive, or anything like impressive. There is space for a man and a cat, maybe a wife – a small, unassuming wife. Little else.

Whoever lives here lives in a subjunctive sort of mood.

You knock at the door. When there is no answer you turn the knob. It's unlocked. You open the door and go inside.

The front room, to the right, is small, with a sofa facing the window, an India rubber plant in a big pot on the floor at the end of the sofa, and a small television set on a round table in the corner by the window.

You go through a dark hall, to the kitchen in back.

There's a bare light bulb in a fixture that hangs down about a foot from the ceiling.

At the table under the light a man sits alone, his eyes downcast, waiting. To one side is a bowl of soup that he hasn't touched. Someone has put it there and told him to eat, but he is not hungry.

On the table in front of him is a pocket novel, which he closes and covers with his hand when he notices you enter.

He is a large man, with the large, rough hands of a fisherman, a logger, a cattle herder, a plumber.

He lifts the book in the palm of his hand and holds it out to you, like an offering.

He holds it so you can see the illustration on the front cover. It shows a forty-year-old bearded man in a pull-down hat leading a pack mule through scrub hills.

The title says Tappan's Burro and Other Stories.

The author, in big red letters, is Zane Grey.

He opens it somewhere in the middle, and reads to himself, his lips moving.

Read it out loud, you whisper.

To your surprise he obliges.

There's something so clear and sweet in his voice, you would like it to last as long as possible.

It's not a rough or deep voice as you might have expected from such a large man. Not a mean voice, but gentle.

These are the words he reads, the words that bring

inexplicable tears to your eyes:

> Sunset - it was the hour of Yaqui's watch.
> Chief of a driven remnant of the once mighty tribe,
> He trusted no sentinel so well as himself
>   at the end of the day's march.
> While his braves unpacked the tired horses,
> And his women prepared the evening meal,
> And his bronze-skinned children played in the sand,
> Yaqui watched the bold desert horizon.

You want him to continue. Go on, you say.

But your voice is harsher than before.

He stops reading. He lets the book drop.

From a little room behind the kitchen you can hear the very faint sound of a radio.

This goes on for a few seconds, then the man says loudly, but not harshly, Will you turn that down.

He turns the whole upper part of his body in the direction of the doorway.

A voice from the other room calls out, Is Mom home yet.

She's next door, visiting.

It's her birthday tomorrow, and I'll bet Charlie won't even remember.

Let Charlie alone.

The man gets up from the table as he says this and goes to the sink.

I'm just saying it, the voice tails away.

The man fills a glass with cold tap water. He takes one sip then puts the glass down.

He stands there with his back to the door, the picture of weariness. A minute passes.

There's silence, then -

Then a young man enters the kitchen from a back room. He wears the uniform of the day – yellow cords and white T-Shirt, a package of cigarettes tucked under one sleeve.

He's excited because he's heading out to meet a girl. He's going to take her to a dance. Her name is Judy.

He pauses a moment. The man still has not turned around.

Do you need anything, he asks.

Do I look like I need something.

I was just asking.

He comes through the doorway where you're standing, brushes past you, and hurries down the hallway and out the door.

The old man is alone. He takes the pocket book from the table and shuffles past you, into the hall. He turns left, into the living room.

He does not see you, either because he is blind or you are invisible.

You follow along, into the living room. You might as well be invisible.

If anyone is living here, it's a sort of hell he is living, as he waits for someone to appear who will never appear.

In his heart there is love, that is what you do not yet understand, and maybe never will.

He still scares you after all these years. This colors everything you say.

Enter into the old man's life.

He is the father, you are the son. The prodigal son. The son who went away and returned one day, his pockets as empty as ever.

He is dying of cancer, and he is waiting for his son who went away to return home. But this son, being the jerk that he is, arrives too late.

He takes his time, he thumbs a ride, he stops along the way, he arrives too late.

The other son, the son who stayed behind, loves the father but the father does not love him, not as much, not enough. They make the best of an unhappy situation.

The old man turns on the television. The screen shows a test pattern. He turns it off again.

What time of day is it. What year.

He sits down on the sofa. He opens the book on his lap, but is too tired to read.

He flips through the pages, from back to front, slowly, absently.

He puts the book aside, on the sofa next to him. He closes his eyes.

Slowly he raises and lowers his hands, lightly hitting the back of the hands to his thighs.

The pain is in the gut, so deep in the gut that nothing but rocking back and forth and steady rhythm helps very much.

The needle helps too, the drugs, the painkillers, when the woman gives it to him.

He keeps telling her he would like more, but she never listens. Maybe she listens, maybe she does not.

She does not give him what he wants. She does not kill him, as he asks her to, with his yes.

One day she will do it, you know she will, you have faith in her.

He sits alone in the dark room, rocking slowly back and forth, slapping his thighs with the backs of his hands.

He has nothing much to say, nothing much to do.

You are not afraid of him now, because you know that his days are numbered. He is mortal like the rest of them.

He is not a god.

He has lost his voice. He has lost his power. He cannot hurt you anymore.

You can leave, there is nothing holding you. You can stay, there is no one telling you to go.

I'll be leaving now, you call out. He comes to the hallway door to say good-bye.

You shake his poor hand, weak now because of his illness, the back of it crisscrossed with puffed up, blue veins.

I hope you'll be feeling better if I see you again, you say.

Why did you say *if*, you ask yourself, when you meant to say *when*. Or did you.

He stares at you. He wants to say something. He has such a sad, tired look, you want to cry.

You do not cry.

He's in trouble. He's lost his way.

If he thinks you can be of any help, he had better think again, because the truth is you cannot.

I'll stop again on my way back through, you promise.

His look tells you that he does not believe you.

Twenty-One

I'm driving south to meet my brother, who lives in a little college town between Lafayette and Indianapolis.

First I'll stop in Lafayette, our boyhood home, explore some places I used to know, look up some people I have not seen in ages. Maybe spend a day or two.

It's just after five. I'm on the outskirts of Lafayette.

First I'll give Anne a call. I'd like to hear her voice.

She is so far away. Canada is so far away.

Canada is a strange land, some towns and a few cities scattered across an otherwise unsettled land. The long, hard winters. The farther north you go the harder they get. The people bright, generous, modest to a fault, more kind than most.

It is the best of places and the worst of places. One day it feels like home, the next it doesn't.

You know what I love about you, Anne told me not too long ago. It's that you're impulsive, you're a little crazy. You're a cultured man who does crazy things. You're intelligent, you think things through, you plan everything down to the last detail, but you make sudden decisions that have nothing to do with logic, just instinct.

Call it instinct, call it a gut feeling. There's logic in that too. Everything I do has a sort of logic to it.

You won't do something crazy and suddenly drop me.

Not too likely. I'd be lost without you.

Because I think I would die.

You mean the world to me. You are my beginning and my end.

I don't like the sound of that word *end*. I don't like the way you say it.

The new highway – new to me – takes me farther away from the city than the old by-pass 52. For a moment it seems that I've driven past the city without seeing it. Without stopping.

Then I see a sign for Battle Ground National Historic Site. I have a chance to regain my bearings.

I know Battle Ground well. I lived here from the time I was six to the time I was twelve. I played in the fields. I climbed the hills. I walked the back roads. I swam in the creeks. I fished in the rivers.

I'll get off here. I'll go back in time. I'll see if I can

remember the way it was.

A place to stay, a bite to eat, give Anne a call, in that order, that's the plan.

Or was it the other way around.

Up ahead is a stop sign. The road comes to a T. I look left, toward Battle Ground. I look right, toward Lafayette.

I have a choice to make. I can remember names, dates, places, facts, surface features. Or I can remember the way it felt.

It was along the back road into Battle Ground that my best friend lived, a boy named Steve Ludlum.

We were in the same classroom for more than a year before we became friends, then there was nothing that could separate us.

I was often at his house, sometimes overnight. The house was on a hill above the road, surrounded by trees, some with swings tied with thick rope to the lower limbs.

If we wanted we could hang there upside down and see the girls in the window, his sister and her friends.

Behind the house was a barn, beyond the barn many acres of woods and fields. There was one field we loved because it was perfect for playing baseball.

The ground was level but rough. The ball would bounce every which way. We welcomed the tricks it played, the smell of the grass, the smell of horse manure.

Sometimes it was just the two of us, sometimes others joined in. We had balls, sometimes big fat softballs, sometimes old, scruffy, torn hardballs.

We had bats with grips almost too big to get your hands around, bats with grips as small as the handle of an axe.

We had mitts, catcher's mitts, old gloves, torn in places, not much better than rags, but good enough to be chasing fly balls, pop outs, grounders, good enough to be chasing our dreams, good enough to make us believe that some day one of us would make the big leagues.

The beauty of friendship is that it dissolves all previous attachments. When I was with Steve I belonged to him and no one else.

We spent hours exploring his large, three-story house. There were rooms I'm sure I never discovered, behind locked doors, up secret stairways.

The downstairs rooms and the front hallway were painted a light color, a creamy off-white. You always felt the sun was shining in even when it was dark and rainy outside.

There was a piano in the living room, a plant shaped like a palm tree on the floor in the corner, a sense of calm.

His mother was a tall, sturdy woman who loved to talk. She was intelligent, knowledgeable, interested in school, sports, politics – anything and everything.

I loved listening to Steve play the piano. Afterwards we'd turn on the radio and listen to the baseball game. We'd hold our breath if our team, the White Sox, were down a run and needed a hit. We thought we could make it go one way or the other by what we did or did not do, by what we said or did not say.

If we held our breath, if we stopped breathing, we could change the course of the game. In our imaginations we could make it happen.

In the farmhouse along the back road out of Battle Ground, Indiana, in our isolation, we believed in the power of the mind to make things happen at great distances, to move mountains if necessary. To win baseball games, at least.

Steve's father was sometimes late getting home. He'd call and say he had work to do at the office. He was involved in some sort of research project at the university, in the field of cross pollination.

Steve did not want to talk about it. He'd fly off the handle if I asked him. His mother would call me into the kitchen. She'd give me little jobs to do – peel the potatoes, cut the carrots, stir the pot of beans.

She made me feel at home. She liked talking with me. Did I have a girlfriend. Did I like school. Did I have any idea what I wanted to do with my life.

After supper I'd follow Steve to his room. We'd sit on the bed looking at his collection of baseball cards. He'd lie on the floor with a comic book, the comic over his head like the wing of a plane he was clutching to.

Being inside Steve's room I was inside his world. I could feel what he was feeling. I could see what he was seeing, the visible world, as well as the invisible world.

From the ceiling hung dozens of model airplanes he had built himself. The walls were lined with shelves of books on military and astronomical topics. His dresser was filled with shirts, socks, underwear, all neatly folded.

His closet held everything else, everything he didn't know

what to do with, not just pants and shirts and jackets, but stacks of comic books on the floor, baseball bats and mitts piled in a corner, a monopoly board, an erector set, basketballs and footballs on the shelf above the jackets, a model train and enough track in a box to make an oval eight feet long.

The fact that often his father did not come home in time for supper he stuffed inside this closet too.

Sometimes Steve would stop at my house but not often. My friends in town were too rough for his liking. We boxed, we wrestled, we played practical jokes, we teased one another, we liked guns, cap guns and BB guns, rifles, we took pride in showing no mercy.

Sometimes, though, on his way to school he'd stop by and we'd play basketball in the lot behind my house, just the two of us, on the hard, bare earth. We'd go on playing even when it turned to mud in the morning sun.

If others came around and wanted to play, if a boy thought it would be fun to tease Steve and push him around, just because he was a little different, I stood up for him.

I was big for my age, not much of a fighter, but enough of a presence to make a difference.

One morning another boy pushed Steve from behind and he went flying headfirst into the tree where the basket was nailed.

He lay crumpled on the ground, touching his hair where it was wet. He looked at his fingertips. He licked the blood.

Roy, the boy who pushed him, was new to town. On weekends he'd go with his father and we wouldn't see him again until Monday morning at school.

I liked to play at his house, which was across the street from where I lived, because his mother played a kind of music that we couldn't hear any other place and because she loved animals and kept a dog and several cats in the house and rabbits in a pen made of chicken wire in the back yard, complete with a little hut where they could sleep.

He was a fat boy who was usually very quiet and kept to himself but when Steve called him a motherfucker his blood boiled and he hit Steve in the stomach and knocked the wind out of him. Then he hit him again, in the head.

He kept saying, you fag, you fag. Nobody knew what 'fag' meant, but it must have been something very bad the way he spit it out.

To make him stop I tripped him and knocked his feet out from under him. When he fell he broke his glasses. Pieces of glass got in his eye.

There was blood under the eye where the skin was cut. My mother, when she came out to see what was happening, said that we had to get him to emergency right away.

Steve and I stayed in the car while my mother took Roy inside to be looked after. Steve started playing with himself and asked me if I ever did. I said no, I don't know what you're talking about.

I'll show you, he said. He wanted me to feel it. I said no. He inched forward on the seat. I said no.

I was watching the door to see when my mother would come out. Come on, be a buddy, he said.

You'll go blind if you do that, I said.

I bet I know who told you that, he said.

No you don't, I said.

He made a little, high-pitched noise, like a cat when it knows it's dying. I couldn't move.

My mother tapped on the window. I got out.

She told me that Roy would have to stay in hospital and have an operation. There was some thought that he might lose the sight in one eye. What I had done was wrong. I should feel guilty.

But I did not feel guilty. I did not feel anything.

Twenty-Two

Steve was a serious boy, a quiet boy, an outsider, mature beyond his years. He could have been a teacher, a doctor, a writer. I loved him as well as I ever loved anyone.

One morning he got it into his head to skip school and ride his bike into town, something he had never done before.

When he reached the end of the road, where it intersected Highway 43 into Lafayette, he stopped and waited for the traffic to pass. My father, on his way home from work, signaled that he was going to turn onto the road where Steve was waiting.

Steve started across the highway. Because he was looking at my father, he did not see the big blue car with white fins coming down the hill in the other direction.

Something got into his head – some thought of what he was fleeing, some idea of what was waiting for him in town, or some vision of a creature running in the woods by the side of the road.

Whatever it was, he stood his bike on one wheel and let out a war cry, enough to spook the driver of the big blue car, who instead of slowing seemed to hit the accelerator.

Father saw what was happening and he did nothing. There wasn't time. It happened too fast.

The car hit the bicycle from behind. Steve hit the windshield, bounced off, and flew into the middle of the highway where he was hit again by another car coming the other way.

My father could remember very little of what happened, he said. He could remember standing at the bottom of the hill, with his hand up to stop traffic. He could remember thinking that if he could just make the traffic stop the boy would be all right.

He could remember turning and seeing four or five or six people standing where the boy must have fallen. He could remember seeing a man removing his coat and covering the boy.

He could not remember tears in his eyes, or feeling sad, or feeling anything. How strange, he thought.

It seemed like a very long time before a police car came, then an ambulance. Traffic in both directions was stopped.

My father waited by his truck until a policeman came over to question him. The ambulance sped away, and traffic began moving again.

My father did not want supper. He sat in the easy-boy in the living room, his arms crossed on his belly, waiting for me to get home.

No one said a word when I came in. No one looked at me. It could have been any other day, marked by long intervals of silence, with no words exchanged, no feelings, no information.

I went upstairs to wash up. I had dirt under the nails, grass stains on the palms of the hands, and both elbows scraped and oozing blood, from crawling under bushes, scaling fences, climbing trees.

I went into my room to change. I could hear them whispering. When I came down the stairs, my mother was sitting on the couch, her lips pressed tight.

Tell him, she said.

He moved his head side to side, as if warding off waves of insects attacking his eyes, ears, and mouth.

I knew him first and foremost, if not exclusively, as someone to be feared. How odd it seemed that he had such trouble finding words to tell me what he had seen.

I'm very sorry, he said.

I had no idea what he was talking about. Words tumbled out that made no sense.

You should be glad you weren't there.

He had no business telling me things I didn't want to hear.

I wanted to go back upstairs. I wanted to run outside. I wanted to climb to the top of my favorite tree. It was so high up, my tree, no one could see me.

I wanted to make time run backward.

My mother, taking pity on him, broke in to say that there had been an accident, and my friend Steve had been killed. Where he was vague, she was clear and forthright.

I didn't know what 'killed' could possibly mean in connection with my friend Steve.

Killed was something that happened to frogs if you shot them, or dogs if they ran under the wheels of a car, or groundhogs if you covered up their hole, or rabbits if you trapped them.

Can I see him, I said, thinking he was in hospital somewhere. At worst he had a broken leg. I'd write something on his cast and we'd laugh about it.

Steve is dead, my mother said, a sharpness in her voice because she could see that I was confused.

I don't care if he's dead, I want to see him, I blubbered.

Talk sense for once, why don't you, my father glared at me.

What do you want me to say. What do you want me to say.

I give up. With this he walked out of the room, his duty, apparently, discharged.

Not once during this exchange did I feel close to him. Not once did he make more than the feeblest of efforts to draw me close to him.

If this was a play where was the hurrah.

If this was a dance where was the uplift.

If this was a poem where was the music.

Twenty-Three

It's getting dark. You drive west, along the back road toward Lafayette, where there's more chance of finding a place to stay.

As you ease your way along you see a car in the ditch, on the other side of the road. You slow your own vehicle, stop, and get out.

The car is at the bottom of the ditch. The driver, a woman, stands by the side of the car. She seems unhurt.

You go down into the ditch to where she is standing. She looks at you but it's as if she doesn't see you.

She's a short woman, an inch or two over five feet, at most. You wonder how she can drive at all, how she can see out the window.

Because of her freckled face and her red hair she looks younger than she probably is. You ask her if she's all right.

She looks at you again with her green eyes, as if she were looking through you. You are surprised at the cold, steady gaze after what she has just gone through.

But, when you think about it, you admit that you do not know what she has just gone through. Maybe it was nothing. A tire blew and when she pulled over to the side of the road she lost control and rolled down the embankment to a stop.

She got out, and waited for help. You happened to come along.

She's well dressed, in a lime-colored pants suit. She works for a company in town, you surmise – a wellness clinic, the Admissions Office at the University, an investment banking firm, Avis Rent-A-Car.

She's waiting for the police, an ambulance, a friend, a colleague, a company car. She turns her back to you, because, it's clear, you have nothing to offer.

This feels like something that happened a very long time ago.

The car is a red Neon, and from what you can see there's no damage done. All four tires are intact.

Maybe she fell asleep at the wheel. Maybe another car cut in front of her and she swerved to avoid a collision.

You climb back up the embankment, and she follows. You offer to give her a drive into town if she wants.

There's something about the spot where she's standing that she likes. She's in no hurry to move away.

I'll wait right here if you don't mind, she says and gives you the once over lightly.

You don't know why you should mind but you do. The more you talk, the more agitated she gets.

She lifts the glossy red leather bag that she is carrying and readjusts it on her shoulder. There is a pad in the shoulder of her jacket that takes the weight of the leather strap.

You stare at the extra-wide lapels of her suit jacket. You press the heel of your hand into one eye then into the other.

They itch. They sting. They're dry. They're red. They're half-closed. Everything is blurry.

That's fine with me, you reply tardily.

She's upset because she thinks she's ruined her pants. Shit! Shit! Shit! She keeps saying because she's spotted a half-inch tear at the knee, where she must have fallen getting out of the car.

She takes several quick swipes at it with her hand, thinking at first that it's a piece of dirt or a fly.

Stupidly you mumble that you are sorry, as if you were to blame. She looks at you again, more closely this time, trying to decide if she should waste her breath talking to you.

Are you a complete idiot.

Five minutes pass, while you wait for help to arrive.

You make a remark about her pants suit.

There's nothing synthetic here, she says. Feel for yourself.

She holds her arm out and lets you touch the sleeve of the jacket. It feels like material of the highest quality – some sort of linen, not some cheap imitation.

She explains that today was supposed to be a wonderful day for 'yours truly.' She was guest speaker at a downtown business conference on 'New Styles in Leadership.'

The room was packed and she could hear the buzz of excitement the moment she stepped out of the elevator. Someone greeted her and ushered her into the room.

But the shocker was, in the front row, sitting as quiet and pretty as she could be, was a woman, a little mouse of a woman, much younger and slimmer of course, wearing the exact same lime-green pants suit.

It serves me right. I wanted to kill myself right there and then. Pull the trigger and blow my brains out. But it was too late. Fatso had hold of my elbow, and she was leading me up to the stage. What could I do.

But when she introduced me, she couldn't even get my name right. She called me Marie. Fuck Marie.

But I've got to get up there and deliver the goddamn goods. I don't even know what I said, I was so furious. I'm sure it was horrible.

She's been drinking, you can tell from the smell of whiskey on her breath. She's a drinker.

Most likely theory is, she was drunk and drove her car into a ditch. She didn't kill herself but maybe she wanted to.

She is older than you thought. There are deep, permanent lines at the corners of her eyes that speak of loss, heartbreak. Sad.

You say the first thing that comes to mind.

I don't know, I suppose some things happen for no reason at all, except maybe just to test us.

She laughs. Right.

You tell her that she reminds you of a girl you used to know.

You kill me, she says, and she turns her back to you.

She's no longer interested in continuing a conversation that is going nowhere.

You let your fingers play over the front of your shirt, over the medal that Anne wanted you to wear – the war medal that belonged to the uncle after whom you were named.

You let your fingers feel the hard bone above the medal, feel the fat of the chest to the left and to the right, feel how the medal fits in the hollow of the chest.

You press it hard into the hollow of the chest.

Some distance away, on the road leading out of Lafayette, you see a police car coming toward the scene of the accident. It's moving at high speed, lights flashing. Red and blue.

You're finished here. You have nothing more to do here – nothing more to say. The woman is unhurt. She's okay, drunk, unhinged but basically – okay.

You did not see the accident. You were not a witness. You know nothing. You have nothing to report. It's time to get going, time to get a move on, time to get out of here.

There is one thing you'd like to know – her name. But it's too late now. She's walking away, up the road toward the police car, that's coming closer and closer.

You cross the pavement, climb in behind the wheel, start your car, shift into gear, inch away.

It's possible you knew her in high school. You had a

girlfriend she reminds you of. It was a long time ago.
  You can't trust your memory.
  There's no reason you should.
  No reason anyone should.
  Beyond the question of trust is the question of, of, of, of.

Twenty-Four

I'm looking for a motel. Nothing fancy – a bed, a bathroom, a cup of coffee in the morning when I wake up.

I'm traveling west on Highway 26, approaching I-65. I come upon several motels very close together.

Comfort Suites is full, but the big sign in front of the Knight's Inn says 'Vacancy' under the logo. I'm in luck.

Under vacancy it says 'All rooms on the first floor, free coffee, free cable, free local calls.'

I pull in here and go inside. There's a young woman sitting at a desk behind the counter, reading a book.

I'm able to make out one word in the title before she puts the book down. The word is 'Religion.' The next word is 'and.'

She comes out from behind the desk, and gives me a big smile. She's glad to take a break from her reading.

She's wearing a long, flowery, loose-fitting dress with a lot of blue in it – a dress more suitable for a dinner out than for a job as clerk at a motel.

Still looking at me with her brown eyes, she puts her hands on her hips and leans back, flexing her back. She's stiff, she explains, sitting too long without moving.

The last thing I notice, after the smile, after the dress, after the color of her eyes, is the pair of glasses she's wearing – small round glasses in wire frames.

I mention the sign that says that all rooms are on the first floor, then add the line I've been rehearsing. I can believe that quite easily, given the fact that there is only one floor.

I've been wanting to do something about that sign, she says, believe me. The reason it's that way is that we have to keep it the same as in the tour book. It's the company's sort of claim to fame.

She winces, and something between a sigh and a cry comes softly from her lips. She lifts one shoulder then the other, then repeats this rolling sort of motion while looking at me.

This seems too private a moment. I don't know what to say. I should leave. I don't move. She has me in a sort of spell.

I've got a really sore back today, she confesses. My chiropractor says the trouble starts when I wake up – even before I wake up. The spine is slightly out of line. Everything I do seems to throw it off a bit more.

Do you have a program of exercises. I can't believe how

practical minded I am all of a sudden.

I do a lot of stretching when I get up in the morning. But I guess the muscles are still weak. She takes her glasses off, looks at me, puts them on again.

I do an exercise called the Cobra that I recommend. You can find it in any book on yoga. Jesus holy Christ, I sound like a preacher.

I must try it.

Sorry, I'm a little tired. I'll take one of your first floor rooms.

Sorry, I'm blabbering away. I'll get a card for you to fill out.

That makes two sorrys. Now I guess we can both go to bed.

Not me, I'm sorry to say. I work tonight.

I take the pen she offers and fill out the little card, the size of an index card. When it comes to the license plate number, I stop, unable to remember.

Not to worry, she says. I can get it in the morning.

Mr. Charles ... I can't read the last name.

I tell her, and she says, My name is Sandy. Nice name, huh, for a night clerk at a motel.

Sandy, sand in your eyes, Mr. Sandman, I get it. I'm so tired it takes me awhile to figure things out. I won't need any sand in my eyes tonight, thanks anyway. Is there a phone I can use. I want to give my wife a call.

There's a phone in your room. Dial nine if you want to call out. Or you can use the phone in the lobby. Use your card. It's cheaper.

The door opens behind me, and in comes Sandy's boyfriend, all pumped up, in a green crew-neck T-shirt that has 'Blast Off' written across the front in white.

He's young looking, at least three or four years younger than the girl. Hey, how's it goin', he says to the girl while looking at me.

I'll just get monsieur here his keys.

I take my cue and leave the two lovebirds alone.

My room is at the far end of the long building – far from the love nest – with a view toward the lights of Lafayette.

I park the Saturn ass backward up against the door, though for the love of God I don't know for what reason.

I have nothing to unpack, nothing to declare except my loneliness and my lust.

There's a double bed, a television, a chair by the window, a table, the standard bathroom. The carpet smells of cleaning fluid.

I open the window above the table. I hear the sound of a siren fading away into the distance.

I decide to wait an hour before driving into town to look for a restaurant. I'm not hungry right now. I've been nibbling at things all day long, on the drive down from Chicago.

Potato chips, rice cakes, cashew pieces, roasted soy nuts, trail mix – you name it.

Okay. First the phone call to Anne.

I'd like some privacy, assuming the kids at the front desk don't listen in.

I sit on the edge of the bed. I think back to our last conversation.

Where was it.

The airport in Chicago.

I remember her words. Don't get me wrong. I could live very well without you. But I would always know there was something missing. No one else would know it but I would.

What is this something that would be missing. Is it the same something I would miss, as a man.

I believe it would be the same thing – or something very similar. Not sex exactly, but something connected to sex.

The closeness, the intimacy. The feeling that you're strong enough to be vulnerable. The feeling that someone thinks about you and worries about you. The knowledge that the more he knows about you the more he cares.

I dial nine, then put the phone down again.

I could live very well without you, she said. She's not just saying she can live without me, she can live 'very well.'

If she can live very well without me, one day she'll forget there is something missing. She'll lose herself in her work. She'll cultivate her friends. She'll travel. She'll re-discover nature. She'll embrace solitude. She'll ask herself what all the fuss was about.

This 'something missing' turns out to be pretty fragile stuff, when you think about it. You don't even know what it is.

I dial nine again, then the number at home. It seems like a long time ago since we talked, though it was yesterday.

I hear one ring, then another. I'm getting ready for the recorded message. My mind's a blank. I have nothing to say. I won't say anything. I'll hang up.

At the last moment I hear Anne's voice. The way she says 'Hello Charlie' is so sweet I put my hand to my head. I'm gone in some place that's so faraway, so peaceful, I haven't visited there in ages.

I've really missed you a lot. As soon as I say it I know it's true. I didn't know it was true until I said it.

I love life on the road – the freedom. Every moment I create my own rules. I could live this way a very long time.

In the way I hold the wheel of the car, the way my eyes are glued to the road, the way I hunger to see what's just around the corner, my body gives me away.

She had a dream last night that she wants to tell me about.

I don't like to listen to other people's dreams, as a rule.

Do you want to hear it or not.

I say sure.

She was at a window looking onto the deck of a house or cottage. Below the deck she saw a river flowing by. It was a small winding river, like the one we saw on vacation once, in northern New Brunswick.

She saw a canoe coming down the river, drifting with the current. Somehow she knew it was her old canoe from childhood, when her father used to take her and her brother to a camp. But I was in the canoe.

I drifted below the window without once looking up. She watched me go by, and she felt sad because I did not look up.

I suppose I could have waved, or something.

Where are you calling from.

I'm in a cheap motel just outside Lafayette, my old home town.

That reminds me, your brother David called. He's wondering where you are, and when he should expect you.

I wrote him and explained all that. I'll be there tomorrow, late in the day.

He was sure you had said today.

No, it was tomorrow. I'll give him a call.

You'd better.

How are you.

Tired. I tried working in the studio, but nothing turned out right. Even the disasters were uninteresting. That tells you something. Sally was supposed to come for lunch but she canceled out. I didn't know what to do with myself, so I went to bed and slept half the afternoon.

I could use some of that. Sleep, I mean.

You love me.

You know I do.

Just thought I'd ask.

What are you doing tonight.

I think I'll go somewhere and have a beer and listen to music. Maybe run into a friend. I'm feeling lonely. What about you.

I thought I'd drive into town and get a bit to eat. I haven't had supper yet.

That's right, we're an hour ahead of you.

I found the medal you packed away as a surprise.

It's for all those reasons I wrote down. But it's also for you to remember me.

Love you.

Love you too.

On this happy note we hang up.

I get a jacket from my suitcase, switch off the lights, and go outside to the car.

It's dark. I can see the lights of the city a few miles away.

Lafayette's a small city, about the size of the city where I live in Canada. There are no very tall buildings.

At this distance, a few miles out, all you can see is a pinkish glow in the haze from the lights.

I stand by the side of the car looking at the lights of the city.

It could be any city. I've been away so many years.

On the highway in front of the motel cars pass by, heading into the city. They make a sound that lasts for a second, then there's silence, darkness, the sound of crickets, until the next car.

Inside one pocket of my jacket is a brochure I picked up at the Art Institute in Chicago. I remember being in the museum and reading this brochure about a planned exhibition of Arab-American art. I do not, however, remember putting the brochure into my pocket.

It's too dark now to read it, or to make out the design on the front cover.

I stand there a moment, my hand pressing the brochure to my chest. I'm not hungry. I'm not thirsty. I don't want to go anywhere, or see anyone.

Twenty-Five

I phone my brother to see about tomorrow, but I get a recorded message. I say the first words that come into my mind.

This is your brother. It's Thursday evening. I'm not far away, you'll be happy to know. Or maybe not.

I'm here at the Knight's Inn. It's just outside Lafayette, where the plan is to get a good night's sleep, no pun intended. In the morning I'll check out the old homestead, maybe call up an old friend or two. I should get to your place around five. If I'm late, it means I got held up. Don't wait supper, all right.

Don't wait supper. Strange the way the words come out. It's too late to take them back now. I suppose they mean something, I'm not sure what.

I sit at the desk by the window, open the spiral notebook I've brought along for just this purpose, and write down what I remember of the day's events.

Raw impressions I'll come back to later, when it comes time to write my book.

Eight o'clock becomes nine o'clock. I hear the cars go by on the highway. There are fewer and fewer.

I become aware of the silence. It's more than silence. It's a sort of stillness that comes with the night when people slow down and the pressure eases. The clock slows. Creatures large and small, visible and invisible, prepare for bed. Others begin the journey into darkness, the clawing and the scratching in the dark, digging deep to stay alive.

I turn out the light to the bathroom, lock the front door, hook the chain, turn on the TV long enough to realize that there's nothing I want to watch.

I stretch out on the bed in the dark. My head is still spinning from everything that's happened today. I know that sleep will not come easily, if it comes at all.

I search for a safe place, where I can relax and drift away, like a boat on a calm lake where there's a mist all around and the sun is breaking through and everything is the color of gold.

I'm thinking about the novel I want to write. The novel I want to write will be like nothing I've ever written before. It will cover three generations, from the grandfather through the father to the son.

The focus will be on the father. The father keeps everything inside, bottled up, and it's only when he opens up that the story of what happened becomes clear.

The trouble is how to get him to open up. Born early in the century, he comes of age in the twenties, is a young man by the time of the depression, a father before the war.

Too old at thirty-two to make cannon fodder, he finds work in the shipyards. He makes babies instead. He is good at that.

To bring the father into focus I'll have to travel back in time to the grandfather. I'll have to find a way to bring the grandfather to life, along with his wife, and the seven children they brought into this world before he vanished.

There are photographs, lost letters, family legends, historical documents - the rest I can make up.

The novel I want to write will have a sense of mystery at its core. It will embrace all the confusion and bewilderment and moments of vertigo that we experience in daily life. It will avoid flowery language.

Flowery language is anything that would invite me to turn away too easily and too quickly from what is disturbing or painful or confusing.

I want to find a way of writing that will take in everything, pain, sorrow, humor, moments of terror, moments of joy, moments that are special because they are ephemeral, smiles from beings who understand that they are dying.

It's because the night clerk was wearing a flowery dress that I'm thinking of her now and imagining what it would be like for her to be here with me.

As she leans down over me to kiss me her breasts move freely under the flowery dress. She smiles when I put my hands up and hold her breasts.

When she was sitting at the front desk, so prim and proper, so wrapped up in her book, I had no idea she had such large breasts. I have the feeling that if I squeeze them milk will come out.

She says her breasts are swollen because she is six months pregnant and if I want to make love to her the only safe way in her condition is to come into her from behind, while she supports herself on her hands and knees.

I read this in a book, so I suppose it's true. She lets me hold her breasts, and I'm not sure how violent she wants me to be.

It seems safe enough.

And this way has the advantage that she doesn't have to

95

know that my cock is bent out of shape – a condition my doctor says is not unusual at my age.

It's not the instrument it once was but it will do.

The main thing is it's still sensitive and this way of doing it puts pressure on the underside of the shaft.

I can stop for a moment, and it's like we are one.

Is everything is okay, she asks.

She's never done it like this before, she says, and I wonder what's the matter with her husband or boyfriend.

Where is he anyway. He was here just a minute ago.

My orgasm feels like it won't ever end. By the time I've rolled over and pulled the blankets up I'm already asleep.

There's no time to feel bad about anything.

In my dream I'm working late on a story that I hope to get published one day if I can ever get it right. In the room with me are several colleagues at the publishing house where I work.

A blond-haired woman whose job it is to sift through the slush pile is looking at what I have written so far, nodding her approval and smiling.

Another blond-haired woman, older and dressed in black leather – our editor – is looking over the younger woman's shoulder and does not seem so happy.

When she sees me at the window, she turns to me with a frown and says, You can't use 'tu' when you're talking to someone you hardly know. Especially when it's a businessman or a politician.

Apparently the whole story is in French, and I have made one mistake after another, mixing the familiar and the unfamiliar, switching tenses, confusing before and after.

Twenty-Six

You have no trouble remembering the address of the house where you lived in the 1950s, during the years you attended junior high school and then high school. And you know, from talking with your brother, that the house has been torn down.

Still, it's a shock to see everything gone, and a parking lot where you used to live, the asphalt new and very black, with bright yellow lines marking the parking places.

Next to the parking lot, in an old house that was once your neighbor's, is a doctor's office. There are tulips in bloom in a border around the house, very neat in packed, heaped wood chips.

A fancy sign, made of plywood with carved wooden letters in gold leaf, stands in the middle of the lawn. Dr. Ronald Smith, Homeopathic Medicine, it proclaims.

It's strange, because this is the last house that your mother and father owned, before your father died.

This is where you sat around the dinner table together, where you played game after game of ping pong in the back room, where you slept with your brothers in the bedroom upstairs, where you awoke to your own sexuality, in a bathtub in the bathroom at the end of the hallway, in a tub of hot water, with a wash cloth that felt like the tongue of a cat and a magazine called *Seventeen*, where the girls were not even naked but had pointed breasts in tight blouses, and posed against tree trunks, or houses by the sea, or rocks bigger than they.

You get out of the car and walk across the parking lot toward the alley in the back. It's early. There are just two other cars parked here – maybe the good doctor himself and an assistant.

Everything is so quiet. Maybe they are inside practicing a little homeopathic medicine, or a little something extra-curricular.

It's here at the back of the lot where there was a garage inside which your father stored his plumbing supplies in metal boxes arranged on fold-out shelves along the walls.

On summer days, when he was away at work, you and your brothers exercised and lifted weights on a mat that you would roll out in the middle of the floor.

You did not mind the dirt and the grime.

You wanted to be as strong as he was. You wanted to have more stamina, you wanted to be quicker on your feet, you wanted to have the courage of your convictions even if he did not have.

You wanted to possess more capacity to suffer, and you wanted to be kinder than he was, to the girls that you hoped to meet one day.

You wanted to be better than your father, better than your brothers, better than your friends, better than you had ever been. If you had gone three days without masturbating last week, you wanted to go four this week.

You would sometimes go with your father on a job. You were his helper, you received his instruction, you absorbed his teaching, you observed and mirrored his anger.

You wanted to do the work as fast as he, even faster. You wanted to cut the pipes, pour the lead, drill the holes, nail the boards, screw the screws, run the errands, put everything back when the job is done.

And when you cannot do what he asks, when you cannot find the exact nut or bolt that he needs, when you cannot find the monkey wrench or the Phillips screwdriver for the job that he is doing, when you let something slip, when you do not know where he keeps the caulking material that he uses to seal the joints between drain pipes – you are ashamed.

You are so ashamed that you cannot find words to express yourself. You are in a place that's hotter than the molten lead that he tips one way, then the other, for you to see.

You are slipping through the cracks in the floor of hell.

The sports, the weightlifting, the straight A's in school, these are ways to compete with your father and outdo your father.

When you do something exceptionally well you receive his admiration – sometimes.

When you play poorly you feel his scorn.

When you fail at the age of twelve to make the cut-off for the little league baseball team, you hide the news from your parents for three days, you are so ashamed.

To play well and know that he is watching makes you proud.

There are moments on the field, knowing he is watching, so sweet that nothing since can compare.

If you come home battered and bruised and with a broken tooth, you pretend it is nothing. You do not feel a thing. It's the way of the warrior.

Your father stands back and says nothing, while your mother looks after your wounds.

You are grown up now. This is the message that you hope you

are delivering, and that she, and he, can find a way to accept.

Friday evenings, before the football game, she prepares a special dinner for you – orange juice, steak, toast with no butter. She calls you to the table early, before the rest of the family, so that you have time to eat before leaving early for the game.

You feel big. You've taken your father's place in her heart, you'd like to think, for one brief shining moment.

The house next door to yours, to the north, is still standing. It was the nicest house on the block, a low, ranch-style house of yellow brick with wide windows that opened at the top, in what seemed to you at the time like a new invention.

The people who lived there, the Korschotts, kept to themselves. Their friends were not your friends.

Sometimes you'd hear shouting in the kitchen window, a car door slamming, and the squeal of tires on the street in front of the house. You'd hear a woman crying in the bedroom window.

But it was none of your business. You kept quiet.

There's no answer when you knock on the door. It feels as empty as it felt forty-five years ago, when you came knocking.

The Korschotts had one child, Becky, a few years younger than you. You felt separated from Becky by many things including age, class, and sex. You were strangers, and you seldom spoke.

But one day after school when you were playing catch with yourself in the backyard as you often did, throwing a baseball high in the air and running to catch it, Becky called your name and asked you to come over.

Though she was not yet ten, she dressed like a young woman, with her dark hair combed down with curls at the neck in the style of the day. She wore a plaid skirt, a pretty blouse, and a sweater with pockets for her hands.

She was so pretty, in the East Coast miniature Sylvia Plath sort of way, that she intimidated you.

In a small voice she said she needed your help. You followed her around to the front of the house. In the driveway two dogs, one on top of the other, were engaged in some sort of fight or struggle the likes of which you had never seen before.

You advanced to within a couple of feet of the combatants. Stop it, you said, in a voice that was more high-pitched than you intended.

The two dogs paused in their agony to look up at you, as if you were a creature from another planet.

The dog on top, the male, was a black and white cocker spaniel. Becky instructed you to grab his tail.

By her tone of voice you understood that the dog on top, the male, was not hers. You got hold of his tail and tried to pull him away.

He cried pitifully, so you let go.

They're stuck together, Becky said.

She was standing behind you, and she was trying to tell you something.

Stuck together, stuck together, stuck together. Her words rang in your ears.

Still, you did not get it. You stood glued to the spot, unable to move, unable to speak, unable to understand what was happening.

You were too confused, too embarrassed to ask her to repeat herself. You didn't even know why you were embarrassed.

The seconds ticked away, until finally the scales fell from your eyes, and you saw what she was talking about.

You felt such a hot flow of blood to your brain that you thought you would faint.

Break it up, you said, this time in a loud, hysterical voice.

The male tried to pull away but could not. He lost his balance and scrambled to get his front paws on the female's shoulders as before.

But it was like falling off a treadmill. Something had frightened the female during her moment of bliss, and she had shut herself tight against the male.

The male had grown to regret the fine form he was in.

The more you shouted at him, the more confused he was. The more you tried to comfort her, the more you frightened her.

She cowered low. The male cried pitifully.

Just then your father drove by in his truck on his way home. At first he did not recognize you, then he did a double-take and almost missed his turn at the corner.

He parked along the street at the other end of the house, got out, and came along the sidewalk toward where Becky and the two dogs and you waited, in suspended animation.

You stood there quite helpless, Becky in front, you behind, the two dogs near the garage door. As your father approached across the manicured lawn, the dogs ceased their whining.

In an instant he fathomed the extremity of the situation and hit on a course of action.

In a low, gentle voice, so unfamiliar to you that you would not have recognized it, he told Becky to get him a bucket. Becky emerged from the garage with a rusty, leaky bucket, which Father filled with water from the hose.

He threw the water on the backs of the dogs. The dogs flew apart. The cocker spaniel ran around the side of the house into the alleyway and disappeared. The female scurried under the door of the garage into the darkness.

In the same gentle voice he said to Becky, She'll be all right.

With this he walked away without even so much as looking at you.

Twenty-Seven

I get back in the car and start toward the downtown. I go along Ferry Street toward an intersection called 'Five Points.'

At the top of the hill that leads into the downtown, drops of rain begin falling on the windshield of the car. Just a few at first, then the sky opens and it rains cats and dogs.

I get the wipers going, put the car in low gear and drive slowly down the hill. There's no one behind me.

At the bottom of the hill the rain is still coming down but not so hard. I traverse blocks of businesses and stores, including one called 'Buck Creek Books.'

I promise myself to return here if I have time.

The downtown looks pretty much the same as it always did. At Sixth and Main is the building where the movie theatre used to be. A couple blocks down is the County Court House, recently sandblasted and cleaned up.

I park on Main Street next to the old newsstand, opposite the Court House. The newsstand is long and narrow, like an alleyway between buildings. I move toward the back, where it's less congested.

I look through the local newspaper, to get an idea what's going on. Strange voices fill the air.

More people enter and move toward the back. I'm shoved right up against a phone booth on the wall next to the back door.

Emergency exit only, it says on the door.

I'll make a telephone call, I decide. Why not.

I'll look up the name of an old friend. I'll surprise him. I'll surprise myself.

There are several Davises but none with the right first name or initial. There are too many Adamses. I was never that close to Norm Copas.

I find the name I'm looking for. Mike Robertson.

I dial the number. I don't recognize the voice that answers.

I haven't seen him or talked with him in forty years.

When I tell him who's calling he doesn't recognize the name.

We went to school together, way back when.

There's a brief pause while he processes this information.

You son-of-a-bitch. No one's heard from you in ages.

I've moved around a lot over the years.

We thought you must be dead or something.

I've been living in Canada.

Cold up there isn't it.

It's about like here, only more so.

What brings you down our way.

Just driving around.

You son-of-a-bitch.

You wanna get together for a beer.

Sure, why not.

Tell me where, I'll be there.

You remember the old A&W where we used to hang out, on Ninth.

The girls would come around with trays to hook on the windows. We'd roll our windows down and try to get them to talk. They'd just smile and walk away.

There's a tavern just across the street called the Igloo. They make the best hamburgers in town.

Sounds great.

I've got some things to finish up here. Meet me there in an hour.

Okay, in an hour.

On Main Street a light rain is falling. I walk east on Main, in the direction of the used bookstore with the interesting name, Buck Creek Books.

The old train tracks on Sixth, where the Monon used to come through, are gone. The pavement is smooth. I see no sign of the tracks, no sign of the old station.

The rain is falling. I no longer know these buildings, I've been gone so long. I no longer know what's going on inside them.

The rain is falling. I walk past the old candy store with its state-of-the-art soda fountain, past the old movie theatre, past the old diner with its juke boxes and booths where the seats and the backs are made of clear green plastic.

The rain is falling. I feel the drops on my face. I feel the loss of old places, old friends, old memories.

The rain is falling. I stand and look a moment in the window of the Sears department store. I see my reflection.

I look through the window, through the reflection, and inside I sense vague movements, glimpse shadowy figures that come and go, discern shapes that withhold meaning.

Inside the bookstore it's so quiet I wonder if there's anyone around. There's no one behind the counter, no one on the main floor.

I ring a bell by the cash register but even then no one appears. I climb a set of stairs to the second floor, where it's equally quiet.

The books on the second floor landing have to do with art, theatre, film, and photography. Farther back there's a narrow room that was once a kitchen. The cupboards are still in place, though now the doors are removed and the shelves are filled with books – cookbooks, gardening books, books about pets.

At the very back is a small room lined with books from floor to ceiling, all in the area of biography and autobiography. There's a window overlooking a yard cluttered with discarded children's toys and cardboard boxes full of old magazines.

Because of the title someone has placed John Le Carre's thriller, 'The Little Drummer Girl,' in among the biographies. If I had a pen I'd write her a note.

I choose a book and make my way back downstairs. The owner is behind the counter – a woman about fifty-five, with white hair and metal frame glasses.

She glances at me, then returns to what she's doing – pricing a stack of hardcover books on the counter.

She looks at each book, front and back, opens it, sniffs it, and writes something inside. She removes a torn dust jacket from one of the books. She glances at me again.

I look through an assortment of old, 'vintage' paperbacks on a table against a wall underneath the steps. Each book is neatly wrapped in plastic, with the sticker price on the outside of the plastic.

I don't see much of interest. The prices are pretty steep. I'm not really into collecting.

I can offer you twenty dollars, the woman calls out. The voice startles me. Is she talking to me.

I look up from the table but before I can say anything a second voice answers from behind a bookcase not three feet from where I'm standing.

I was hoping I might get twenty-five. A young woman in a yellow raincoat, her hair wet and stringy from the rain, steps out from behind the bookcase.

She approaches the counter, to within a couple of feet, where she stops, as if at some invisible barrier, and stares at the bookshop owner.

The owner says that twenty dollars is all she can offer.

The young woman says that that does not seem like very much.

The owner says it's the best she can do.

The young woman, still not moving forward or backward, concludes that she doesn't have much choice. But she is not happy and wants that to be clear.

The argument fizzles before it gets really hot.

The storekeeper removes a roll of bills from the pocket of her skirt and peels off a twenty. The young woman takes the money and asks if she should sign something.

Her tone is less than friendly.

No, that's not necessary, the storekeeper says. The young woman leaves.

I make my way to the counter to pay for the book I've chosen, crossing whatever invisible barriers lay in my path.

The woman moves her glasses down on her nose and looks at me for the first time. It's a searching look – a severe look.

She's about to say something but stops short.

I'll just take this one book, I say, giving her a ten. She gives me six dollars in change.

Enjoy, she says, a big smile on her face, which surprises me.

I do not necessarily feel there is anything false about this smile.

Her eyes have a sparkle I hadn't noticed before. Again, she seems on the verge of some sort of intimacy. She keeps looking at me without let-up. She does not want to let me go.

It could be that I'm her first paying customer of the day.

Twenty-Eight

When I get to the Igloo Mike is not there. It's too dark to read, so I sit at a table, order a beer and wait.

I wonder what 'things' Mike is working on, these days. When I knew him, in high school, he wanted to be an artist. I wonder if that dream ever came true.

I recognize him immediately when he comes in, though it has been forty years. He's not a tall man – five foot ten, five foot eleven – but he's strong, with a neck like a bull, arms and shoulders of a fourth or fifth generation farmer.

He wanted to be an artist but what he excelled at was sports – wrestling and football in particular.

I stand up when I see him, gladder than I've been in a long while. He has a large face that has an unshaven look even when he's just shaved. Bright merry eyes.

We shake hands. It's good to see you.

What are you having. Curtly.

A German beer I like a lot. Beck's.

Mike motions to the bartender to bring him 'the usual' – a dark beer on tap.

We sit down at the round table, in two chairs next to each other, facing a window that looks out on the parking lot. The window is dark, with imitation stained glass.

I look at him, and don't know what to say. The crew-cut is gone, the hair is brushed straight back, it's long enough that he has it tied in back.

Big burly man with his hair tied in a knot.

There's a swelling in the side of his face as if he has a sore tooth, or a cancerous growth.

The bartender comes with Mike's beer and sets it down without a word. I don't usually drink during the day, Mike says, downing a third of the glass.

Rules are made to be broken, I like to think.

Remember when we used to stay out all night driving around the countryside, tanked out of our minds, it's a wonder we didn't get killed.

We almost did a couple of times.

He takes another chug from the glass and sets it down very carefully on the table. I don't know about you, but my father almost killed me a couple times when I came in late.

Me too.

The thing is, he was a boozehound. Killed him in the end.

I liked your old man. I'm sorry.

Remember the time he holed up in a motel and wouldn't come out. Said he'd rather kill himself than go back to that bitch, my mother. He had a gun and said he'd shoot the first fucker that got within forty feet. He got that way when he drank too much. He didn't mean it.

I remember.

Mike motions to the bartender to bring another beer.

We pause until the beer arrives in a new tall glass. The foam spills over the top of the glass and drips onto the table.

Mike bends over the table and sips foam to stop the spillage.

He pats his mouth with a paper napkin.

You boys want somethin' to eat, the bartender says.

It's the way he says somethin' that catches my attention. He is a tall man with a big belly, long, stringy hair, and a soft, pleasant voice. A gentle man – easy to like.

I'm not really that hungry. Can I get a plate of French fries.

No problem, he says.

I'll have some fries too, Mike says, and bring me one of your awesome burgers.

Your father drove me out to the motel. What I remember is the way he held the steering wheel, tightly with both hands, one hand on each side of the wheel, and how he moved his hands up and down in quick, nervous little movements, his arms bent a little, but still stiff.

It used to drive my mother mad, the way he held the wheel so tightly. She claimed it was bad for the steering column. Dad said she didn't know what she was talking about.

He was extemely quiet. He waited until we were almost there before asking me if I knew what was happening. Sure, I knew what was happening. My goddamn father was threatening to blow his brains out. I told him I was afraid my father would leave some day and never come back.

What did he say.

He just kept on driving and didn't say anything. It was as if my words had not yet reached the part of his brain where he could make sense of them.

What happened when you got to the motel.

My father was meek as a lamb. He must have seen us drive

up. Your father got out and just stood there by the side of the car. He was extremely calm. He had an air of authority, I don't know if you know.

We could see my father in the window, the barrel of his rifle sticking through a big hole in the glass he'd punched. But somehow we knew he wouldn't shoot. He respected your father too much. After a while he opened the door and came out. Not a word was spoken. We were safe again. Your father being there made us all feel safe again.

Twenty-Nine

Mike leaves the table and goes outside to have a cigarette. I finish my beer and go in search of the men's room. He is back at the table, with a fresh glass of beer, when I return.

I'm taking the afternoon off, he says, for old time's sake.

When I was coming into town I came across a car in a ditch. There was a woman standing by the car who reminded me so much of Bernie Davis, I was sure it was her. But when she spoke there was a southern drawl that I just don't remember. Could it have been her.

Bernie Davis doesn't live around here anymore.

I used to have a terrible crush on Bernie Davis.

It was more than a crush. You were sick.

Maybe I was, I admit.

You stalked her, man.

True.

They should have locked you up before you hurt someone.

I would've gone willingly.

The woman you thought was Bernie Davis was probably Mary Doyle. They look so much alike they could be sisters. The same red hair, the freckles, the green, piercing eyes. Mary lived in Kentucky for about twenty years after graduating. My wife knows her. Ex-wife, I should say.

Why am I not surprised to hear that Mike is divorced. I didn't know.

We had twenty decent years together, then five years so bad we wanted to kill each other. We have extremely different ideas about life. I love to travel, I always have. The funny thing is, the older I get the more important it seems. Nathalie would rather stay home and look after the garden.

I tell him that I share his love of travel, but I wonder how he finds the time.

His job, he explains, allows him to work six months a year, then travel the other six. It's the perfect situation in a way, except that the job sucks.

Where do you like to travel.

The last couple years I've been spending most of my time in Florida. I've got a trailer on some land out on Key West.

I remember somebody called Mary Doyle. She was a grade or two behind us. I think she was in the same class as my brother.

She was a skinny girl then and she's a skinny girl now, as flat as a pancake. But she was a good fuck. Man she was hot.

He's bragging his head off, the way he used to, and I don't want to follow him down this road. She was stuck up, as I recall. Nobody you could really get close to.

The fries and the hamburger arrive. We smother everything in ketchup, and fall silent a moment or two because we're both hungry. The French fries are hot and crispy and very good.

What about you, Mike says. You married or what.

Second time around, I answer, sitting up.

Welcome to the club. He can't help laughing the way he used to, out of one side of his mouth.

Tell me about the job.

The job sucks, as I said. We publish a little book every fall for the university crowd, with information about the town, where to eat, where to shop, where to party, that sort of thing. What I do is go around to various businesses in town and bargain for the advertising dollar.

Don't sound like much fun.

Bargain is too mild a word for what I do. I beg, I plead, I cajole, I get down on my knees, I use all my powers of persuasion. The book comes out around mid-September. By the first of October I'm ready to pack it in and head south. I drive some place new every year, maybe Roanoke, maybe Charleston, maybe New Orleans. By the first of November I'm in Florida, living the life of Riley. I'm also responsible for graphic design.

The graphic design part sounds like something just up your alley.

After a few years you get lazy. It's basically the same thing, year after year.

Maybe one of these years you won't come back.

I've thought about that. When the time is right, when I still have my strength, I'll take to the road. I'll live the way I want.

You have children.

A son and a daughter. Both grown up, living elsewhere. Nothing to hold me here.

What's it like in Florida.

Florida's a ball. Everybody's extremely relaxed. Where I am in Key West there aren't that many people. You can walk into town, nobody bothers you.

The thing I like about traveling is leaving everything behind.

All the worries and concerns that used to seem so important. You leave the old self behind and when you come back everything has changed and yet nothing has changed.

While I'm talking Mike devours his sandwich. I have the feeling he's not listening, even though what I am saying is the same thing he's saying, or something very close, using different words.

I shut up and look around, first at the India rubber plant in its light green plastic container, then at the window with its fake stained glass design. Lines of silver separate patches of red and green and blue, with just enough transparency to the glass that shapes and movement in the parking lot outside are noticeable.

What about you. Mike is done with his sandwich except for the crumbs and bits of lettuce and raw onion that litter the table in front of him.

What brings you down this way. He holds up his glass of beer in front of him as if in a salute, in a way that suggests that he's all ears. But if he finds anything I have to say of interest it will be a great surprise to me.

Doing research for a book.

What kind of book.

I'm not sure if it's going to be a novel or a memoir. It's supposed to be the story of my father's life, and everything that flows from that, before and after.

Hmmm.

The key event is when my grandfather disappeared in Chicago in 1927. My father was nineteen.

Lordy, why do you want to go and dredge it all up again. We all have these memories and things we'd be better off forgetting.

I think there's a sort of fault line that runs in the family. Something that makes us want to run away from all the commitments and responsibilities we've taken on. My father held out against it by pure force of will but at a tremendous cost to himself and to everyone around him, including his children.

You're afraid it's in you. Is that what you're saying. Now he's sitting up and taking notice.

All my life I've been leaving, moving on, starting over. Already at the age of four I ran away from home. I love Anne, but I just think it's time to move on.

When the words are out, like the lie about my father I told on the airplane coming down, that he was going on ninety when he's been dead for forty years, they seem like fateful words, words I might like to take back but can't.

They have a life of their own. They express something that was in me all the time that I didn't know was there.

Sometimes I have the feeling I'm not really living.

What you say makes sense to me, Mike says. Just the way you say her name tells me you love this Anne. But love sometimes can really tie you down.

I want to do some traveling. I want to be alone for a while. Maybe Canada is not the best place for me now. They look after you too well in Canada. It's too safe. Where's the risk in that.

Mike raises his glass to propose a toast. Here's to risk taking. Here's to the open road.

He's smiling as if I've just made his day all the brighter with my babbling.

I didn't even know I was going to call you when I did. Now I'm glad I did. I'm beginning to understand what I'm doing here. Why I'm here.

Mike finishes his glass and stands up. It's dark inside the tavern, much darker than before. Dark clouds are coming in again, with more heavy rain.

We shake hands across the table. It was great to see you man, he says.

Let's get together again.

Sure, why not. I don't think he means it.

I'm heading south for a few days to see my brother. After that, I don't know what's going to happen.

It's the journey that counts, not the destination.

I'll remember that.

He leaves. I sit down again at the table. I sip the last of my beer. I relish the silence all around me.

I repeat to myself the words I've just spoken but can still barely believe.

Did I speak the words, or did the words speak me.

Thirty

I'm in a fog the rest of the day. I don't know who I am, the loving husband or the cheat and the runaway. It's not even up to me to decide, but events.

I want to get moving, get going. I think if I go to bed early I will get up early and have a head start.

But it does not work that way. I'm awake at midnight, and I can't sleep. I toss and turn, unable to tell what is a dream and what is something I'm remembering for the first time in a long time.

I'm in a bookstore, browsing among the stacks with no particular aim, killing time. Anne is in another part of the store, searching for a book she's long wanted – a historical novel set in Ethiopia by a French writer the title of which she cannot remember.

There's no one else in the store, other than Anne, me, and the clerk behind the counter who after greeting us has resumed reading his newspaper. It's peaceful enough, until two young men in T-shirts and baggy pants enter.

I smell trouble, but I'm still surprised when one of them pulls a gun and demands cash from the clerk.

Anne is nowhere in sight. I suppose she's seen what's happening and has found a safe place to hide.

I'm able to slip out through a side door and return home, which is a few blocks away. I'm so tired from the stress of events that I fall asleep on the bed.

An hour passes, maybe two. When I wake up I'm alone in the house. I remember what happened in the bookstore. Anne could still be there, in some danger. She could be lying hurt in the store where I left her with the thieves.

She could be dead for all I know.

I return to the store to find out what has happened. I feel sad when I think that something might have happened to Anne because of my negligence.

Just as I'm about to enter the store I wake from the dream.

I'm awake but only half awake. Something terrible has happened while I was sleeping. It takes me awhile to remember where I am, in a room in a motel outside my hometown, Lafayette, in my home state, Indiana.

I wander in and out of the bathroom. I open the curtains. It's dark outside. I'd like to go back into the dream. I'd like to find out what happened. I'd like to reconstruct the sequence of events, and follow it to the end.

Sitting in the chair by the window with my eyes closed, I can picture the door of the bookstore. It's a plain white door. The doorknob is white porcelain. I turn the knob. The door opens, and I go in.

There's no one at the desk, no one among the stacks of books in the front of the store. Hello, I call out.

Hello, comes the reply, like an echo. A young man comes forward from the back of the store, three or four large format paperback books tucked under his arm.

Are you the owner. I shake my head.

Strange sort of place, he says, where there's no one around to take your money. He sets his books down on the front counter and prepares to wait until someone comes to take his money.

Why doesn't he walk out of the store with his free gift of books. I might be tempted. But apparently this never enters his mind.

I'm looking for my wife. In answer to my statement it's his turn now to shake his head. We both have cause to be puzzled.

It's as if the store and everything in it has been left in our care, to protect or not protect according to our whim.

Maybe she went looking for you, he suggests.

No likely. I shrug my shoulders.

He's wearing a name tag around his neck, suggesting he's in town for a conference on, say, the collapse of fish stocks in the Great Lakes, or the relation of excessive harvesting of the forests and flooding in the rivers of the northern tier states.

Or he's escaped from the nearby hospital for the criminally insane.

There's a twinkle in his eye and a few days' growth of beard on his face, so I lean toward the latter option.

The name on the tag is Sam.

Inside a glass counter by the front desk are the more valuable books in the store. There's an illustrated 'Alice in Wonderland' from around the turn of the century, open to an illustration showing Alice at table with the Mad Hatter. The colors are light, transparent reds and greens such as you might see on the wings of dragonflies.

Sam picks up a newspaper the clerk left behind on the desk and starts reading.

I'm about to walk away when Sam says, By God I wish I had the brains to write something like that.

He's so carried away that he taps the paper with the back of his fingers, and spit flies halfway across the floor to where I'm standing.

He reads a few lines to himself, then comments out loud, knowing he's caught my attention. Beautiful, beautiful, Jesus Christ, man, you've got that right, whatever the fuck your name is. I couldn't agree more. The whole direction of our civilization is wrong. Call it the American way of life if you will.

He stops and waits for me to say something.

When I don't, he continues. It's a rather stupid way of life, in my opinion. You've always got to have more, more. There's no future in that.

Maybe it's the American in me, but all I can think of to say is, I don't agree. It might be a stupid way of life, but I don't really see an end to it.

Sam disregards my comment and goes on reading. Get this, get this, he shouts. The man's a genius. I admire their democracy, he says, but they have no tradition, and that's something that's bound to predetermine their behavior. A second thing is technology - TV addiction. Man, you got that right.

Before I can utter any platitudes about the post-literate universe, the leveling effect of the new technology, media illuminations, global communication as total terror – the clerk re-enters the store and takes up her position behind the counter.

She's returned with a cup of coffee and a bag of potato chips. The coffee, which she sets down on the glass counter top, is in a very tall white plastic cup with some sort of design on the side. It's in red, and looks like it says *Mock One* but I'm probably seeing things.

She opens the bag of chips, eats one chip, then sets the bag aside before turning and looking first at Sam, then at me.

I recognize her as the girl who was at the desk of the motel the night before, when I checked in, and who seemed so interested in the French philosopher Foucault.

I'd like to buy these three books, Sam says. While she looks after this purchase, I wander through the back rooms looking for Anne. I have no idea where she might be.

I leave by the same side exit as before.

Thirty-One

You are on the road, driving south toward the little college town where you went to school and where your brother did too, and where he teaches to this day. Nothing much has changed along this road, after forty years.

You can remember every twist and turn along the way, every house, every railroad crossing, every tree.

You stop a moment in one of the villages along the way, to drop a note to Anne in a mailbox. There was a post office here, which had always seemed an anomaly, the village was so small and insignificant.

It's still small and insignificant, and now it has no post office too. In those days you would often post letters in the village when you did not want anyone to see you. It's hard to imagine what you might have had to say that was so important that you had to keep it a secret. But you thought it was.

There's a rest area by the side of the road, with a picnic table that looks newly painted and grass that looks fresh and green. You stretch out in the grass and close your eyes a moment.

Far away you can hear the whistle of a train and you remember that there are train tracks that run right through the middle of this town. At one point along the road the tracks cross over from one side to the other.

You fall asleep in the grass by the side of the road, and in your sleep someone calls your name. The voice feels like it is coming from a long way away.

Get up Charlie, there's someone here who wants to see you, the voice says. You recognize it as belonging to Jack McAnally, your roommate at college.

Your father has driven all this way to see you. The least you can do is get up.

He's waiting outside the door of your room, in a much larger room that is like the waiting room of a doctor's office. With a stern look he asks you if you know what time it is.

It must be about eight o'clock, you answer in a sort of daze.

He tells you to think again. It's eleven o'clock. Don't you have classes.

You answer him, saying that classes have been cancelled for today. This is pure fabrication, which you know very well, but it seems easier to lie than admit that you have overslept.

He wonders why you don't ask him why he is here. Don't you want to know.

Not really.

A woman named Rita called the house. She said she was a friend of yours.

Not really a friend.

She said you left town without saying good-bye. She said she's written to you several times but she's got no reply.

I don't owe her anything.

The least you could do is be courteous enough to reply.

I liked it better when he didn't talk to me, you think to yourself.

She worked in an office at the plant where I had that job before I quit.

I never understood why you quit.

I had to. I'll explain some other time.

He clears his throat the way he always does when he wants to say something important. She seemed to be hinting that there was something going on between the two of you.

It was all in her mind. Anyway, what does it matter.

He gives you a look that says, Why don't we talk about this outside. You put on a pair of running shoes and follow him out of the dormitory, down the front steps to the sidewalk below, and around behind the building to the parking lot in back where he has parked his car.

Your great fear at this point is that he will ask you to get in the car and come home with him.

Tell me about this woman, he says in a voice that makes you wonder if he has not indeed taken a sudden and unprecedented interest in your well-being.

There's nothing much to tell. She had a crush on me. She invited me to her house once, to meet her husband. Her sister was living with her at the time, because she couldn't stand being alone with her husband.

We sat around the table and tried to make small talk. It was very awkward. The husband was this little mouse-like figure that everyone ignored. I felt bad for him. Rita had fixed her eyes on me because her husband was such a big disappointment in the sack.

Did she ask you to go to bed with her.

You can see what he's getting at, and you realize that you have already said too much. After all, it is your life to live, not his.

You shake your head like mad.

You're not lying to me. His voice is suddenly much deeper, as if this is the question that will finally settle the matter.

No way. This is not a very convincing denial. In fact, you don't even buy it yourself. But it does serve to end the discussion.

There is really nothing more he can say to you.

You have closed the book on this particular exchange, and you suspect, even then, that there will never be another.

Thirty-Two

You're a little old to be doing this, don't you think. Monkeys do it, baboons do it, but how come you are still doing it. If there was ever an argument for the tripartite brain, this is it, the skin of the glans as soft as clouds on a summer day, but the thoughts that float up from your reptilian past as hard and unforgiving as nails.

According to the early advocates of the theory of the tripartite brain a monkey, if you bring him into a room and put him face to face with his own image in a mirror, will spontaneously ejaculate.

But there's no need for you to worry, you have seen your own image in a mirror a few too many times for this to happen, even naked, unless it's coupled with the image of a pretty woman, or at least the memory of an image. So take your time and try to concentrate.

It's because of a pretty woman that you are here now in the men's rest room of the local diner, under the light, looking at yourself in the mirror, worried about who might be just outside the door, waiting to get in, and at the same time not worried.

Who's to worry when the stakes are so high.

The big surprise is that even though your penis is crooked from years of use and misuse there's no pain involved, no discomfort. Just the opposite.

It's bent because of a lump in a blood vessel, mid-shaft, that has the same effect as tying a knot around your wildest dreams. But the dreams are just as wild, and nobody ever told you not to do it.

There's a name for your condition but you always forget what it is since there's nothing to be done about it anyway. It's pretty common.

You were sitting at the counter, ready to leave, but embarrassed because you had no appetite for the soggy French fries you had ordered, when you saw her coming through the door and heard the way she laughed when her boyfriend, pushing up against her from behind, said, I'm the last one to complain about tight squeezes.

She did not say anything to you when she sat down, just to your right. She handed her jacket to her boyfriend, who took a moment to place it on the back of her chair and brush away the dust and the dandruff. Once settled, they leaned close, giggling like children and whispering things that you could not decipher.

She was talking in a language, French, that you do not understand but have long wanted to, even more so now that she is here. What you remember best is the way she fiddled with her belt and had trouble getting it adjusted to the right notch.

Apparently, she had a tender stomach, and she had to let the belt out when she sat down. She did not look pregnant but who knows. You were almost touching, your leg against her leg. Your black denim against her light, pre-washed jeans.

The top two buttons of her blouse were open, and her breasts were small and white, much whiter than her hand when she held it there, even slipping it inside, vainly trying to contain her laughter.

Her boyfriend, apparently, was a wit, and kept her constantly entertained. Her blouse was cream colored, and you thought it was probably silk, though you could not be sure. You would have had to feel it to know for sure. You would have had to reach out and touch it and feel it, and you did not dare.

All this time she had not yet looked at you.

You tried reading the pocketbook novel you had brought along but found it hard to concentrate, she was sitting so close.

You closed the book but still she ignored you, leaning toward her boyfriend, at the same time moving her leg till it touched yours. When she did this, you could feel the electricity.

You busied yourself looking at a few family photographs that you had brought along for the journey and kept tucked into the pocketbook. The woman fell silent a moment and when she spoke you knew she was speaking to you. But it was in French and your French is not very good.

You made a gesture with your hands, turning them palms up, to indicate that you were willing to make the effort, if she would just speak a little more slowly.

She repeated the same question, and this time you could just make out the words, C'est ton père.

She leaned in closer, looking at the photograph on the counter, a studio photograph of your father taken on the day of his graduation from high school, with everything in one shade of brown or another.

Yes, you said, but I don't really speak French.

When she glanced up from the photo her face was older than you had thought, from the way she moved and talked and laughed. There was a hint of something desperate in her look. That's all right, she said. Do you mind.

Go ahead, have a look, by all means, if you insist.

In the photograph your father has a sweet smile and there is no hint of the weight problem that was to plague him most of his life. His eyes are soft and heavy-lidded, foretelling much sadness.

She asked if he was still alive. You lied and told her yes, very much alive. He turns ninety in November, you said.

To speak of death at such a moment seemed gauche.

She leaned in even closer, just as you were wishing she would, and it looked like one breast would pop out of the black lacy bra pushing it up from below.

It's hard to imagine that man, she said, tapping the photo hard with her middle finger, ninety years old.

You liked the way she was so demonstrative with her middle finger and you liked the way she emphasized the word *hard*. And the way she leaned toward you, touching your shoulder, letting you see her breasts, wanting you to see her breasts.

In the mirror now you see your face and there is something different in the look in your eyes, because you are remembering the way the woman talked to you and the way she leaned against you.

It's hard to imagine. It's hard. It's hard. You keep repeating these words to yourself, and they begin to work their magic.

You switch to your left hand because with your left hand it's easier to reach the spot just under the glans, a little to the left of the slit, where it is most sensitive.

You look into your eyes, and you see how the green is surrounded by a ring of blue and how the blue infiltrates the green, the more excited you become.

You remember something else she said that you wish she hadn't. I wish my father had lived to ninety. There were some things we needed to talk about.

You were going to ask her what kind of things, but she had already turned away, reached into her bag, and taken out something that looked like a vibrator, but that turned out to be a puffer. She tilted her head back and sprayed something into her mouth, then closed her eyes and sat very still.

Her boyfriend knew, from experience, that when she did this it meant that she wanted to be left alone with her thoughts. He sipped his coffee and kept quiet. He avoided looking your way.

You excused yourself, and made your way past the two of

them, around the end of the counter and into the men's room.

You don't have very much time now because there are people waiting outside the door. You can hear them talking back and forth. Someone is knocking on the door.

Just a minute, you shout back. You try to forget what she said about her father and remember again how she leaned against you, and how you could see inside her blouse, and how you could almost feel her breasts they were so close.

You position yourself over the toilet bowl so that when you ejaculate it will not spill all over the floor. The water is blue and because you are already beginning your descent there are ripples and waves in the water.

You can feel the floor shaking and you are not even sure you will be able to remain steady on your feet. When you look into the bowl and listen to it, really listen, you can hear the air being sucked out of the bottom and drawn down into the abyss below.

It's hard, it's hard, this fix you've got yourself in, but you don't see how you can stop now. You can see inside her blouse and the nipple is hard, and the other one too, and your cock is hard, and the look in your eyes is hard and unforgiving. It's reptilian.

You are one cold-blooded son-of-a-bitch.

Someone outside the door says, Shit!

You growl, Fuck you!

A man's voice calls out, with a gravity to it that makes you guess that this is not just any old voice. It is the owner's, or, at the very least, the cook's. It reaches into every nook and cranny of the diner, even into the washroom.

It seems to you, given the circumstances, incredibly calm. At the same time, it possesses an authority that is beyond question. You know that you had better listen, you had better do as advised, or there will be a price to pay.

Just thinking about it makes you feel smaller. For once in your life, just once, you'd like to get that monkey off your back.

Fuck you! you hear someone say, and you know it is you because you are looking in the mirror and you can see the way your lips move and the way they spew forth the words, the way a fish out of water gasps for oxygen.

Fuck you! Fuck you! Fuck you! you keep saying, and you no longer know if you are talking to yourself, or to the owner, or to the cook, or to your own father, long buried in the hard earth.

And then, just when you think you are never going to get done in time, it's over, and it feels like the top of your head is about to come off.

Thirty-Three

Everything is spinning, and I'm better off just sitting here awhile in the car. I'm not thinking straight. I'm thinking about Bernie Davis. I'm thinking what if she had not refused me, what if she had changed her mind and stayed behind and married me.

I'm feeling dizzy and tired and sleepy and I'm beginning to see things in a new light, things that may have happened in one way but could just as easily have happened in another.

She thought she loved Bill Eylens and she would spend the rest of her life with him. But he played her for a fool, and she cast him aside. She did not and she could not love him anymore.

I didn't call her for a while, or try to impose myself in any way, because I knew she was feeling miserable because of Bill Eylens. But one day we chanced to meet, and everything fell into place.

We began to see each other. I studied to become a high school teacher, choosing history and economics as my areas of special interest. Bernie and I dated all during my years of study, and when I found a job teaching at a high school near Gary, we got married.

Almost from the start things began to go wrong. Our life together was not what I had thought it would be. Some days I felt trapped and doomed to mediocrity.

We were very different and the differences began to claw at the surface of things, like a bird trying to get in at the window. Bernie was short, red haired, freckled, a firebrand. I was tall, slow to form a definite opinion, given to long pauses.

She always wanted to be doing things and meeting people. I liked to stay at home, and read, and watch the news, and go to bed. She would get angry because I always had my face in a book. If I was not reading, I was watching a basketball game on television, or a hockey game. If I was not watching television, all I could think about was sex.

All right, I said, let's try an experiment. You choose a book and we'll sit down together and take turns reading to each other. I'll read for ten minutes, then you'll read for ten minutes, then we'll go to bed.

I was young, I was naive, I thought that if we could find something to do together then we might feel closer. But Bernie always fell asleep halfway through my reading, which was bad for morale, and even worse for our sex life.

Our apartment was in an old building that someone had bought, fixed up, and then opened again at double the rent. We had a kitchen, a living room, and a long hallway with two bedrooms and a bathroom at the end.

Everything was new, the kitchen was spacious, the walls were white, the floors were oak parquet, and everything felt empty. Bernie kept her things in the main bedroom, and I kept mine in the spare bedroom, which became my office.

She was a compulsive shopper, something else I didn't know until after the fact, and the big walk-in closet was soon filled with dresses and coats and more pairs of shoes than there are months in a year.

When she was out with friends, shopping, or having coffee, I liked to walk into the closet and feel the cottons and the satins and smell the places she'd been and the people she'd seen.

Her best friend was a smoker and more my type actually. Her name was Peggy, and she was dark, and she had a funny way of walking, as if she were dragging the weight of the world after her.

I always knew when Bernie was out with Peggy because I could smell the smoke on her clothes in the closet. I'd stand there smelling Peggy and wondering what it might be like married to Peggy and if it would be the same sort of disaster as it was with Bernie, different only in the details.

Sometimes I couldn't sleep and so I'd get up in the middle of the night and work at my desk in the spare room.

What sort of thing did I work on. I was writing a novel and it had something to do with what I was teaching at school in my combined history and economics class. I was trying to go beyond the usual analysis of the stock market crash of 1929, beyond the idea of cause and effect, and talk about the way it had ruined lives.

In my novel I was going to have two families, both recent arrivals to the big city (Chicago), and follow them through that ten year period from about 1925 to 1935. One family survives and grows, and the other does not. The men have been friends since high school. One man turns to alcohol and in the end he kills himself. His friend can do nothing to save him.

It was a depressing idea for a novel, and when I got tired of sitting there staring at the blank page, I would get in the car and take longs drives into the country. Bernie would be snoring in the bedroom, and nothing could wake her, not even if I gunned the motor.

I could drive the car into a tree and she'd sleep right through it. Something was missing in my marriage, and I was trying to figure out what it was. I would listen to the music on the car radio at four o'clock in the morning and I would know what it was that was missing even if I could not put it into words.

I would listen to Morgana King singing 'A Taste of Honey' and all I would want is to keep on driving and never come back.

Thirty-Four

The town where David lives and teaches is not far away. I enter the town from the north on the new state highway. I drive along a strip of motels and fast food outlets and various businesses that goes on for at least a mile. I'm immediately in the downtown area, which amounts to a total of nine square blocks.

The courthouse, which occupies the center square, is smaller than the courthouse in Lafayette, less impressive than I remember it when I was here. The businesses downtown are small, specialized shops, a newsstand, a salon, a video store, etc.

The old Woolworth's, opposite the courthouse, is now converted to offices of a communications and public relations company, the only recent renovation in sight that looks up to standard.

Just out of the downtown I turn right on the street that takes me past the main entrance to the campus, past the President's house, past a new building I don't recognize, past a row of fraternity houses, into the residential part of town where David lives, just beyond the campus, going west.

David has a large house on a large lot, a five-bedroom house with a garage attached, much too big for his wife and himself now that the children are grown up. He keeps saying he wants to move to a smaller place but never does.

It's April but, unlike at home, the trees are in leaf and even the lilac hedge that runs along one side of the property, from the sidewalk to the garage and all the way to the back, is only a week or two from being in flower.

There's a note on the door which says 'Hello Charlie, I've gone to the store. Come right in. Love, Evelyn.'

The front door is locked so I walk around to the back and try the back door. It opens into a spacious kitchen that has a tile floor the color of white roses, with a rectangular counter in the middle that can be used for food preparation and quick meals when everyone is on the run.

A cat appears out of nowhere and begins crunching dry cat food from a bowl placed just next to a door that leads into the basement. She's a thin black cat and doesn't seem concerned that a stranger is standing three feet away from her in her own house watching her, at least not too concerned, in the manner of cats.

There's no one home, so I wander upstairs. It's been years

since I visited, but I imagine that I will have the same bedroom as before, a small bedroom at the top of the stairs that previously belonged to one of the children. It's some distance from the large master bedroom at the other end of the hall where David and Evelyn sleep.

A towel and washcloth have been laid out for me on a chair by the foot of the bed. The top drawer of the dresser has been emptied for my use. In another drawer are some clothes that I left behind the last time I was here.

There's a black cotton turtleneck, the kind of thing I do not wear anymore. There's a long-sleeved shirt which is also black but which seems more to my liking. It's neatly folded as if just freshly washed and ironed. It has the feel of cotton.

There are several other pieces that once belonged to me, including a pair of pajamas, an undershirt, and an assortment of mismatched socks.

Underneath everything is a little container, a few inches square, made of a clear thin plastic, inside which are some leaves of something that must be a kind of tea, light brown, crisp and curled, looking as good as the day it was packed.

Next to this is an identical plastic container inside which is a Chinese cookie, half eaten, with the round teeth marks plainly visible. There is a thin brown icing on top of the cookie, the same light brown color as the tea leaves.

It's hard to know how long this half-eaten cookie has been here in the drawer. Possibly since my last visit.

I do not see any sign of mold. It's safe, I think. I'm hungry enough to take the chance.

It has an almond taste that I love. I wonder why I can't find a cookie like this where I live in Canada. Maybe I haven't tried hard enough. It's very good. I take another bite.

Down the hallway is the bathroom I've been looking for. Though small, no substitute for the main bathroom off the master bedroom, this one does in fact have a bathtub, as well as the usual sink and toilet.

Everything's been remodeled and brought up to date. Wood paneling, brass fixtures, water efficient toilet.

There's something else funny about the toilet. It's not fixed to the floor but moves depending on where I direct the stream of urine. By degrees I can bring it from its original position next to the sink to a position just behind the door to the hallway.

Unfortunately, there's a towel hanging down from a rod near the door. Before I know what's happening the towel goes in over the edge of the toilet bowl and gets soaked. That spoils the game and shuts off what was beginning to feel like a stream of never-ending piss.

I push the toilet by hand back to its place by the sink, which for some unknown reason is a much more difficult maneuver than the original one.

It zigzags across the floor and it's hard to keep under control. It keeps swerving.

I wash out the towel in the sink and hang it to dry over the curtain rod.

Thirty-Five

There's a noise downstairs, so I know someone is home. I look around, satisfied that everything is in order.

Is that you Charlie. I recognize Evelyn's voice from several recent phone calls. I feel I know her though I've yet to meet her.

She and David have been together almost five years. The last time I was here, with Anne, a little over five years ago, Evelyn was a name we heard, sprinkled in the conversation, the wife of a friend, an artist, a distant rumor.

I know the story of how they met and formed a couple, and I'll get to that in a little while. For now I'll just say I'm glad to be here, in the closest thing to home I think I'll ever feel again in these United States of America.

Evelyn is in the hallway, at the bottom of the stairs, draping her coat across the back of a chair. As I come down the steps she looks up at me and says, David's at a meeting.

She's shorter and thinner than I imagined, and there's a wariness in the way she looks at me that I would not have expected. She has straight black hair that she cuts short, like a man's.

It's great to see you, I say, putting my arms around her and giving her a kiss first on one cheek, then the other. She finds this way of greeting awkward, and she laughs her infectious laugh.

I've heard this laugh on the phone before and because of it I knew I was going to like her.

Come in the kitchen, she says. There's someone I want you to meet.

I've already met your cat.

Actually, we have two cats, she says as we move into the kitchen. The one you met was probably the black one, Shadow. Oliver's the shy one.

In the kitchen a man is sitting on a stool at the counter with his back to me. He's sipping red wine from a glass and does not seem to hear us. He has a bag over his shoulder, the same shape and color as the one Evelyn placed on the floor by the chair when she came in, but twice as big.

Evelyn says something and the man looks around at me without changing his expression – an expression that suggests fatigue at the end of a long day's work.

He would like to get it over with, whatever it is, and be on his way.

He's an arts journalist and the reason he's hovering around Evelyn like a cat around a patch of catnip is that she has just won a commission to build a sculpture at the entrance to a new pavilion at the Art Museum in Indianapolis. He's writing an article on her life and work.

As she's introducing us, he slips on a pair of silver-frame glasses to get a good look at me. She introduces him with just one name, Lindsey. It's not clear if this is his first or last name.

I am her 'brother-in-law Charlie who lives in Canada.'

I've never been to Canada, Lindsey says. That may have to wait for another lifetime and probably another life form, but from what I hear it's very nice up there.

This strikes me as both insipid and inane.

I doubt if nice is the right word. There are places that are very beautiful, and places that are so wild, so forbidding that you feel struck dumb.

I sound like I'm selling the goddamn place.

It's a big country, is what people find so hard to grasp.

I guess big – in every sense of the word except perhaps the one that counts – sort of sums it up.

Along the southern edge, as we like to call it, it's a lot like the States, but then what it has are these great stretches of land to the north where no one lives and no one would want to live, except a few natives and a few other hardy souls.

I don't seem to be able to shut up.

I would think foolhardy might better describe them. He smiles, feeling he's hit the bull's eye.

Evelyn comes to the rescue by suggesting we move upstairs to see her work space. It's here, she explains, that she does her sketching and comes up with her ideas. Her studio, where she sculpts, is in the country.

Her room is behind a door I missed when I was up here nosing around. While Evelyn shows Lindsey the drawings on her table I scan some of the titles of the books on the shelves.

They talk in low voices, as if discussing matters of great urgency. Once in a while Lindsey jots something down in a notebook that he carries.

I sit on a sort of sofa at the far end of the room watching all this and feeling superfluous. Near extinction.

After a while I put my head back and fall asleep.

In my sleep or half-sleep I can hear Evelyn's laugh and Lindsey's repeated use of the phrase 'what I really like' followed by something said in such a soft voice I can't make it out.

They could be talking about their next tumble in bed.

Or maybe they've pulled out a hidden sofa and they're doing it while I doze and dream.

The next thing I know Lindsey is pulling at something behind my head and shoulders on the sofa where I'm sleeping.

I've fallen asleep with my head on his coat where he threw it when he first came into the room ahead of me. He is tugging at it and saying 'Sorry man' at the same time.

Now is my chance to say something clever and show him unforgettably the brilliance of my mental process, but I've lost my glasses and can't think straight.

Even when I find the glasses they are caught in some sort of material that looks like a shawl that some peasant woman in remote Uzbekistan might wear.

I work to free the glasses, but without success. I'm afraid to pull hard, in case it's something else that belongs to Lindsey.

Lindsey shakes hands with Evelyn and turns to leave. I stand up, still without my glasses, but he's gone before I can think of anything to say.

Thirty-Six

Evelyn asks me about my trip. She asks me about Anne. She says for the second time how glad she is to see me. She asks me about my children.

They're fine, I say. Mary's running the bookstore while I'm on the road. I haven't seen Alan in a while.

Where is it he's living. I keep forgetting. We're in the kitchen preparing supper, waiting for David to arrive home.

New York City. He's got an apartment a few blocks from the Guggenheim, though he claims he's never set foot inside. He's very much his own man, very independent, which is just another word to describe the fact that we don't talk. Maybe once every four or five months we'll get together for a meal.

And what about Anne. She's got two children, right.

Three. Can I do something.

It's all right.

You're doing all the work.

Here, you can open this can for me.

I open the can of water chestnuts. She drains the water from the can, dumps the chestnuts on a cutting board and slices them into halves.

There, that's done.

She's planning a stir-fry for supper. She has everything ready to go, in various bowls and plates on the kitchen counter, pieces of chicken in a dark sauce, slices of red pepper drying on a paper towel, cashew pieces, strips of green Chinese lettuce.

What about a glass of wine.

A glass of wine would be great.

We sit at the counter, on the high, soft stools, and sip white wine. I ask Evelyn about the project she's working on.

I almost didn't get it. A friend called and told me about this competition I should know about, in Indianapolis. I don't know why, but I hadn't heard about it, There's a new pavilion at the Art Museum having to do with the fabric arts, and they want a sculpture out front, as a way to announce the building.

I like this sort of public art. It's where the money is. So I drove over and looked at the building. I've always been interested in the fabric arts – quilting, costume design, wall hangings, that sort of thing. When you ask why, the answer is simple. Because the artists are mostly women.

Edward Lemond

I think it's great, that we have a building where you can go in and even if you don't know the names of the artists you can see some of the things they did that are really wonderful. To me it's a sort of 'Memory Pavilion.' It's a way to remember.

I like that idea, a 'Memory Pavilion.' What a great image.

There's a wonderful book I came across recently, by an author called Francis Yates. It's all about memory as an art, an idea that goes back to the Middle Ages – actually way before that.

Funny, I've just been doing a lot of thinking about the idea of memory. What I'm finding is that I don't seem to have much of a nose for memories. Sometimes they come to me but it's pure chance when they do. I'll be walking along and something will happen and maybe this will make some connection to something in the past and then the memory will come back.

Proust talked about that. He called it involuntary memory. It's involuntary, that's the catch. What Yates is talking about is more like a skill that can be learned. What you do is construct some sort of building, or maybe a wheel, or a grid. You can sketch it out on a piece of paper, or you can do it all in your head. Then you place your memories inside.

You do this carefully, with key words or some sort of sign system, or something to remind you in what room, or what part of the grid you've placed the memories. Then you always know where to find them. The hard part is coming up with a sign system, or some way to keep all the keys sorted. It's sort of like finding your way through a maze.

Tell me about your piece. What's it like.

It's not like much of anything. It's pretty abstract. What I want to do is give shape to the idea that nothing is ever completely lost.

I'm trying to imagine what that could be like.

First of all, it's big, over seven feet high, monumental. It will be placed right by the entrance to the building, and when you stand next to it it's like it has tree-like limbs shooting up toward some place where all memories, everything that's ever happened, could be stored.

Walking around it, you feel a certain fear, because what it's pushing toward looks unattainable, barely conceivable. It's very solid, made of limestone – actually limestone that comes from Quebec in Canada, with a thicker grain than Indiana limestone.

I don't try to control the shape. I let the stone speak to me.

It's a sort of tall tree with a trunk that is splitting apart and that has such a tactile quality that it invites you to come close and touch it. But at the same time it is so big, so monumental that it keeps you at a distance. And so when you go into the pavilion you are ready to touch and be touched, ready to be drawn in.

The suggestion of a tree trunk might give a suggestion of motion, sort of like legs that lead the visitor into the building and into this new world of unknown masterpieces.

I hadn't thought of it like that. I suppose that makes sense, legs, yes, legs that will take you in, and keep you going, into the dark places. Interesting.

Maybe we could drive out to your studio and I could see for myself. What about tomorrow.

I'd love that. I'd love for you to see my studio.

David is late, and the two cats are getting impatient waiting for dinner. They circle and rub against Evelyn's ankles. The black one begins to nibble Evelyn's toe because she's slipped off one shoe and she's flexing the foot back and forth on the bottom rung.

Premature, premature, Evelyn keeps repeating to the cats, bending down to their deafness.

My guess is, they will get their fair share of the chicken stir-fry when the time comes.

Oliver, who is the orangest cat I've ever seen, lets me reach down and stroke her, down around the soft underbelly.

She almost never lets anyone touch her, Evelyn says. I'm impressed.

Maybe she knows I'm not a stranger.

Evelyn wants to have a little fun at my expense but doesn't know how I'll take it. She looks at me, hesitates, smiles, grimaces, stiffens her back.

It's remarkable, the family resemblance. I speak as an outsider. There's something about the shape of the eyes and the smooth forehead that definitely runs in the family. And the same small nose that makes you both look much younger than you are.

Now the black cat, Shadow, is scratching at the back door.

I think she's just fed up waiting and wants to go out.

But we hear the sound of a car door and Evelyn says, Ah, there he is now.

It takes me a second to realize she means David.

I'm on my feet, looking out the door, as excited as any ten-year-old kid waiting for his best friend to show up to play.

PART TWO

Thirty-Seven

I'm remembering the poem Charlie asked me to read at his wedding. It wasn't even a poem – it was one of Thoreau's meditations on nature. But he fixed it up like a poem – and it read like a poem. I love and could embrace the shrub oak.

All the other readings were from the Bible, so this was a nice touch. It was his way of saying, Here I am, in Church, it's not my Church, I do not believe in the teachings of the Church, but I do believe in ritual, ceremony, community.

He was always clear about what he did not believe in, but not what he believed in. He was always moving, changing, shifting, drifting, and I think half the time he didn't know who he was or even where he was.

Meeting Anne was the best thing that ever happened to him.

It changed our relation – as brothers. I could feel it right away. We were no longer so intensely jealous of each other. He wasn't trying to out-do me or put me down. He was in love, and it had nothing to do with me. It was not a competition.

I was the odd man out at the wedding, reading Thoreau – no getting around it. I thought, Hell, let's have a little fun, so instead of shrub oak I said, I could love and embrace your beautiful maple trees.

After all, here I was, in Canada, for the first time. Maple trees everywhere, on signs, on billboards, maple syrup for breakfast, even the flag had a fucking maple leaf. But it must have come out sounding pretty much the same – nobody batted an eyelash.

But Charlie found it amusing, and we laughed about it afterwards. I still remember it.

> I love and could embrace the shrub oak
> With its scanty garment of leaves rising
> Above the snow, lowly whispering to me,
> Akin to winter thoughts, and sunsets,
> And to all virtue. Covert which the hare
> And the partridge seek, and I too seek,
> What cousin of mine is the shrub oak.

How can any man suffer long.
For a sense of want is a prayer,
And all prayers are answered.

Strange thing to say at a wedding, but I wanted to do it because it was for Charlie. It was the first time in a long time, since we were boys, that he wanted me do something for him, something that close to his heart.

The day before the wedding we drove to one of the beautiful beaches in the area, to get away from the frenzied planning. Ruth had rented a car, and I drove with her. Charlie sat in the back with our sister, Ellen. Anne was coming in another car, with Elizabeth and some of the children.

Our brother Fred had died not long before, and we could see that Ruth was still hurting so much. She felt alone – not even sure if we really wanted her there. When she felt alone, she tended to talk too much – and too loudly. Nobody could stop her.

She thought it was great that Charlie and Anne had planned the ceremony so carefully and gone to the trouble of printing a program for us all to see. She kept glancing at Charlie in the rearview mirror and weaving back and forth on the highway.

Her smile, which was like a sneer when she was in one of her moods, feeling insecure, kept getting bigger and bigger, until she finally confessed that she found the lines from Thoreau confusing.

Better explain that one, dear brother, she said.

Charlie took the question seriously. What he's saying is be open. Be present. Be aware. Don't re-fuse but fuse.

Yes, but how do you open yourself to a shrub oak. There's not much there to excite the mind. Or are we talking about some sort of weird sexual practice.

Charlie looked at me. What do you think Dave. Would you rather read something else.

There was no way I was going to back out at this late date – I had read it and memorized it and begun to like it. But what surprised me was the new feeling that came over me like a fever – I love and could embrace this brother of mine. For this I credit Anne's magic.

The reception was at the house – seventy people gathered in groups in different rooms and on the back deck and in the big tent in the backyard where the children would come in and sit at the tables and play games, no more than for a minute or two, then disappear upstairs again where they would laugh and say what they really thought.

I wandered into Anne's studio, a converted garage, and found a supply of beer and wine that looked like it had not yet been touched. I must have been drunk because when everyone began proposing toasts, I stood up and said what was on my mind.

I might not be an artist, I might not be sophisticated like some of the people here, I might be a country bumpkin from the Midwest, but I love this brother of mine.

Charlie was sitting on the sofa with Anne, and for a few seconds he just looked at me as if he had never seen me before. His eyes got bigger and bigger, and he licked his lips the way he does when he knows everyone's looking at him. All he said finally was, Get outta here you idiot.

Then everyone started ribbing me, calling me country bumpkin, pumpkinhead, clown, fool, hoser. The one who really got after me was Ruth, who was high on something – maybe just the fact that Charlie had been so careful to include her in everything.

I would have liked to hold her and tell her that we all missed Fred just as much as she did. But I'm not sure we did.

There were more drinks all around. Everyone was feeling high. Someone spilled a bowl of grapes, and the grapes rolled over the table and onto the carpet. It was a red carpet with Persian design.

People began picking up the grapes from the carpet, blowing on them and eating them.

People were laughing and hugging each other. In the living room two strangers were sitting next to each other on the sofa and the woman broke the silence by saying, Sorry, I didn't get your name.

When I looked around, they were embracing and rolling together on a blanket on the floor. The woman kept saying, Excuse me, excuse me, while she laughed and clutched the man even tighter.

I went up the stairs in search of the bathroom. In a room down the hall some of the kids, girls as well as boys, were gathered around a screen playing a video game. It was some sort of war game – you could hear the noise of the explosions.

I opened a door that I thought was the bathroom but that turned out to be a spare bedroom. Charlie's daughter, eighteen years old, was on the bed in the arms of a young man I recognized as one of the musicians who had been hired to provide music on the back porch. Here he was – providing more than music.

In the bathroom I looked at myself in the mirror. There was more white in my beard than when I left home – or maybe it was just the angle of the light coming in the window.

Several stray hairs stuck out half an inch beyond the others.

I looked inside the cabinet for a pair of scissors. Something in me said, Don't be silly. Everything's all right. Call it the Ravages of Time.

I closed my eyes and moved my head left then right. There were popping sounds in the neck, in the upper spine. I felt dizzy and held on tight to the edges of the sink to keep from falling. I said to myself, Relax, don't worry. You've had too much to drink. You got carried away. Everything's all right.

But later, when I fainted and broke two ribs, I learned the hard way that everything was not all right.

Thirty-Eight

All through dinner Evelyn has that funny little smile she gets when she's trying to figure out what's going on. I'm glad to see Charlie but not as glad as I thought I would be. I like him better when he is with Anne.

He gives me a big hug at the door but I'm not sure he means it. With Anne you always know she means it. Charlie gives you the feeling he is keeping something back – guarding something.

It's like we were back to the days when he was twelve and I was ten and he had to keep me in my place. His great fear was – I would take his place in mother's affections.

It's not exactly like we are Cain and Abel here. First of all, I'm still here, so Charlie didn't finish me off, though I think he wanted to once or twice.

True, he's been a wanderer most of his life, and he must have had a mark on his forehead because he should be dead by now. And he ended up in Canada, a little east of Eden, in the land of Nod – where you might very easily nod off if it weren't for the fact that you were freezing your ass.

Evelyn has made the chicken stir-fry that I love so much – with almonds and black bean sauce. White rice. A clear sauce flavored with garlic and lemon juice. Charlie asks about the meeting I've just come from.

There's nothing much to tell. The department is hiring, and we've narrowed the choice to three candidates. All in their thirties, all published, all committed to working with undergraduates. All women – as it happens. It's a toss-up.

Choose the one who will light up your fires, Evelyn says. It's a pretty quiet bunch over there right now.

Evelyn thinks we're all just a little bit over the hill in the religion and philosophy department.

As long as the other departments are still functioning, Charlie says, and it takes me a second to figure out why he's giving me a big fat wink.

No problem in that department, Evelyn says with a trace of a smile – the inscrutability bit that she's so good at.

Charlie would like some elaboration, but he's not getting any.

And how's Anne. I'm the one asking, since Evelyn's fallen silent. We haven't seen you guys in such a long time. Too bad she couldn't make the trip with you.

Charlie tells me the same thing he's probably already told Evelyn – that Anne is so busy these days getting the gallery ready, she couldn't take the time.

How long has she had the gallery.

He holds up four fingers.

As long as she's finding time to do her own work, Evelyn says.

The wine goes down pretty easily with this sort of talk, so by the time we've all had a first helping of the stir-fry the bottle is empty. I leave them to it and head down into the basement looking for another bottle.

I take out a nice sauvignon blanc from California I've been saving, which will go with the salad that Evelyn's made. The salad is in the teakwood bowl that Charlie and Anne gave us as a gift last time they visited.

Evelyn is telling Charlie about a musical project she's been working on the last few months. She belongs to a group of amateur musicians, one member of which has composed a musical setting for some of the words from The Song of Songs. They're planning a performance this Mother's Day, and everyone is invited.

Eat, friends, and drink, until you are drunk with love, is the idea.

I'm involved, against my better judgment, doing research on the rare fruits mentioned, and on the stories and legends associated with the various plants – the mandrake in particular.

The music, needless to say, is going to be lots more fun than the research.

Pomegranates are mentioned, as well as grapes and dates, various spices, myrrh and aloes, henna and spikenard, saffron, sweet-cane, and cinnamon. Things that have come down to us as commonplace, like milk and honey, and wine, were part of the culture then too.

The words go like this:

> Let us go early to the vineyards
> and see if the vine has budded
> or if its blossom has opened,
> if the pomegranates are in flower.
> There I will give you my love,

when the mandrakes give their perfume,
and all rare fruits are ready at our door.

The story of the mandrake, however, is not commonplace at
all, but dark and tangled. Just like the root of the plant, which
grows deep in the dark earth, and has the tangled, new-fangled
shape of a very twisted human being.

We're not quite sure, some scholars say, if the mandrake that
we know today is the same as what's mentioned in The Song of
Songs. When you pull up the root you can hear the voice of a
human being shrieking in agony, and you might go crazy if you're
standing too close. Or you might faint and fall down, dead on the
spot.

Charlie wants to dig up his roots, and this seems to me as
foolhardy as pulling up the root of a mandrake – you just might go
crazy when the ghosts start shrieking. Better stand back. Better
find a dog to do the dirty work. Better tie a rope around a dog's
neck, the other end around the mandrake and get the dog to run
very fast in the opposite direction.

Maybe the fact that he's taking notes and he's going to write
about what he digs up is a way to keep his distance and keep his
sanity. Writing could be thought of as the dog that does the dirty
work of taking us down deep to places where otherwise we might
not come out alive.

Charlie says he's semi-retired from the book business. This
semi-retired business sounds to me like he's just giving himself
license to do what he's always loved – traveling, moving from
place to place, leaving everything behind.

I've a sneaking suspicion he's in the process of leaving Anne,
without even knowing it. He left his country, he left his first wife,
he left his girlfriend – no reason to think he won't leave Anne
when he gets that feeling in his blood, that yearning.

He scouts for books and when he's got a few boxes, he ships
them back. His daughter runs the store now, which must please
him no end. He and his daughter were very close when she was
growing up. You could see it in the photographs he sent –
Christmas photos, birthday photos, photos taken in summer on
one of those nice beaches they have up there.

After university she decided to try her luck in New York City,
as so many Canadians do, and for a while she was very distant.

She had less and less to say to her father. She was finding her own way. He had to respect that. Fathers do – what choice do they have.

Charlie's not sure why his daughter came back. She had a boyfriend who suddenly disappeared from the scene, so it's a good guess it had something to do with that. She does not want to talk about it. All she will say is that she got tired of the politics – the lies – the propaganda. Living in conditions of constant fear.

She says the worst thing was she couldn't tell if the fear was well grounded or not, Charlie explains. Half the time it seemed there was good reason to be afraid, half the time they were just screwing with your mind. And when you tried to talk about it and say, wait a minute, we don't have to live like this, you were told to shut up. Sometimes you were threatened.

It must be nice for Anne, Evelyn says, and when Charlie obviously doesn't understand what she means, she adds, I mean to have Mary there, for company while you're away.

Anne has many friends. Anne never wants for company. I don't worry about Anne.

I'd worry about my wife if I were away for a couple of weeks.

Charlie looks at me with a kind of blank look I've never seen before. You don't know Anne.

We've finished the salad and half the bottle of sauvignon blanc. I help Evelyn clear away the dishes while Charlie pours himself another half glass of wine. Evelyn's made a crème brûlée for dessert, with an almond glaze on top instead of plain brown sugar. It's so cool and so delicious that we all just shut up for a while and enjoy the sensation in the context of a sudden blissful silence.

Thirty-Nine

Evelyn has work to do after dinner and disappears upstairs while Charlie and I tackle the dishes. We feel light-headed after three or four glasses of wine each. The cats, clever enough to stay out of our way, run up the stairs after Evelyn.

I make a point of being extra careful with the dishes – this is when I sometimes get carried away and start dropping things. I wash and stack while Charlie dries. In this way I can slow things up and set the pace.

Slow things down.

I can grab hold of the edge of the sink if I feel dizzy. I can stop what I'm doing if things start spinning.

Charlie knows about my recent illness, my time in hospital, and the recent scare – a mild heart attack. Under doctor's orders I'm allowed to teach part-time. Charlie doesn't seem too concerned.

He keeps telling me I should deal with the 'underlying problem.' Deal with it man.

Screw that. He doesn't have to keep telling me. I know what the underlying problem is. It's diabetes. That's easy. I seemed to have inherited it from our grandmother. Charlie, as far as we know, is unaffected.

With Evelyn upstairs Charlie feels it is safe to ask, How are the children. I have not talked to any of my children in weeks, months, so my reply is a pathetic, As far as I know they're fine.

The two older have moved recently and eventually they'll tell me where they are. Maybe.

Helen, the youngest, is in Chicago, where she works as a journalist. If I call, she'll talk.

I have to think back fifteen years to a time when I got along with my children. Evelyn was married to a man named Richard Robinson who taught comparative religion. Richard was a bright, energetic man, who charmed everybody he met. He was small, probably no more than five feet four, with a big rounded forehead.

Balding already at the age of thirty. Interested in many things – art, music, philosophy, photography, yoga, and much else.

We were soon good friends, the four of us – Richard and Evelyn, Elizabeth and myself.

Then Evelyn had a second child with Richard, and Elizabeth

and I followed up with a second and then a third. We were all so busy with the children, and so surprised and delighted to find that we were now the grown-ups, the ones making the decisions and taking the responsibility, that we didn't feel the ground moving under our feet.

The first obvious sign of the ground moving was when Evelyn announced that she was going back to school to take a degree in art. The implication was that she was not going to be defined by the role of faculty wife. She wanted something more – though what this more was, it's safe to say, was not clear to anyone – including Evelyn.

The first time I knew I loved Evelyn was one day when we were talking on the telephone about taxes. Evelyn was doing her own tax return for the first time, and she didn't want to ask her husband's help.

Richard did not know how to help. He'd have to do it himself. He had that kind of mind. He was 'good at numbers' as people say who hate numbers. He was good at anything that involved research, weighing pros and cons, doing a cost benefit analysis, taking things apart and putting them together again, making lists, working up a balance sheet. He liked that kind of thing and whenever he had a chance he'd jump at it.

Evelyn's income was up from the previous year, though still modest – four thousand dollars from the sale of her art. Her expenses had remained constant, but she thought there must be a way to juggle things and make them come out right.

In the middle of the conversation she paused to add up some numbers, and in the silence while she worked away at the numbers I could hear her breathing and sighing in agony. Those sounds, so intimate, like a cat calling for its young in a dark basement, penetrated deep into my brain, and I think I have never felt closer to a human being.

In the end I advised her that she would be inviting an audit, and it would be best not to claim a loss this year.

I didn't deny what had happened, but I also didn't act on it for a long time. Then it wasn't even that I acted on it, but we just happened to meet downtown in a coffee shop where we both had stopped for a break.

I don't remember what we talked about, only that we could have talked for twice as long. Suddenly we both realized what was going on and we got up. Maybe if we both got up and walked away right now, that would be the end of it. Maybe it would be better if that were the end of it. But no.

We'd meet at Evelyn's house, mornings when Richard was teaching and the children were in school. Sometimes we'd walk in the park behind the house, just two friends walking in the park. What could be more innocent.

But apparently people can see things with their own two eyes and draw conclusions. Someone went to Elizabeth and said, Did you know your husband is seeing another woman.

Elizabeth was never not anything if not direct. When I came home she was sitting on the couch – there'd be nothing for dinner tonight. I went into the bedroom to change. She followed me in when I didn't come out.

I remember I was sitting on the edge of the bed reading a book of poems when she came in. She sat down in the chair opposite me and just looked until I stopped reading. I couldn't think of anything to say. I muttered something that didn't make much sense but it was the trigger she needed.

She accused me of having an affair with Evelyn, which of course I denied. I spent the next week trying to find a way to make things come out right. But instead it all came undone very quickly.

I was never in love with Elizabeth but I admired her. I liked the rebel streak in her – that fascinated me. She was fierce and relentless, when provoked. This is what I had learned early on, though perhaps not early enough.

Having children softened her hard edges and I think for the first time in her life she was able to love deeply, without holding back. Her love for me, if it was love, did not go very deep, I knew that, but we had always thought that we could live with that, because of the children, and because of the life that we were building together.

We had just bought a new house, and now Richard and Evelyn were thinking about buying a new car. Being Richard he had done all the research, gathered details no one wanted to know about, and presented them to us in columns marked For and Against.

He had narrowed the choice to three specific models - one American, two Japanese. But here he got stuck. When he looked at all the pros and cons they canceled each other. Evelyn bugged him, wanting a decision. Richard said she should call up 'her friend Dave' and get his opinion.

You seem to put a lot of stock in what your friend Dave has to say. Take him for a spin and see what he says.

I was already in a spin, and there was no getting out of the spin I was in. We drove the first model around the block, the second model around town, and the third model into the countryside, where we parked and kissed for half an hour.

Evelyn is a small woman, of Oriental extraction, and I've always feared, with my two hundred plus frame, I might crush her in the heat of the moment. But she's very quick and strong in everything she does, and she kissed me hard and deep and cut my lip. Where was this passion coming from.

I liked it – being floored, almost knocked out. I bit back but she was not really playing this game. She wanted to tell me something, as if telling me would fix it. I can't live with him anymore. It's like living with a calculating machine. There's this buzzing going on all the time. You don't know what it's like.

I asked her about the children.

I'll ask Richard to leave. Let him think about it for a while and he'll have to agree that I should have the children. Let him do the research.

But Richard developed an unexpected stubborn streak and refused to listen to anything Evelyn had to say. He refused to leave the house and find a place of his own. He refused to think about the question of who should have custody.

For the sake of the children, he said, stop what you are doing. If you don't stop what you're doing, that will be all the proof I need that you're an unfit mother.

Evelyn laughed at him and said she refused to be bullied. His attempt to smear her name was pathetic.

The scene we all dreaded and that we all seemed to be waiting for to settle the issue took place on a Friday, around the dinner table. We often had dinner together, the four of us, at the end of the week. It was a habit we had fallen into. We were the closest of couples. This time it was Richard and Evelyn's turn to have us over.

Elizabeth, who was the unpredictable, the explosive one in the mix, did not say a word all during the meal. After a while we stopped pretending that we didn't notice. She hardly touched her food, and flatly refused dessert.

I'll make the coffee, Evelyn said, retreating to the kitchen.

Nothing for me, Elizabeth said again, even louder.

With Evelyn hiding in the kitchen all small talk had come to a halt. We listened to Evelyn moving the dishes around, grinding the coffee, feeding the cat. We could hear the coffee begin to bubble. The three of us sat at the table, not moving, avoiding looking at each other.

Time slowed, like great black oxen in a field. We fidgeted. How long would she be. Maybe while the coffee was bubbling she'd step out the back door, start walking and never come back.

A sort of paralysis had got hold of us. Everything was out of focus and obscure – past, present, future. There was the feeling that everyone involved was much smaller in talent and ambition and accomplishment than we had suspected.

Some machine was at work that seemed to have a mind of its own. No one knew where the switch was, to shut it off, or throw it into reverse.

Finally Evelyn came back in, with three cups of coffee on a tray. Elizabeth stood up.

With the movement of her body in rising her long black hair, which was tied loosely at the back of the neck, ballooned at the sides, like the jaws of a cobra in full attack mode, and this had the effect of framing her face and setting the high, delicate bone structure on fire.

She had a way of speaking clearly in moments of high emotion. Her words seemed especially intended for my ears, but the unforgiving look in her eyes took in the lot of us.

That was it. We were finished. I found an apartment near the campus, from where I could walk to work. Evelyn moved in. Richard and Elizabeth began seeing each other, to no one's surprise. It was a great scandal, for about a month.

One day they appeared together at the door of the apartment and announced that they were leaving 'this stinking little town.' Elizabeth was taking the children with her – there was nothing I could do.

Evelyn fought for custody in the courts and proved to be the more convincing – even with the black mark of infidelity against her. Richard could have the children every second weekend, for two days. He was very bitter.

They settled in a university town a hundred miles away, far enough that we seldom saw them, close enough that they always seemed to be hovering over us. Jobs were not hard to find in those days – universities were expanding and there was a shortage of teachers. He was a good teacher, I'll give him that. Students loved him, because of his energy and his interest in everything.

But it wasn't long before we began to hear rumors that he was drinking a lot and making a fool of himself at faculty gatherings and late night bars. This did not sound like him at all. Then one night very late he showed up at the door and demanded to see his children. Evelyn told him never to try a stunt like that again.

One day I answered the phone and could not recognize Richard's voice he was so drunk. Evelyn would not take the phone. Tell him to sober up and then we can talk, she said.

I felt sorry for him. But when he kept calling and kept calling, I told him where to get off. Just fuck off, I said.

Evelyn was afraid to let the children go with him, even for a weekend, because he was drinking all the time. He'd come into the house and you could smell the alcohol on his breath. He did not try to hide it. You couldn't hear his laugh anymore – it was gone.

In the end even the children turned against him. The younger, just ten, would come home crying from her visits. The older, fourteen, was silent, and very angry. The man he knew as his father no longer existed.

Eventually, Elizabeth too lost patience with him and found a place of her own to live. She had three children to bring up, and if he wanted to straighten up, fine. If not, then too bad. She would not put up with a man whose major contribution to the household was waking everybody up in the middle of the night with the sound of his vomiting in the toilet.

None of this would have happened if you hadn't wanted to sleep with his wife, Elizabeth said to me, the day she called to tell me of Richard's suicide.

I didn't feel that I needed to take on this extra burden of guilt.

You decided to leave. It was your decision. Nobody made you do it. All the while I was saying this I was wracking my brain trying to remember if this is the way it had actually happened.

Elizabeth would not let me see my children when they were

growing up. Whenever I called, she would say, I'm not talking to you, and she would put the phone down.

She blamed me for what had happened and said that she had nothing more to say to me. The children had the benefit of one side of the story only, hers. With a little poison sprinkled in for good measure.

Helen, the youngest, was least swayed and still visits me on occasion. She has found a way to walk the line between mother and father and keep her balance. She is afraid of nothing – even a mother's wrath.

Sometimes I feel I'm falling from a tall building. On the way down I'm conscious of everything I've lost, everything I no longer have – beginning with the children.

I have no one to blame but myself – I know. I was a half-hearted father at best. I did try to think about what was best for my children, but so often ended up with no conclusion – in a sort of fog. My first and last thought was always for my own well-being – all the other thoughts in between, the shadowy thoughts, added up to nothing.

What I did not understand was how closely my sense of well-being would end up depending on which road the children took.

Charlie is calling up the stairs to Evelyn, to ask if she wants coffee or tea. I can hear Evelyn's door squeak as she comes out of her room and crosses to the top of the stairs. What kind of tea, she asks, in that soft voice she has, the note of gladness in it because we've taken her away from some work that is not going anywhere.

It's some sort of herbal tea. Ginger something.

I'll have tea. She goes back into her room, while we get the tea and the coffee going. The tea takes a few minutes to steep.

I open a can of cat food and fill up the two cat dishes, one for the Shadow and one for the Orange Fluff Ball. At the sound of spoon on tin they appear out of nowhere – suddenly I am an important presence in their lives.

Charlie arranges cups and saucers on a tray, along with the teapot, a little glass with an inch of honey, and three spoons, and I follow him up the stairs – this big brother of mine who has his own share of troubles.

Forty

I have not seen Evelyn's room this tidy in months. She's cleared the stack of books and papers and drawing materials from the big table by the window so that we can sit here and look at some of the old photos Charlie has brought along.

Charlie, standing behind us, places the photos on the table between Evelyn and myself. Then he stands back and lets us form our own impression – without comment.

Evelyn's eyes light up when she sees a photograph of Charlie at four years of age. It is a small, dark photograph with serrated edges, and a black mark on the back where it's been ripped out of a photo album.

Charlie is sitting on a step in front of the house in West Lafayette where we lived, briefly, in the 1940s. Behind him is a long walkway leading to another set of steps just at the door. One corner of the house juts out, with windows showing above his head and an evergreen bush below one window, at shoulder level.

He's sitting with his hands folded on his knees and his feet planted firmly beneath him, against the bottom of the step. The coat he's wearing is buttoned up tight to the neck and seems to be the thick material of a duffle coat. The hat, with a little bill in front, is pulled down tight over his head and ears. It could be made of felt or corduroy.

Everything, from step to house to bush to coat to hat, is in some shade of brown, from light to dark.

But it's the look on his face that makes Evelyn lean close. The lower jaw juts out as if he is in a high pitch of anger about a point of principal – anger about being made to sit quiet like that, or anger at something somebody has just said to him, off camera.

His mouth is half open and maybe he's missing a tooth or two. It could be a shadow – it's hard to see. He's squinting in the sun and fury flares in his eyebrows.

When you look at that mouth a moment, close up, he's ready to kill somebody. His shadow, which is half again as long as he is himself, tapers off to his right and back a little.

On the sidewalk are some chalk marks – an arrow on the step below him, pointing in, toward the house, another arrow on the step he's sitting on, some other letters or numbers on the sidewalk behind him that his little body obscures.

It looks like a set up for a game of hop, skip, and jump.

You don't look very happy, Evelyn says. When Charlie does not say anything, she turns her whole body and looks up at him as if she's got a stiff neck from sitting all day at the drawing board.

I don't have a good memory of those years, Charlie says. I suppose I was just as happy and just as unhappy as the next kid. I know I did try to run away from home a couple of times. I was only four or five. That tells you something.

Evelyn tells him that she ran away from home once, when she was eight. Until she was eight, she did not know that she was different. Then one day all her friends seemed to turn on her at once. They started teasing her and calling her awful names. Mellow Yellow. Little Miss Saigon. Here Comes Slant Eye. She was on the outside, and they made sure she understood.

Kids can be merciless, Charlie says. Especially when they know they've got you cornered.

What about you. Why did you want to run away.

I don't remember. Maybe it was just the sense of adventure – wanting to see new things. That seems to be very strong in me.

Charlie takes another photograph from the envelope and places it on the table between us. He takes a good look himself then stands back to let Evelyn and myself in closer.

The three boys – Charlie, myself, older brother Fred – are sitting on the running board of a car. Ellen, our sister, stands near the huge, round front fender, looking toward Father who is standing off in the distance, at the rear of another car.

The picture is taken so that it feels like we're looking uphill toward Father. This is an illusion of the camera – the street is level in front of the old house.

It's a photograph that is full of action. Charlie has both of his pudgy little hands around his right knee and his head is turned in the direction of the camera – he is the only one not looking toward Father. He could be looking at the camera or past the camera, at something happening behind the camera.

His eyes are half closed so you can't see where he's looking. Maybe he's turned that way because he doesn't want to look at his father – unlike his three siblings. Or maybe somebody over there has just said something to him.

His mouth is rounded, puckered. It looks like he's ready to say something to break through the false sense of everyone posing

– the words Fuck off take shape.

He's five years old in the photo and already fat – a problem that would plague him on and off all his life. He's dressed in shorts and a short-sleeved shirt that's too tight.

I'm wearing shorts with suspenders and a T-shirt. My legs are stretched out straight in front of me and I'm looking toward Father. You can see the back of my head and my puffy cheek.

I'm squeezed in between Charlie and Fred. I'm three years old – maybe four. I'm the one who seems to have the least to do with what's going on here. I'm getting squeezed out.

Isn't he sweet. Charlie says, his finger touching down for a second on Fred who is sitting in the middle of the picture, between Ellen and me. He's wearing dark shoes, low socks, shorts, and a T-shirt with the sleeves rolled up to the shoulders. He's sitting very straight, with his bare legs set square and steady.

His left hand is on his left knee – with his elbow almost in my face. His right arm is extended and the right hand placed gently on Ellen's shoulder. You can see his face in profile. He has that sweet smile that he had all his life and that was as close to the beatific as you would ever want to see.

Ellen seems to be moving off toward Father, and Fred is either holding her back or telling her, Steady as she goes. She's wearing tiny black and white shoes, the right one just slightly off the ground, in mid-step.

Her face is turned completely toward Father, though her body is seen sideways. She has the same very light hair, almost blond, that I have – whereas Charlie, Fred, and Father all have dark hair.

The way we are sitting on the running board, and the way the photo is taken, from below, we do not even come up to the handle on the door. Off in the distance Father seems huge, his head rising up above the windows of the church in the background.

He's dressed in long pants, a short-sleeved shirt that's too tight and he has both arms out just a little in front of him, as if he is about to raise them to catch Ellen as she comes flying his way. His face is half in sun, and he seems relaxed and happy – just waiting, nothing to do.

He was a big man, Evelyn says. Big in every way. He seems to be having some trouble keeping his weight under control.

He struggled with his weight all his life. Every few years he'd just balloon right up.

I'd say he's a kind man. There's a soft look in his eyes. It's pretty obvious that he's fond of this ragtag assortment of ruffians. But at the same time he seems puzzled. He seems to be asking himself a question. How do I look after this tribe of wild Indians and what if we have another one or two, what then.

I suppose this is the question that was always in the back of his mind, because he never did make enough money.

Somewhere along the line they decided, to hell with family planning. We'll just fuck our brains out and live with the result.

I think he felt trapped – more and more trapped toward the end of his life. He had this big family to provide for, and very little money.

He liked his work, and he hated it. He was good at what he did – he was a skilled tradesman and he had no reason to be ashamed. What he didn't like was to be on call six days a week – seven days when there was an emergency.

He never worked on Sunday. Sunday was his day off. Remember, we'd all get in the car and go driving. Sometimes we'd drive around the countryside. Frankfurt, Lebanon, Attica, all those exotic sounding places that were nothing but little towns, like ours, in the middle of endless corn fields. Sometimes we'd visit Uncle Bill and Aunt Pat in Indianapolis.

I went with Father once on an emergency call. Some important person at the university had a burst pipe in his front yard and it was flooding. I remember the telephone ringing, just as we were all heading out the door to get into the car for our Sunday drive.

It was Aunt Dot. Father didn't say anything, just listened. His face got redder and redder. I remember he was so mad he slammed the receiver down. She must have said something that really got under his skin. She had a way with words that he found irritating. She could skate circles around him.

He didn't get angry very often, but when he did, watch out. My most vivid memory remains the time he got so angry with me he hit me. He only hit me this one time but it killed my love for him forever. I was ten years old.

Mother had called me into the kitchen, and asked me to run some errand for her. Some friends were coming over, and I pleaded with her to get Ellen to go. No, Ellen was doing something else. Couldn't she go herself. No. Couldn't she wait till later. No.

Well, I'm too busy, I said. Father was washing his hands at the sink, just home from work. The way he saw it I was talking back to Mom, and with no warning he slapped me on the back of the head.

It was like my head was exploding. I looked around because I didn't know what it was. Never sass your mother, he said, and you can bet I never did after that. And I never felt free around him again, to speak my mind. If he asked me a question, I would answer it.

But I never really talked to him again. Even when he was home dying, and I was living at home that summer after my first year at university, I never really talked to him. I found ways to avoid him.

Charlie falls quiet a moment, thinking back. I remember harsh words being spoken, but never being hit.

It was nothing. He didn't knock me down or break any bones. He didn't hurt me. That's what I kept telling myself. But I never forgot the sting of it – so I guess it did hurt. I was wobbly on my feet the rest of the day. I had to grab hold of things to keep from falling down.

Ever since that day, when I've fallen or when I've felt the desire to fall, I see the look in his eyes when I turned to him after he slapped me on the head. I trace everything back to that look. It was a wild look – an unforgiving look.

Ever since that day I've had a great longing to fall, to let gravity do its work, and to forget everything I know and everything I believe about myself. But it's so hard to find the time and the place to make it happen.

Maybe he hit me when I was very young, and I've suppressed the memory.

For a long time I held it against him. But now that I've had the experience of being a father I don't judge him so harshly. He wasn't the best father, but I was not very good either. I was worse – I abandoned my children.

Evelyn looks at me sharply. You did not. She took them. You didn't know she'd be so spiteful. We've had this discussion before.

Lot of things I didn't know I should've known.

And don't tell me your falling episodes have anything to do

with your father. It's because of the diabetes, and the sooner you start taking care of that, the better.

Where did I get my diabetes, if not from my father.

Your logic escapes me. Evelyn gets up from the table. I feel like a drink, she says. She moves toward the door, into the hallway, with Charlie close behind.

Give me something stiff, put me in the groove, what are you waiting for, she sings like a drunken sailor. I turn off the lights and follow them out.

She's at the bottom of the stairs, already disappearing into the kitchen. Charlie is waiting on the top step for me to join him.

I see him clearly for the first time this trip – a big man with a white beard, leaning against the railing, sort of swaying back and forth, his eyes half closed, dreaming, in no hurry to go anywhere.

It makes me feel dizzy as I approach him, seeing him standing there as if balanced at the end of a diving board, the edge of a cliff, the ledge of a window on the ninety-fourth floor of a skyscraper. Why do I want to surround myself with images of people falling.

In my dreams people are forever falling down stairs, slipping on ice, fainting on stage, tumbling from windows. I'm not alone. It feels good knowing I'm not alone. Everybody's falling. Some faster than others.

This really happened. In a departmental meeting I stood up to say something and even as I was standing up I knew I had nothing to say. I remember saying to myself before I fainted, What a waste of energy and talent. Sit down and shut up.

The next thing I remember I'm lying on a stretcher, with straps across my shoulders and my midsection, being carried by four firefighters to an ambulance parked half on the sidewalk, half on the lawn in front of the building, lights flashing. There's one at each corner, struggling to keep me at a level as they come down the stairs.

Geez, he's a heavy one, one of them keeps saying.

Whoops, almost dropped him there, another says. Sorry.

It's okay, I've got him, no need to worry, a third chimes in.

I don't know if they are horsing around or what.

The insulin treatment works, as long as I remember to follow instructions. I have dizzy spells but I know how to deal with them. Don't stand up too fast. Know when to say no. Know when to stop.

Half the problem is not knowing when to stop. Always pushing, pushing. When I fall I have the feeling of being distant from everything and everyone. Far from home. Lost in space. Nowhere at all. I'm not even sure if I'm still alive. It could all be a dream.

As we come down the stairs we get a glimpse of Evelyn crossing the hall into the living room with a tray on which she's arranged a bottle of something, three liqueur glasses, and a plate of those unsalted rice crisps she's taken a fancy to.

Charlie is assigned the place of honor at the end of the coffee table, facing the fireplace, a wicker chair with a high back and wide flat arms, shaped like a king's throne. Evelyn gives me the nod to put on some music to listen to.

I choose an old record that I picked up at a secondhand store a few years ago called Chet Baker Sings.

Forty-One

I like Chet Baker for the same reason I like Billie Holiday. It's the same thing when you look into someone's eyes and there's nothing there, it doesn't matter how beautiful they are if all you can see is a blank wall. An empty stare. But when you listen to Chet Baker or Billie Holiday the words and the music come from such a deep level of experience, anguish, and emotion that you know it has to be true.

Maybe Ella has a better voice – one of the purest voices ever. Toward the end of her life Billie's voice was a shadow of what it had been. Tired. Burdened. Beaten down. But she feels it and that comes across. Chet Baker gives you the same feeling.

I Love Too Easily, he sings in that thin flat voice of his that seems to be choking back the misery of years of sleepless nights and wrong choices. He's living on the edge and the only reason he'd ever lie to you is to get a quick fix.

If he decides one day to throw himself from the balcony, all you can do is wish he'd found a way back inside, to the music and the melancholy.

It's not late but it's been a long day. Charlie has his eyes closed and I don't know if he is sleeping or listening to the music. He moves his fingers ever so lightly on his knee tapping out a rhythm so it must be the music. But maybe it is not the music I'm playing but some other music that no one hears but him.

I'm thinking to myself, why have I stayed in one place all these years, while Charlie is the one who's never lived in one place more than five years – always on the move. But he seems to like it where he is in Canada and maybe he's settling down. But I remain to be enlightened as to why. They say in winter it's not unusual to see minus thirty, minus forty. My toes turn black and blue when it gets that cold. They fall off.

I went to college here, then came back to teach and never left again. Liked it here. Never wanted to live anywhere else. I wonder why that is.

That was thirty-five years ago. More than that, counting the student days. Many years teaching. Head of the department twice. Dean of the College for five years. Teaching again now full time. It adds up. Holy shit!

Even during sabbatical years I didn't go far, except that once, when my marriage was falling apart.

My marriage. It was always a precarious thing. From the beginning I knew there was something missing. Some spark. Some glue. I did not love my wife but I thought maybe one day I would. Never happened. Took some time to sink in. I admired her – so I pressed on.

Having children woke me up to what deep feeling is all about. So I was in a bind. I knew what I felt and what I didn't feel. Some sort of new arrangement would have to be made. In the meantime there were the demands to be a father to my children. This can take you only so far – say until the youngest is nine or so. Then you begin plotting an exit strategy.

I wanted to get away as far as possible from everything that was going wrong. We no longer slept in the same bed – and it wasn't too hard to figure out what this meant. If she wasn't sleeping with someone else, she might as well have been. I might as well have been.

When I talk to Evelyn about this, she just shakes her head. Evelyn has strong views about marriage.

This is what I know about love. It's tested every day. If you let anything come between you, the smallest thing, it's like a wedge and it will drive you apart.

That's the thing about wedges – they get bigger and bigger.

Every day you have a choice to make, to love more or to love less. If you choose to love less, you chip away at the foundations. Eventually the whole building comes down.

Evelyn has strong views, yes, but what I love about her is that she doesn't mind if you don't agree with her. She's not afraid to put her ideas to the test. She says what's on her mind.

I lack her spontaneity. I have to think things through and make sure I've got it right before I open my trap. But more often than not as soon as I open my trap I find out that what I thought was airtight is full of holes after all.

It's the give and take that's the key to finding a balance. This is what I keep forgetting.

Evelyn wants to know if we have any plans for tomorrow. Charlies says he'd like to see what the downtown looks like, then drive out to Evelyn's studio and have a look around.

Evelyn says she'd like that. She's got some work to do, and we, meaning Charlie and I, could arrive later – around two. The place needs a good cleaning out, she says, looking at Charlie. Why don't you get Dave to take you somewhere for lunch. There's a place called the European Bakery that we like a lot.

Don't bother cleaning up. That's part of the deal. Artist at work. That's what I want to see.

I'll just clear out a few things so you can get in the door. It really is a mess.

Chet Baker is singing 'You'd Be So Nice To Come Home To,' and I'm humming along. Evelyn gives me that look which says, I miss you too and I hope you won't stay away too long.

You guys have probably got things to talk about, she says and heads upstairs.

Charlie's very tired and can hardly keep his eyes open. We listen to a few more songs. We pass the bottle of Grand Marnier back and forth. A handsome bottle it is too.

The last song is so scratchy that I get up and put the record away. I put on a CD I've been listening to a lot recently – Keith Jarrett playing 'Standards in Norway.' Keith Jarrett at his most relaxed – just taking it easy.

Charlie starts telling me about a dream he says has been bothering him all day. I'm in the bookstore, upstairs, in a little room where we keep the children's books. The books are scattered about over the floor, more chaotic than usual.

I notice a little creature on the floor, no more than a few inches tall, but very strange, prehistoric, like something you'd see in a movie. It has a lot of bright colors in its design, greens and reds. It's alive and it lets me pick it up, sort of perched on my finger.

There's a woman in a room just outside the children's room, looking at books about natural history. I ask her if she knows what sort of animal I've got, but she shakes her head and backs away, afraid. I carry the creature down the stairs, and I'm able to get a good look at it as I go.

The thing I notice most easily is the large tongue that's protruding rigidly in a mode suggesting either fright or threat. It frightens me a little because I don't know which it is, but I continue on my way and the creature lets me.

You're in the dream, standing downstairs among some other books. I go to you for advice as to what to do. Do you think I should take it outside and let it go. Your reply is that it is not ready for the outside. I should first spray it and subdue it.

With this in mind I release the creature into the front display window of the store. A crowd collects and watches in amazement as the creature climbs the window and begins gnawing at a vent in the ceiling, looking for an escape. When this fails, it breaks the window and gets out.

It has powers I never suspected. Frightening powers. Before they are fully on display I wake up.

Telling the dream seems to release Charlie from the fatigue he's been feeling for the last hour. He sits on the edge of the couch, waiting for my response. I guess I'd wake up too, and pretty fast.

The thing is, it was so real. There's a prehistoric animal living inside me. Now what does that tell you.

I'll say what I said in the dream. It's not ready to be released.

If it's prehistoric I don't think it wants to be released. It's more comfortable in the background. But the question is, How do I live with it.

The same way we live with everything in us that's primitive. We just have to know it's there.

Okay. Here's something primitive for you. I'm thinking about leaving Anne.

That's news.

There's no good reason, I don't know why, I just think it's time.

Shocking news.

The thing is, I still love her. But I don't think I'm going back.

You're thinking about it, but you're not sure.

No. It just hit me yesterday. Bolt of lightning. Very primitive.

Just because it's primitive doesn't mean it's the right thing to do.

Never said it was.

Just because you get some idea in your head doesn't mean you have to act on it.

Remember the quote from Blake. 'Better to murder an infant in the cradle than suppress a desire of the heart.'

Boy, you really mangled that.

But you know what I'm talking about.

I don't think I do. The way you're talking sounds to me not just foolish and stupid but wrong.

Ah, here we go. Brother to the rescue.

You're way too old to be rescued. I'm telling you what I think.

All right. Go ahead. Tell me.

It's stupid because you've done it before and you ought to know better. It's foolish because you won't find what you're looking for by leaving Anne. It's wrong because you really love her but you're willing to throw that away.

Continue.

I'm almost out of breath, the feeling is so intense. On the road. Wonderful. You get this momentary feeling of freedom. This rush of adrenalin. You see things new again. And then what. After a while things aren't so new. You stop a moment and look around. Nothing has changed. You're still the same. Same hunger, same desire. You're not free. You pause, you listen, and what do you hear. A familiar sound. You listen again. It's the sound of prison doors closing.

Let's assume you can tell the difference between shit and shinola. Let's assume you're not a piece of dried-up potato fungus that doesn't know fuck-all. If freedom is what it's all about, where do I find it.

You find it right where you are. You open your eyes and it's there. It's all around you. It's in you. It's everywhere. It's nowhere.

When I open my eyes all I see is the same tired faces. I'm bored. I'm not living. I'm sort of just waiting around. I might as well be dead. When I begin to feel this way, I know it's time to move on. Time to heed the call. Gentlemen, start your engines.

You talk like you're ten years old.

Charlie sits back on the couch, stretches his arms out wide, yawns. Maybe that's it. Maybe I just never grew up.

Wham! He shuts down, and I know I've touched a nerve. Maybe the wise thing would be to shut up but no, that would be too easy. Or maybe it's like a game and I've got the advantage and I don't want to give it up. What are you running from.

It ain't like that at all dear brother.

Well what is it then.

I'm tired. I think I'll head up to bed.

He stands up and I follow him into the hall. He turns and looks at me, and his eyes are not just tired, but blurry, like clouds moving over water.

I don't know what to say and mutter something stupid like, Sorry. You know me. Compassion of a rock.

He's already very far away and says, Remember me in your dreams.

I can't think of anything else to say, and I know he's not listening. Sleep well brother. He's already halfway up the stairs.

Forty-Two

Evelyn is up before me. She takes her shower and gets dressed. She whispers in my ear, Is everything okay. I thought I heard you and Charlie arguing last night.

Everything's fine, I mutter, and then she's gone. I hear the car, and I know she's left for the studio. She wants to get the studio ready for Charlie's visit. She worries too much. Charlie doesn't care if it's cluttered.

I sleep another hour or two, and in my dream I am in Paris, driving around in a black limousine with two black musicians I've only just met, looking for a nightspot near the Eiffel Tower that I've been telling them about.

But for some reason we can't see the Eiffel Tower among the tall buildings visible all around us, and we end up in a seedy part of town. Maybe this isn't Paris, I think, because of the unusually tall buildings – skyscrapers.

Don't stop here, I say, it's too dangerous. They ignore me, and one of the black guys gets out and goes into a doorway and down some steps where there are loud voices. He doesn't seem worried and I say to myself, maybe that's how it is when you're black.

He appears again in the doorway and motions for us to follow him. I wake up.

Charlie's sipping coffee at the kitchen table, reading the paper. He's already meditated, walked two miles, showered, written in his notebook, and read a chapter in the pocket book he's brought along, by a Canadian author I've never heard of – Tim something. Finney. Finley.

I'm the slowpoke today and can't seem to wake up.

I'm standing at the stove heating skim milk for my coffee the way I like it, in a bowl, like the French, when Charlie announces, Says here that Jack McAnally died last week. I remember Jack McAnally.

He looks at me to make sure I'm listening.

He played football. Running back. Broke his ankle in the Heidelberg game.

Jack was head football coach here for many years.

I didn't know that. See how out of touch I've been.

Played professional ball for ten years, then turned to

coaching. Did well the first few years but then had one bad season after another. Here's a man who always did love a drink but now he began to drink to escape. Got himself fired, which ain't easy around here, and drank some more. Doesn't say it in the paper but he shot himself.

That's too bad.

I sit down at the table across from Charlie, with my bowl of coffee and a piece of toast. Didn't you room with Jack, your first year.

Actually, just the first few weeks. I had applied late to college, after a dismal summer working at the GM Plant in Indianapolis. The only empty bed they could find me was an upper bunk in Jack's room.

What was he like at that time.

He was two years ahead of me. When I first knew him he was already a big man on campus. The main thing I remember is that I never got any sleep when I stayed with Jack because Jack stayed up all night talking with his friends. I was new, so I didn't dare say anything. Finally I got a room with another freshman in the same building and it was like waking up from a nightmare.

He graduated from college the year I enrolled, so I just had a glimpse or two of him before he left to play pro ball. I think it was the Packers he played for. He made quite a name for himself.

Yeah, it was the Packers, I remember that.

Anyway, he played professionally for about ten years – before injuries forced him out. He wasn't a big star or anything, but he played in the big leagues, that's something. In the meantime I was back here teaching – staking out my own little piece of turf. I was here when the decision was made to hire Jack.

He didn't have much experience, a year or two somewhere in Wisconsin, coaching at the high school level. But the program here was so strong, he did well the first few years. He had everything – a beautiful wife, three children, a job he obviously loved, a team that was so good that once or twice we made it to the national playoff.

What happened.

His oldest boy died in a fire. It was very sad. The boy was autistic but just the most loveable child. One day we had a bad storm and the power went out. The boy lit a candle and went into his sister's room to keep her company. He was very protective of his sister. But the sister got up after a while and went outside to sit on the front porch with her parents. He must have knocked the candle over in his sleep. By the time the smoke reached them sitting on the porch it was too late. Jack never got over it.

You know when I was driving down yesterday I stopped in Battle Ground. I wanted to see the old home, and the school we went to, and the cemetery where the soldiers are buried, and the places where we used to play.

The moment I turned off the highway and headed down that back road into town the thing that really jumped out at me and stuck in my mind was the time my friend Steve was hit by a car and killed. He was just eleven or twelve at the time. Not as old as Jack's boy. He was my best friend. Sometimes it seemed like my only friend.

The strange thing is, I didn't feel much of anything when he was killed. One day he was there, the next day he was gone. Life went on. I was too young I suppose.

I remember when that happened. What was his name.

Ludlum. Steve Ludlum.

Your best friend dies, and you don't feel anything. It tells you something.

It's the way we were brought up. Absorb the pain. Don't complain. Keep your mouth shut. Be stoic.

I remember once someone closed a car door on my fingers and I didn't say anything. I didn't cry out. It was second nature not to cry out but to stifle it. I'm not sure who closed the door but I think it was Aunt Pat. I loved Aunt Pat, everybody did, and I didn't want to do anything to lose that love. Like look like a sissy. Very carefully I knocked on the window to get her attention. She was astonished when she saw me and I pointed at the door, but I was proud.

Pride goeth before a fall.

Yes yes yes. Just keep reminding me.

I don't remember Steve very well. He was your friend. I was a couple of years younger and you didn't want me tagging along.

I didn't know you wanted to tag along.

Be that as it may. But I do remember Steve's parents. Before the accident his father was a scout master. We used to meet at the farm. He'd show us around and we learned about farm life. Difference between a bull and a steer, that sort of thing. Then we'd go back to the house and have some of the wonderful cookies that Steve's mother made. Peanut butter, chocolate chip, oatmeal. I can still taste them.

It wasn't too long after the accident that we moved to Lafayette. I didn't hear much about the Ludlums after that.

They made the news a few years later – but I think you had already left for college. Old man Ludlum left his wife and married his secretary. It was a big scandal at the time. Seems he had been seeing this secretary all the time, and this is what Steve vaguely suspected when he got on his bike that day and started into town. At least he never had to find out what a cheat his father was.

I think he might have preferred to live with the knowledge.

What do you say, should we head into town. A few things may have changed since you were here. Though I suspect very few.

Ready when you are.

Forty-Three

Charlie has on a green jacket with a hood – in case it rains. In his green golf pants and green jacket he looks like the jolly green giant and laughs like him – from the belly, deep and low. He looks his age – no spring chick.

I've got a fold-down umbrella no bigger than a baton just in case. The sky's gray and it looks like something's brewing.

We cut across the campus. It's mid-morning, Saturday – no one about. We walk down the middle of the street, between the gymnasium and the student union. On the left as we go – The Scarlet Inn. On the right – Haenisch Hall. Straight ahead – The Chapel.

Since Charlie graduated forty years ago nothing much is new – except the gymnasium and the Fine Arts Center, located across the central mall by the north entrance.

With its white decorative entranceway the Fine Arts building stands out from all the others, like the one member of the family who dresses up because she's socially ambitious and she's clever enough and good-looking enough to get away with it even while she ignores the discord that she creates.

Charlie wants to get a closer look. We circle the mall – past The Chapel and past the old Administration Building.

The Fine Arts Center houses a 275-seat concert hall, a 350-seat theatre, two air-conditioned art galleries, and numerous classrooms, studios and recording rooms.

Music was always important, Charlie remembers, but not funded very well. It was mostly the glee club. What the hell does that mean, glee club, when you're living on a budget that amounts to peanuts. When we had concerts they were in the chapel. The art gallery consisted of a couple walls in the administration building. The drama department used the gymnasium whenever they were expecting more than twenty-five people to show up which wasn't that often.

We had some great concerts in that old chapel. Fischer-Dieskau, van Cliburne, Cleo Lane. The one I remember best is the time Lotta Lenya was here, singing songs from Kurt Weil. The Three Penny Opera. The Golden City of Mahagony. The balcony was full. There were people hanging from the rafters. I don't sing, but Kurt Weil I come close to being able to sing.

Charlie opens the door to the concert hall – a door that looks like all the other doors on the main floor but only deceptively so. It's like those caves in Kentucky where you step inside and suddenly the space opens up and you can stand up straight and breathe.

The ceiling is thirty or forty feet high. Below on the stage they're busy getting ready for the concert that's scheduled for this evening.

I've seen the poster announcing the concert – four recent graduates from the music school in Bloomington are on tour, doing selections from Mozart's opera, Cosi fan tuti. It's going to be taped for broadcast – already workers are laying black wires across the front of the stage, down the steps, out the back door.

We stand at the top of the stairs watching the activity below on stage. It's very quiet. The workers know exactly what they're doing and don't need a lot of talk. You like opera, I whisper to Charlie.

Sometimes.

Well, Mozart, you can be sure the music is gorgeous.

I love everything he wrote, including the naughty letters.

What do you say, let's get some tickets. I'm sure Evelyn will come.

Charlie starts down the aisle toward the stage. Yeah, great, he says, plunging ahead. I can hardly keep up. We're going down, down, down, into some sort of pit, and it's like we're leaving the outside world far behind.

I introduce Charlie to a couple of the technicians I recognize. One of them says, Canada, eh. I was in Toronto once, hell of a city. But before we can explore his take on Canada and on Toronto, Ray Little, chair of the music department, walks over.

Ray's in charge around here – and sometimes you'd think he was running the art department too. He's a tall man, as tall as Charlie, but bigger, rounder, with a head just as big and round as his belly, a long face made longer by thinning, whitish hair, so that the forehead is impressively broad.

Around here Ray's word is final – he's God. But a God who also agonizes when things don't go right. Who suffers like the rest of us. Who delights in telling stories about the times when things do not go right.

Hey there, he says, and gives me a vice-like squeeze with his big hand. He could be a lumberjack.

Hey yourself. I'd like you to meet my brother, down from Canada. Charlie, this is Raymond Little. We pronounce it like Ray-man. Music teacher, conductor, choir master, organizer sans pareil.

Glad to meet you, Charlie says but his look says he's not so sure.

I guess I'd better watch out what I say if you're from Canada. I hear you people up there have a pretty low opinion of us Yanks these days.

I don't know about that. I suppose we have a different perspective.

It's like you're on the outside looking in. Things always look different.

I'd say it's more like we're living on the margins and we get a very good look at the way power is used and abused. We also tend to have a bit more sympathy for the underdog.

Touché, as the French say.

I'm standing right next to Charlie on stage – facing Ray, who has a smile on his face I've never seen before. I put my arm around Charlie's shoulder to calm things down. I have a feeling they will come to blows if this goes on much longer.

Most people around here couldn't care less what Canada has to say. Ray is the exception that proves the rule.

Yeah, that's right, Ray says. In my case it's not hard to understand. My mother's family came down from Canada a few generations ago. She was a Gautreau, but when they arrived in the Boston area they added an x to their name just to confuse the Yanks.

A lot of Acadians came down to Massachusetts to find work.

That's what I've been finding out.

There's a village just outside Moncton, New Brunswick called Gautreau Village. I've been through there a few times on the way to an old lighthouse at the end of the road where you can see the river with its great tidal flow joining the Bay of Fundy. I think they spell it without the x.

I've never been back, though I've had the chance once or twice. I guess for me the past is something I'd rather leave behind. Look to the future, forget the past, that's my philosophy. The past is a graveyard. Maybe I should. Go back, I mean. But these days I have a feeling that my welcome in Canada would be a cold one as soon as people found out where I was from.

We like Americans - we just don't like your politics.

I notice you say we. Sounds like you've bought the whole pacifist package, hook, line, and sinker.

Pretty much so.

Too bad. I wonder what you'd do then, if some fascist dictator came knocking on your door, threatening to blow up your buildings.

The point is there's not, and there never will be, because we're not out there fucking around with other countries.

Ray scratches the back of his head, and on his face there's a puzzled look. I'd never thought of it that way. Gee I'm glad you're here to enlighten me.

I don't claim superior wisdom.

What I see is other countries wanting to be like us, coming to us looking for a helping hand.

Your helping hand usually ends up in the other guy's pocket, digging deep for all the loose change you can shake free. What I see is a country bent on empire. Against all its better instincts.

Whoa, you two, I have to break in again. It's too early in the morning to start banging heads.

Charlie takes several deep breaths, as if he's just run a four-minute mile. A technician taps an overhanging microphone to see if it's live. Ray walks over to have a word with this same technician. Charlie looks at me with a sort of startled look – the color gone from his face. I return his look and shake my head.

Let's get out of here, I say to myself. Ray's a friend – at least he was.

I don't suppose you've totally sold out for tonight, I say to Ray when he walks back across the stage to where we are standing, near the top of the steps.

He looks at me, wondering if this is a Freudian slip and something worse. Last I heard we still had a handful of tickets.

I'll talk with Evelyn and see if she wants to come. We'll probably see you tonight.

Hold on a second. Let me see what we can do about that. He pulls a packet of tickets out of his back pocket, pushes the rubber band back, and peels away the top three tickets.

Here, these will put you in the middle of row 'M' – best seats in the house.

Very nice of you Ray.

My pleasure. Just knowing your big brother came all the way down from Canada to take in our little production makes my heart glad.

Charlie's embarrassed and doesn't say anything. They shake hands. I go first, and we start down the steps.

We're about halfway up the aisle toward the door at the back of the hall when Ray shouts, Down with tyrants!

Charlie looks back and waves at Ray feebly. He has a sick look on his face – the look of defeat. Ray strides across the stage and is about to disappear in the wings when a light dawns in Charlie's brain and he shouts back, Down with empire!

His voice fills the hall. Ray looks around, flabbergasted. I put my arm around Charlie's shoulder and with a little assistance we move up the aisle. He's shaking – I don't know if it's laughter or tears. His eyes are closed and his mouth stretched wide, lips together. I push open the door and we step outside.

Forty-Four

Charlie half-walks, half-runs along the pathway behind the Arts Center, away from Ray's angry shout, Down with Tyrants, and I find myself struggling to keep up. Funny how fast things spin out of control when you're talking politics or religion or former wives or anything half buried, half dead. You don't know what you're saying until you say it. It just comes out. Then it's too late.

At the stoplight at the northeast corner of campus Charlie looks at me and says, What was that all about. He shakes his head – as if he's been deep diving and his ears are full of water that's lodged there stubbornly.

Ray's like that. Very strong opinions. The light changes to green, and we cross – green man in a green jacket in a green light. Now we're grinning.

Jesus, I thought he was going to bite my head off.

What you don't realize, dear brother, is how much things have changed in the last couple of years. The climate here is very bad. This comes out sounding like a wife who says she's being beaten on a regular basis but she doesn't want anyone to know – while at the same time she's begging to be rescued.

We're early for lunch at the European Bakery, so we sit for a while with a cup of coffee. There's a nice table by the window that's free. It's small and round. The window is made of an opaque, wavy glass, wrapped in bands of metal. There's a light green tinge to the glass.

Outside, the day is gray, dull. Across the street we can see the county courthouse – the stone a light, honey brown. It's a quiet Saturday morning – not much traffic.

Charlie's itching to hear more about the political climate and keeps giving me that look that says, Go on, spill the beans. I'm saved from this unpleasant task by some commotion across the street.

A police car stops across the street and we watch as two policemen get out of the car and walk toward a man who's pissing very publicly in among the high-growth cranberry bushes along the side of the county courthouse. They give him a push from behind and you can see him turn and say something like, Hey, get your hands off me.

He zips up and starts walking away, across the street, toward the café where we're sitting. He comes into the café.

You can tell he's mad, and he says as in a dream, Boy, does that make me mad. I've got rights too.

He looks at Charlie, as if at an old friend. What do you think, should I report them.

Damn right, Charlie says.

The man sits down at the table with us. He's wearing a raincoat – black, crisp, and new-looking, with buckles on the shoulders and a belt of the same material. Coming across the street with the coat flying out behind him he looked like a wild man – a bum. But up close it's a different story.

There's a twinkle in his eye, and a laugh that says this is no one's fool. I've seen that look before – and that laugh.

Haven't I seen you before.

Maybe.

I've seen you on TV.

I play DaVinci.

Now I remember. Charlie, don't you get that show in Canada.

We make that show in Canada.

So DaVinci, what brings you to our town.

He brushes his hair back with both hands – hair that's too long, too wavy to be stylish. He's a man who doesn't care that much about style – off screen.

He has the look of a little boy – mischievous and pugnacious at the same time. But what's striking is that he's a much smaller man than he appears on TV. Still good-looking – but smaller. More restless – edgier.

I used to know a girl from Indiana. She was from around here, and we were supposed to get married in that very courthouse across the street. But she changed her mind at the last moment. Decided she wasn't ready to settle down in quotes. First she had to do some traveling – see Europe.

I told her Fuck Europe, but she went anyway. So I was just passing through town and thought I'd stop and piss on that old courthouse. That old cunt. Excuse my French.

I think he's making it all up but Charlie says, Christ, I'll bet that felt good.

DaVinci laughs. What, you had a similar experience.

Very similar. Including the trip to Europe. I've got to see the world, she said.

Now it's the world is it. Not just Europe. He looks at Charlie, then at me. Well I'll be fucked.

It's eleven and lunch is being served, so we order the soup and sandwich special. DaVinci says he's got to be on his way and won't change his mind though we ask him to stay. We'd like to hear more. His parting words, at the door: Try the dark cookies with the green filling. I had some this morning. You won't be able to stop eating them. Taste of mint.

Charlie disappears into the bathroom – to continue the pissing theme. DaVinci drives off in a sports car with the top down – a little two-seater that's either an antique or the latest thing going.

The soup is delicious – an apple zucchini soup with a taste of ginger. The bread is whole wheat, fresh, a meal in itself.

Charlie's gone an awfully long time. His food is getting cold.

Forty-Five

Charlie's always disappearing. It's the theme of his life – no wonder he wants to write about it. Everything revolves around Charlie and his disappearing act.

Do I sound bitter.

My first memory is sitting up with mother the night Charlie ran away from home – at the age of five. Three times she commanded, Go to bed, and three times I crawled back into her lap, complaining I can't sleep because of all the voices.

Father was on the phone with the police, and Mother was on the phone with her sister. I made myself invisible, which was my own sort of vanishing act. No doubt I overdid it – that night and for the rest of my life.

They found Charlie around eleven and delivered him back to us safe and sound. What does he get for keeping us up half the night and scaring everyone shitless. Mother's tears of joy, Mother's great big hug, and a cup of hot chocolate.

How is that supposed to teach him anything. The pattern is set and all his life Charlie has been disappearing without a word – always coming back, always coming back, always coming back, and always managing to get some sort of reward for his troubles.

So I'm bitter.

I'm the one who stayed behind and took care of things. For instance the time Father died and Charlie was taking his sweet time getting home. Hitch-hiking!

Where was Charlie when we needed him. Somewhere on the road between Anderson and Marion – with his thumb up his ass.

In other words – nowhere to be found.

I remember this.

At the age of five, in the dead of winter, Charlie runs away from home, seduced by a neighbor boy two years older, an experienced and avid shoplifter who sets Charlie up as a decoy and a patsy.

At the age of ten, in Battle Ground, Charlie takes up smoking and gets so high on tobacco that he passes out under the bridge at the edge of town. No one can find him. Mother's frantic. The

police are called in – again.

At the age of sixteen he meets a girl and falls in love but she's not interested. He starts staying out late, and one night he does not return. A search party finds him asleep in the rafters of a half-built church a mile away. His reason for being there. In the rafters, under the open sky, he feels closer to God.

At the age of eighteen, after little more than a month at college, he vanishes without a trace – and the next we hear he's dockside in New York City, seeking passage on a boat to South Africa. Why. He wants to become a missionary, though he has absolutely no training in the field. Why. Because Bernie Davis, the girl he's unable to get out of his mind, had once talked about wanting to be a missionary in Africa.

At the age of twenty-two he drops out of first year medical school and is nowhere to be seen for the next five months – swallowed up in the Haight-Ashberry pseudo-revival.

At the age of forty-four, after 16 years of marriage and two children he has been extraordinarily close to, he decides that now is the time to find his way in life, his 'path.' It's now or never, he tells himself.

Today, after twelve years with Anne, when they seem perfect for each other, he thinks it's time to move on. He's feeling 'caged in.'

That's the short list. I imagine that every day, in his mind, he's trying something new, leaving something or somebody behind, moving on, with no intention of ever returning.

But here he comes.

Maybe our minds do follow parallel lines because the first thing he says is, You know, it just occurs to me, I haven't spoken to my daughter since I left.

He's going to give her a call and see if everything's okay at the store. There's a phone near the front door that's free. It's close enough so I can hear the few words he has to say, in reply to her questions.

I'm fine, what about you. Who. Sorry, I forgot to tell you. He said he'd be coming in with a box of books. Price them, and divide by two. Credit only. No cash. Take it or leave it. That's right.

Mary gives a full account of the week, including the regulars and the crazies, to which Charlie responds mostly with grunts and finally with, Not her again. Tell her we don't buy Bibles. Not now, not ever.

Then Mary says something that brightens up his voice. Really. That's great. Well, I'm so glad. You too.

With this he hangs up and comes back to the table. Mary told me to tell you she's planning a trip of her own one of these days. She wants to see you and everyone before it's too late. She's afraid you're going to die off on us, one by one, like flies.

Tell her not to count on it.

Charlie pulls his chair up to the table. Anne's invited Mary over for dinner. They've never been very close – so I'm glad they'll have a chance to talk without me being there.

How is Anne.

She's still very much alive and kicking, God bless her. Mary feels divided in her sympathies. She can be very aloof, which hurts Anne no end. So maybe it will do some good – my absence.

So explain this to me again. Mary takes over the bookstore, Anne becomes like a second mother to Mary, and you go your merry way.

Charlie ignores my inquiry as to his intentions, my slam against his plan, and picks up his sandwich.

It's hers if she wants it. He means the store.

And if she doesn't want it.

She can sell it.

What if she can't sell it. I don't suppose a person makes much money selling beat-up old secondhand books.

He glares at me but says only, We do all right.

I put my glasses down on the table and shut my eyes. I'm sorry, I say.

You're my brother. I expect you to give me hell. What are brothers for.

I'll remember that. I leave Charlie in peace to finish his sandwich. I signal the waitress for a refill on my coffee. Outside, on Main Street, a parade is going by.

Girls, eight or nine years old, dressed up as cheerleaders and baton twirlers, march by in happy disarray. Older girls, in their late teens, or early twenties, follow in plain clothes, most somewhat to very overweight, looking stunned, much less free and easy compared to the young ones.

A fire truck inches along, with two firemen inside. Boys ten years old, in full football uniforms, but wearing sneakers instead of cleats, traipse along behind the fire truck, not sure what they are doing in a parade on a Saturday morning when they could be playing a deadly serious game somewhere, on some battlefield.

I try to remember when I was that young and that lost.

Forty-Six

Evelyn's studio is a few miles out of town, in an abandoned mill by a creek near the boundary of a state park. She shares the building with a man who looks after the trees in the park.

His job is to prune in a timely manner, and cut back when necessary. He keeps his tools, his power saws and his chains, on the ground floor, while Evelyn's studio is on the floor above him.

He also keeps a horse in a stall at one end of the building. During the summer tourist season he will hitch the horse to a wagon and drive people through the park, to see the trees and the wildlife.

I don't know the workman's name but everyone calls him Brother Leo because he used to live with the monks at Gethsemeni in Kentucky where he helped out in the kitchen and in the fields.

His eyes light up when he sees me. I can tell he's been having what he calls one of his off days. He's standing in the door of the mill, and he's not going anywhere.

No one gets through without his say so.

Guess who I've brought along. I make a gesture with my arm, as if to introduce Charlie to a roomful of people.

He looks Charlie up and down, and pretends he doesn't know. He has the face of a peasant woman in a Rembrandt – long, lumpy, leering, laughing – and shy, laughing eyes that keep looking away.

Your long lost brother from Canada, he says, unable to keep the secret to himself.

Why do you say that. I never said long lost.

He looks lost, I think.

Charlie is embarrassed. He doesn't know what to say. Brother Leo shakes his hand and will not let go.

Finally Charlie says, Once I was lost and now I'm found.

But now Brother Leo's attention is diverted by something behind us. You go on up, he says. No charge for Professor Edwards and his guests.

A male pheasant has settled on the ground outside Brother Leo's door, and when it sees us stopping to gawk, it flies off again, with a great flutter of its wings and a loud squawking.

Brother Leo steps outside the better to see it on its way.

The bird is the important thing, in his eyes. We have ceased to exist. I show Charlie the way to the ladder that takes us up and into Evelyn's studio.

The only way to get there is through a trap door. This has one big disadvantage – she has to use a hoist attached to the side of the building to get her larger pieces up and down.

The advantage is, the studio's free, it's large, it's solid, and there's ample storage space. She doesn't mind the extra work, hoisting blocks of stone up and down the side of the building – she loves a good challenge.

Come on up! she yells when she sees who it is. We climb the ladder and find Evelyn in a foul state of mind because the piece she's working on is dismal, beyond hope – a failure.

To her mind.

Pretty awful, wouldn't you say. She nods in the direction of the wall where she's hung a huge piece of plywood, ten feet by twelve, which she has painted, gouged, painted some more, and festooned with cast-off bolts and nuts and pieces of band saw to make the point that nothing is ever completely lost or abandoned.

The paint is the same dark rust-brown as the cast-off metal, with a hint of red. It's true that it's dismal.

She always says the same thing about her works on plywood. Dismal. Dismal. But she keeps coming back to them.

I keep telling her she should stick to what she does best, and what gives her the most satisfaction – the limestone sculptures. But she won't listen to me. All I can say is, It needs work.

That's what he always says. Evelyn turns to Charlie who stands there transfixed – as if he has never seen anything so huge and dark and ugly and so powerful at the same time.

Sometimes he says, I think it's redeemable, as if I've committed a sin and need to beg forgiveness.

Evelyn, tell Charlie how you lucked out with your studio here.

He wants me to stop raving. Gladly. There, I've stopped. No more raving. See.

Charlie shakes his head but can't think of anything to say. Is she totally stark naked mad, he is asking himself.

I want to assure him she is not but sometimes I'm not so sure. She says, The concept is really quite simple. I get free studio space, unlimited access to the power tools down below and a place in the main building in the park to exhibit my huge, ungainly, unsightly but redeemable works of art, and in exchange I agree to create one large sculpture each year for the state park people to do what they want with. Stick it up their ass if they want.

Show him the piece you're working on, I suggest.

Evelyn leads us to the other end of the long room, where there is a huge piece of limestone, more than seven feet tall, cylindrical, with the faint suggestion of arms pressed close to the sides, but nothing else.

The stone, even unworked, has a beautiful coloring to it, a light yellow, as if coming from within. This one they want to set up on the hill above the lake. I'm afraid someone will come along and give it a push and the whole goddamn thing will roll down the hill into the water.

On the floor next to the limestone are two rusted metal rings that presumably, one fine day, will encircle the stone, like belts. She has done this before.

Charlie is in a sort of daze. The kind of work you do is so different from Anne's. Yours is large, monumental. Hers is small, intimate. She uses boxes, and inhabits them with found objects. I guess that's what you have in common. You like found objects.

That's the way we crazy women operate, we don't like to see anything go to waste. No siree.

Nobody will dare push this down the hill. Not with those metal rings.

You think so.

Nobody will touch it.

She gives him a strange look – not sure what he is implying. Then she takes a deep breath and says, You must be tired, you two. Let's have a cup of tea and get out of here.

The building is old, and Evelyn's studio is one long bare room, but she has everything she needs – electricity to run all her various power tools as well as boil water, a miniature fridge to keep things cold, table and chairs in case company comes, a chemical toilet so she doesn't have to run to the main building every time, and a horse on the ground floor making noises so she won't feel lonely.

While the water is boiling and Evelyn is putting out cups and saucers and a plate of cookies I give Charlie a guided tour of the rest of the studio – including the loft Evelyn's built where she stores all but her largest works – they fit underneath the loft.

Okay, gentlemen, she calls us back. Tea is served. Get back in here, I'm lonely.

We're all suddenly at a loss for words. We sit quietly sipping a peppermint tea and eating chocolate-chip cookies. We can hear the horse moving around below – clomp clomp clomp – bumping into the wall, snorting.

Brother Leo is in the yard at the side of the building, below the hoist, calling for the pheasant to come back. I'm lonely, lonely, he sings, I was born to be lonely.

I can see how Evelyn would find this comforting, after pounding away in isolation with hammer and chisel for hours on end. Better a mad hatter than a blank slate.

It's after three and Evelyn wants to drive Charlie into the park and show him a couple of her sculptures from previous years, one just outside the main building, one down by the river.

Why don't I take the car and head home, I suggest, and you come later with Charlie, after you show him around. That way I can get dinner going. I'll have time to do a little shopping.

Clever, Evelyn says though I can tell she doesn't mean it.

I leave the two of them to their devices, climb down the ladder, and head back through the woods to the car. I turn and wave to Brother Leo when he shouts after me.

Evelyn's purse is on the passenger seat where she forgot it – she's always forgetting things.

It's a nice-looking purse – an Anne Klein.

It's a wonder no one has broken in to steal it.

Forty-Seven

It's nice to be by myself for a while. I open the window and let the fresh air blow in. It's great. I can breathe. I can forget about Charlie. Forget about Evelyn. Forget about everything.

It still seems like I understand – nothing.

It begins to drizzle, so I roll up the window again. I turn on the radio to the opera hoping it's Cosi fan tutti but it's The Flying Dutchman instead.

Love and betrayal, love and betrayal – everywhere you turn.

By the time I do the shopping and stop for a bottle of wine and a six-pack of beer, they are home ahead of me – much to my surprise.

Charlie hands me a beer. We decided to skip the walk down to the river. Too many damn kids swarming the hillside.

Evelyn comes down the stairs, in a white shirt and blue jeans. She's wearing a pair of white tennis shoes, and looks just as thin, energetic, and ready to go as ever.

I'll get supper, I say. Why don't you and Charlie sit out on the porch for a while.

I'll take a beer, she shouts, though she's three feet away, in the kitchen door. I don't know what's got into her.

Luckily the back porch is screened in and keeps the rain out, so they can sit out there while I get things going in the kitchen.

Poached salmon, boiled potatoes, sautéed in butter with parsley, steamed Brussell sprouts with a sauce of butter, sugar and crushed walnuts – nothing too complicated. Evelyn has already prepared the salad and the dessert – an apple crisp.

While the salmon poaches I sit with them on the porch. It's a warm, humid, sticky day. We sip our beer and laugh about nothing in particular.

The heavens open and the rains come – a deluge. This is the kind of weather that spawns tornadoes in this part of the country, at this time of year – mid-April.

We sit there another minute, marveling at the intensity of it, then move inside. We're getting wet – through the screen, with the wind blowing in.

Evelyn calls for the cats to come in but they don't respond. The rain is too heavy – they've found shelter under someone else's porch.

We move into the dining room. I open a bottle of red wine. Evelyn serves the salad – a Greek salad, with Feta cheese, white onions, black olives. The salmon, poached in maple syrup, is perfect.

By this time we're all a little drunk – though with Evelyn you can never tell. She gets just as juiced with her art as with alcohol.

The conversation comes around to our sister Ellen – when was the last time anyone saw her, or talked with her, or had any sort of communication with her.

When no one else can remember, Evelyn finally claims the honor. It was last summer – her birthday. I said to myself, what the hell, I'm just going to call the little bitch. If she hangs up, she hangs up. But as it turned out, we had the nicest talk.

It was as if we had never broken off communication. Of course, we haven't heard from her since then, have we dear. Odd, I just called you dear – I haven't done that in ages. I hate the word. Don't mind me, I'm a little tipsy.

Let's give her a call, Charlie suggests.

Yes, let's do! David, you dial the number, and we'll all talk. That'll teach the little twit.

Do you think we can manage to just cool it a little and not make the poor girl even madder than she is.

Evelyn slaps a hand to her chest. I'll behave myself – don't you worry.

I dial Ellen's number, and when it rings and when I realize that I don't have a thing to say, I hand the receiver to Evelyn. Evelyn gets a very serious look on her face, then puts a finger to her lips to suppress a giggle.

Ellen! It's Evelyn! Shit! Evelyn lets the phone slip down until it's pressed against her left collarbone. Screw it, it's the bleeping machine. David, you have anything to say. Better do it quick.

I've got the phone again – and I still do not know what to say. So I say the first thing that comes into my mind. Ellen, this is your brother, David. I love you. I know we haven't talked in a long time but I still love you. I hope you're living exactly the life you want to be living. It doesn't matter what anybody else thinks. Charlie's here and I know he wants to say something too – before this machine cuts out.

Charlie is waving his hand back and forth like he's on a boat leaving for a month-long tour of the outer Hebrides. No, no, I don't want to talk, he's saying, but it's too late.

It's me. Charlie. Sorry I missed you in Chicago. Hope everything's all right. We just had this crazy idea we'd call you. I'm here a few days with David and Evelyn. I wish we could get together some day and talk. We used to have such good talks. I hear you, I hear your pain, but I feel it too. Don't you know that. I remember the poem you sent me. When was that. You came to the funeral – when Fred died. We walked around the block. Is that the last time we talked.

Goddamn it Ellen, if you're there, pick up! Anyway, you sent me your poems – the ones you mentioned at the funeral. I like them very much. You were the only girl in a family of seven. The boys got all the attention. I didn't see it that way – of course. I remember you were the one who got the trip to Florida. Anyway, there was one poem about Father. You called it 'The Legacy.' I memorized it. Hope you don't mind. The thing is, your memories are so different from mine. Here goes.

> What was your need, the hunger denied.
> Were you lost when your father abandoned his tribe.
> The loss of your place as the child in his eyes
> sent you searching the sky for the hows
> and the whys. No voice in the world
> could ever express the emptiness within
> that you brought to our nest.
> Your presence charged the air,
> The potential of your anger drove us inside.
> Anger you hoarded as your sole domain,
> none you left to us ...

Charlie stops – not because he forgets but because the answering machine cuts out. He holds the phone away from his ear. That's it. We tried.

Damn right. We tried.

Where's Evelyn.

She went looking for the cats. They've been out all day. It's not like them to miss dinner. They get into terrible fights if they stay out late. Especially Shadow.

Let me do the dishes. It's the least I can do.

I'll get the coffee going.

I feel bad. Actually I feel like a goddamn asshole.

It's got nothing to do with you, brother. We just don't know why she won't talk to us – something happened.

We hurt her in some way – we don't know how.

She'll tell us – one day.

Forty-Eight

Shadow is usually the hard one to get inside – the adventurer. But this time he appears first. Here's one, Evelyn says as she drops him inside the kitchen door and disappears outside again, in search of Oliver.

The rain has stopped – the wind too. Is this the lull before the storm.

I put out a bowl of water and some food for Shadow but she shakes herself, splattering everything, and runs upstairs. Don't you just love cats, Charlie says. They make you feel like such fools.

Charlie works awhile in silence. You can tell when he's thinking hard – he gets a certain look, the eyes get narrow and become fixed, the lips curl in, one hand points up, the other straight across.

I don't say anything. I wait. But when he finally does speak it's only to say, I'm really looking forward to the opera tonight.

It's not really an opera. Just excerpts.

Did you ever notice when cats get in a fight, they go right to it. They run at each other screeching and there's no doubt it's a fight. With dogs you can't always be sure. Sometimes they sniff each other and you think they could be friends, then one will snarl, the other will snarl, and before you know it they're trying to tear each other apart.

Humans are even more subtle. Maybe the word is devious. It may start with just a few words. Or the way a word is inflected.

I can't remember the last time you and I had a fight.

We should be fighting right now by all accounts.

What do we have to fight about. Anyway, you're my brother. I haven't seen you in three years. I don't want to fight.

Come on, there must be something. Remember the way we used to fight – before you found religion.

His eyes are closed. He's drying Evelyn's best piece of china with his eyes closed. He's remembering what it was like to have a really good fight, one he would win naturally, being bigger.

I remember how he used to egg me on. He could make me feel so dumb I'd lash out, which was what he wanted of course. It's an old game he still likes to play. What are you talking about.

I went to Church because I was in love with Bernie Davis.

That makes me a fool, I'll admit. A fool in love. You went to Church because you actually believed that shit.

What you had for Bernie Davis can hardly be glorified by calling it love.

We used to have fun – before you got religion. Sometimes we'd fight but it was all in fun.

Maybe it was fun for you. Put the goddamn plate down before you break it.

You were such a righteous little prick there for a while. Nobody could do anything when you were around.

And you were a horse's ass. Still are, for that matter.

Go to it, brother.

The thing that gets me is this talk about leaving Anne. Lucky fucker to meet a lady like her – and here you are, brainless, clueless, talking about leaving. You think it's something you have to do. It runs in the family. Horseshit. The only thing that runs in the family is that you're an asshole.

You're the asshole. With your big house, your big job, your big little college that no one's ever heard about, your big bully of a country that's going to the dogs.

Wait a minute. Don't lay that one on me. I'm not buying into this shitty little government anymore than you are.

You're also not buying out of it. You just sit there on your ass – pretty damn comfortable.

Now it all comes out. Mr. High and Mighty, looking down on us poor slobs from puny insignificant useless fucking Canada. I'm sure things are soooooooo fucking different up there.

The door opens and in flies Oliver, soaked to the skin, his fur flat and stringy, all the bright orange color washed away. More like a wet rag than a pet.

He shakes himself all over the floor, the side of the stove, and halfway up the wall behind the stove – before disappearing down the steps into the basement. Doesn't dare look me in the eye.

Evelyn is inside the door, leaning down, pulling off her rubber boots. One look at us, one glance, is all she needs. What's going on here, she says.

Charlie hands me the dish he's been drying for the last five minutes and says, Nothing much. A difference of opinion.

Don't let him kid you. This has got nothing to do with his opinions or my opinions, or his ideas about shit as opposed to my ideas about shit. That's too abstract. One of us is holding a deep-seated grudge, that's the long and the short of it.

What grudge. You're my brother.

Exactly. Two brothers. One mother. One over two equals one half. Who wants to settle for half a cake when he can have it all.

Fuck your cake. I don't even like cake.

I'll remember that the next time you try to take my head off.

Shake.

All right. To set Evelyn's mind at rest, more than for any other reason, we call an end to the slinging match and agree that we'll get on with the evening.

Evelyn pads across the kitchen floor barefooted, muttering something like, Whoever breaks one of my best plates pays. Try saying that three times.

She gives her funny little laugh, more like lips snarling, then disappears up the stairs. After a decent interval Charlie follows her up the stairs to change.

There is a debate going on in some far corner of my brain as to whether I can go as I am. The jeans I'm wearing, besides being comfortable, are the right color for an evening out – black. The red cotton turtleneck is iffy – granted. But if I top this with the tweed jacket, gray with a hint of brown, pure virgin wool – I'll get by.

If I look like a skunk, I'll go as a skunk.

Forty-Nine

The people I think I recognize in the lobby turn out to be somebody else. There's a tall man at the bar who could be Ray but when he turns my way, drink in hand, he has a white beard cut very short and his face is red the way Clinton's face used to be red because of the disease he had – I forget the name of it. Maybe he still has it but who cares.

There's another man looking at a painting hung on the wall who is the spitting image of a boy I knew in high school – Larry Vanderweilen. But of course it's not Larry – Larry's dead.

Finally I see someone I know is real though he himself, because of his rapidly progressing Alzheimer's disease, has lost the sense of his own identity. Lewis Gillen taught physics in the old days, before becoming President.

Charlie recognizes him at the same instant that I do. No, Charlie says when I suggest we go over and say hello to Lewis. He makes a motion with his hand, moving out from his belt, to show he means it. What can you say to a man with Alzheimer's. Charlie would rather not chance the embarrassment.

Instead, he starts a conversation with the man looking at the painting, the man I mistook for Larry Vanderweilen. The circle around Lewis breaks up and Evelyn and I make our way through the crowd to shake his hand.

Lewis was always thin but he's even thinner now. He has a long face, and his eyes have a startled look. His hair is white – wispy.

The only reason he's here is that Linda, his wife, much younger than he, insists on bringing him out. He's in the beginning, or middle stage of Alzheimer's. She wants him to stay 'active' – whatever that might mean.

He was our most beloved teacher, and it's not pretty to see him like this. It's not just that he was a brilliant teacher, he had what few people have – purity of heart. At least this still shines through.

Charlie is near the door, ready to go in. He is standing alone, looking lost. I leave Evelyn in conversation with Linda and head across to get Charlie going in the right direction.

I give him the ticket for the seat by the aisle. You've got the long legs, I remind him. We'll join you in a minute.

I leave the crowd and go in search of a washroom. The washroom on the ground floor has a line-up of people waiting to get in. Up the stairs on the second floor, next to the door to the student lounge, I find a smaller facility.

I flip on the light as I go in. A young man is standing at the urinal as if he has been waiting for me – expecting me all the while. I say the first thing that comes to mind. Are you a student here.

He's in the computer sciences, and to hear tell of it he has never had the privilege of taking one of my classes, though he hopes to in the near future. Maybe the class in comparative religions, he thinks.

I don't bother to tell him that I do not teach a class in comparative religions. You don't remember me, do you, he says, while he stands there for an inordinate length of time making loud splashing noises.

I have to confess I do not.

You saved my life once.

I'm very glad to hear it but tell me, you've piqued my curiosity, how. Now it's my turn to make loud splashing noises.

It was my first year here – my first week. I was feeling very bad – very homesick. I was going up the steps to the Dean's office to tell him I was quitting when I saw you come out of the men's room.

What a prick I said to myself. There was something about the way you looked, so self-absorbed, so sure of yourself, I just couldn't stand it.

I followed you along the hallway and down a different set of stairs. You heard me following you and looked around. The stairs creaked. I guess I must have had a scary look, because you took off down the steps like a bat out of hell.

I had a screwdriver in my hand, I admit, but I don't know where it came from. I shouted after you, I'm dangerous, I'm dangerous, and I guess I must have felt I was. But you would not look around.

There was nobody downstairs at the main desk, so you went right on through and out onto the street and started mingling. It felt like a fire drill. Maybe it was.

You stopped and waited for me. You reminded me of my uncle, the way you looked at me, with your soft eyes. What are you so angry about, you said. Nothing, I said. Where did you go to school, you said. Kokomo, I said.

I've never been to Kokomo but I like the way it sounds. Whenever there's a chance to say Kokomo, I say Kokomo. I wondered why you cared. Suddenly I felt very calm, and I realized all I wanted was for somebody to say a kind word to me.

Kokomo, ka-ka, kill the bitch, I didn't care. I started to walk away. You raised your hand. I thought you were waving good-bye. I waved back.

Then I saw you were holding something in your hand – a stone. You were waiting for me to come back and have a look.

It was a beautiful stone – shaped like an egg but elongated at one end, as if pulled on, stretched like silly putty, big enough to fill the palm of your hand.

The color was unusual – a light brown, almost cream, crisscrossed with streaks of white. It seemed to glow. Here, take this, you said. It belongs to you.

You placed the stone in the palm of my hand. It was cool, smooth, soft, almost like velvet – not polished. I didn't know what you meant when you said it belonged to me.

I remember a young man following me down the stairs, you said. He kept repeating the same phrase over and over again. But I don't remember the business about the stone.

I still have it.

I'm glad if I was able to help.

This doesn't make any sense, because I've never taken a class from you, but you're my favorite professor. Before I can say anything the boy is gone – out the door.

I'm alone in the men's room. Below, in the pit, I can hear the orchestra tuning up.

It's past eight – I'm late. I'm the last to take my place – three seats in, next to Evelyn. The lights dim, and the curtain goes up.

There's a first rush of excitement, as the music begins and we have a moment to fasten our eyes on the scene before us. This moment of beginning, with its great expectations, is, to me, the definition of happiness.

The setting is stark, bare, minimal – a black-leather couch, a black-leather armchair, a table and a beat-up old lamp with a gaudy red shade that has strands of what seem like gold filament unraveling.

The overture begins slowly, with a calmness and stateliness that could presage almost anything. Then come dark, dramatic Giovanni notes that give way to a sense of playfulness.

The music rocks me, like the sea rocks a boat, back and forth. I feel like I'm floating, in a vessel full of holes, on a sea that's being whipped up by a master puppeteer who is up to his eyeballs in mischief making.

After the initial excitement I feel sleepy, and I fight to keep my eyes open. I dose and dream of my own bed at home, until something jerks me awake and I find myself outside a coffee house in Naples.

Two young army officers, Fernando and Guglielmo, are standing near the table, next to the red lamp shade, sipping their coffee. I go back to sleep. Evelyn nudges me with her elbow when she sees me nodding off.

The woman in the seat to my right places her arm on the armrest, claiming that space for herself and forcing me to sit up and shift a little in my seat.

It is a remarkably thin arm with a fine red fuzz on the back that seems to glow in the dark. An arm so thin, so fragile, yet so much a part of her. She, the rest of her – a vast unknown – so close and yet so far away – I do not think of mounting any sort of challenge.

There's nothing to do but jam my own arm, fat and hairy, down and across my lap, letting my belly bulge above.

I lean forward across Evelyn's line of vision and catch Charlie's face in profile. It's startling, because what's familiar, at least what I thought was familiar, seems so strange.

It's the same profile as my own – the same slanted forehead, same slightly protruding brows, same small nose, not a pug nose but almost, same lips, same chin that disappears into the folds of the neck.

The difference is that I'm a few pounds heavier – more than a few if the truth be known – and so everything gets multiplied.

Something happens. Don Alfonso, a philosopher, rises from the couch and begins teasing the young men about women's lack of faithfulness.

È la fede delle femmine come l'araba fenice, he sings. Women's faithfulness is like the Arabian phoenix. Everyone says it exists, where it is...no one knows.

The two men agree to Don Alfonso's wager. They will pretend to go off to war and be killed, then come back disguised as 'Albanians' to test the women's resolve.

I've heard it before, sung with gusto. These two young singers do not seem to know the difference between pretending and pretending to pretend.

The first appearance of Fiordiligi is like a wake-up call. Even before she sings a note I'm sitting up and paying attention. What I like is the way she comes on stage, and the dress she's wearing.

It's a magnificent white dress, with long sleeves that reach almost to the white kid gloves. Her hat – also white – is tipped forward on her head, with a fine white lace behind. Her hair is thick, wavy – and blond.

Mi par che stamattina volentien farei la pazzarella, she sings. I feel this morning I'd gladly play the madcap. I feel a certain fire, a certain ticklishness in my veins...

Dorabella answers, To tell you the truth, I also feel something new in my spirit. I could swear that we are not far from our wedding!

Too bad, sweet Dorabella, that you are singing in the dark and don't know that your man has decided to play a dirty trick on you. Your wedding day will have to be postponed – and many bitter tears shed.

Dorabella bores me too, I don't know why. Halfway through her first aria, implacable longings that stir me, I'm fading and tuning out.

I want Fiordiligi, only Fiordiligi, and finally, after a few more preliminaries, which feel like so much foreplay, I'm as excited as everyone else when her big moment comes – her first aria.

Come scoglio immoto resta... As the rock remains unmoved against the winds and the storm, so this spirit is still strong in its faith and in its love. That torch was born in us, which pleases and consoles us; and death alone will be able to make our heart change its affection.

Not every death is a real death, dear Fiordiligi. Some are staged. Don Alfonso is like those trickster gods in native mythology.

Better watch out, better not shout.

There's something so sad, so tender in her voice, the moment I recognize this quality I feel a chill run up my spine. To feel this kind of tenderness is to feel a sense of oneness with someone, so that your fate is bound up in his fate or her fate.

The wonder of it is to feel, if only for the space of an hour, that there exists a world in which love is not just real but outweighs and outlasts every other emotion – every other consideration.

Guglielmo continues to irritate, with his Non siate ritrosi ... Don't be shy, charming little eyes, send two amorous flashes here for a moment. Make us happy. Be loving with us, and we will also make you very happy.

You are playing with fire, Guglielmo, and your fine eye might get blackened, and your fine nose might get knocked out of joint if you don't watch it.

Now we are heading toward the end of Act One. Dorabella and Fiordiligi are being sorely tested. Pity the poor darlings.

They sing a duet that begins, Ah, che tutto in un momento ... Ah, how all in a moment my fate was changed. Ah, a sea filled with torment is life for me now.

Fernando and Guglielmo pretend to take poison and cannot stop laughing at the silliness of it all. They think it's a fine comedy to see how the women suffer – all for nothing.

At intermission Evelyn stays behind and strikes up a conversation with the tall, thin, red-haired woman who was sitting next to me. In the lobby Charlie veers sharply right when he remembers that this is where the bar is. I go up the stairs in search of the bathroom.

This time there's a line-up but no sign of the boy with the screwdriver. I can piss in peace and quiet.

When I come back down Charlie's waiting with an extra glass of wine in his hand. This is great, he shouts, above the din. Music, wine, everybody talking and laughing.

Eat, drink, and be merry. Forget your troubles.

What troubles have you got. You don't have any troubles.

You know, the war. People getting killed. I end up very loud on the word 'killed,' and people look around.

Charlie wraps his arm around my shoulder. Here comes Evelyn, he whispers. Who's that gorgeous woman she's with.

She was sitting next to me. It was as if she was there and not there at the same time. I didn't ask her name. I didn't dare say anything.

Here they are. We turn and pretend surprise as Evelyn and her new friend cross the lobby and come up to us.

Guess who this is, Evelyn says.

She's as tall as I am, thin as a rail, and much younger than I thought she was when she was sitting next to me – her arm on the armrest, quiet as stone, sphinx-like.

She's wearing a green velvet jacket with silver sparkles. The red of her hair is even redder against the green. The hair is long, reaching the small of the back – very straight, very sixties.

Talking with Evelyn has brought her to life, as is so often the case with Evelyn. Her name is Angela and she could be Chinese, she could be Inuit, she could be anything.

She has a way of looking at you, her head turned a little to one side – shy, as if she's been hurt many times. She's small-boned, with a small, narrow head that looks even smaller because of the way the hair is combed straight back, tight to the skull, and because she's so tall.

All we can do is shrug and stare, stare and shrug. Evelyn says, She's Guglielmo's wife, and I'm quickly trying to sort out if Guglielmo is the large, pot-bellied man or the shrimp who looks like he's still in his teens – the baritone or the tenor.

Our Guglielmo this evening is an imposing figure, with a chest and belly surpassing my own, and I am trying hard to imagine this thin woman in the same bed or even in the same room with such a grotesque individual.

Say something, stupid.

I'm really enjoying his performance, I spout, and redness spreads across my face like ink across an ink blotter as it sinks in that what I have said is not just stupid but a lie.

Charlie comes to the rescue. I felt when he was taking the poison and pretending to fall down dead that he really put his heart into. I don't understand Italian, but I could hear the word disperato loud and clear. For one brief moment he was no longer pretending. Love always has something desperate about it, and I thought he captured that very well.

I know he feels that way when he sings, she says in a voice that is calm and measured and presents such a contrast to the general state of frenzy in the lobby and in my chest.

He enjoys the mischief making but it hurts him too, because he really does love his Fiordiligi desperately.

To be a singer must be like being a lover in that respect, I say, in an attempt to redeem myself. Always reaching for something that seems to be just beyond your grasp.

The bell calls us back. Evelyn makes a point of walking with me, murmuring, Slow down, slow down. Charlie escorts Angela to her seat and proceeds to sit next to her, so that when I finally take my place I have Evelyn to my right, and the aisle – the dark, the void, no one, silence – to my left.

Charlie's sitting tall and pretty, his hands on his knees, puffed up like a pigeon in heat. Whenever she says something, he leans in close the better to hear her.

It doesn't take much – a grunt or two – to keep her going. She's a talker. He's all ears, all eyes – and all thumbs.

Everything's a blank for the next half hour. I've shut down and the only thing I want to hear after this is Fiordiligi's great aria, Per pietà, ben mio, Have pity, my love, forgive the error of a loving spirit, which I've been waiting for all night.

Like the scene in the film, The Whale Rider, when the girl gets on the back of the whale, this scene with Fiordiligi all alone and lost, crying, My courage, my constancy, will sever this wicked desire, always brings tears to my eyes. It touches something so deep that it's not possible to hear it and remain unmoved.

Soon of course she gives in. She's lost – she's riding the whale down to her death. The word ascoso – hidden – takes her down to such a depth of despair that it's either die or give in, and she gives in.

She has more courage, more constancy than Dorabella, but not endless courage, not endless constancy. In other words, she is human too, and the lesson the men are supposed to take from this is that women are just as fallible as men and it's best not to pretend otherwise.

I deceived you, Don Alfonso says, but my deceit was undeceiving for your lovers, who will be wiser now. The lovers are reconciled. The women say they will be loyal and adoring, always and forever. The men say they believe them but they know enough not to want to test it – ma la prova io far no vo'.

Everyone's happy again, and the chances that love will last are much improved.

Even before we reach the lobby the singers are there, to greet us on the way out. Guglielmo himself, whatever his name is, Jason or George or Bob or Bogman, is surrounded by well-wishers.

He's got his arm around his Angela, who seems content to bask in his glow. Everyone's drinking red wine.

Charlie plows straight ahead, through the crowd, to the door. He doesn't wait for us, he doesn't look around to see if we're following – he's like a man desperate for a cigarette.

It's unusually warm for April.

The sky's covered in clouds. Things feel close and darker than usual even though there are buildings all around with lights in the windows.

Across the way, at the library, there seems to be an empty head in every window.

At the student union the cleaning people are busy shutting down one floor after another – beginning from the top.

Wolcott Hall, the main student residence, boasts half-naked figures as they come and go behind semi-transparent curtains.

Evelyn remembers that she's left a coat at the coat check, so she goes back inside.

Charlie remains silent as we wait. It's hard to tell if he's laughing or crying, smiling, or holding his gut in pain. His expression is enigmatic – the eyes half shut, the mouth wide, the bottom lip drawn in.

I watch him, knowing he doesn't like to be watched. He goes across the street and walks into the area of clipped grass where so much activity takes place during the day – touch football, soccer, demonstrations, boys meeting girls, boys meeting boys.

He looks up into the sky and wonders why it's so dark when we're surrounded by buildings that are lit up and busy. I ask myself the same question, until I realize it's because the street lights have been turned off – as an energy saving measure.

Evelyn takes a long time because of the line-up. I stand a few feet away from Charlie in the area where most of the rough and tumble games take place. The ground is bare in spots.

It's warm enough that I can feel the ground moving under my feet – smell the grass being chewed up – see the ball come spiraling down out of the sky.

Open your arms. Cradle the ball as it falls.

I'm standing close behind him. I can hear his breathing. I can hear the way he catches his breath, holds it, and spits it out.

I'm such an asshole, he says, shaking his head.

What are you talking about.

You've got to be an asshole to risk losing it all. Like that Guglielmo. Talk about assholes.

Before he can say anything else, I hear my name being called.

It's so dark where we're standing that Evelyn does not see us.

Dave, Yo, Charlie, Wait up. We walk back to where she's calling, on the curb in front of the arts building. She's saying good-bye to some friends who are walking away in the opposite direction – toward the parking lot behind the building.

Who was that.

That was Sally. She has a new girlfriend.

Maybe she'd like to come with us for a drink somewhere.

I don't think so. She said she was very tired.

Everyone is walking away, in different directions, heading home.

The three of us decide to go somewhere for a coffee and dessert, rather than drinks.

Fifty

The place is called Boomerang's, and it is behind the Courthouse, around the corner from where Charlie and I had lunch. It's much busier and noisier than usual at this time of night.

I recognize several faces from the theater we've just come from – including all four singers – at a table in the middle of the room, each one sitting with a spouse or partner, including the red-haired beauty, Angela, who keeps touching her Bogman on the shoulder and forearm and whispering in his ear.

Ray is with them, and Ray's wife, Belinda. With her green velvet jacket, her sparkling eyes, and a laugh that's as loud and deep as a man's, Angela is the center of everyone's attention.

We are about to leave when someone says there are still some tables on the second floor. A group of us splits off and heads up the stairs to see what it's like.

We've never been to the second floor – it's only recently been opened. The stairs are toward the back of the main floor where you would never find them if you weren't looking.

The space up here is larger than on the main floor, and it's much quieter. It's so quiet that Evelyn shushes me when I ask her where she wants to sit.

The tables are arranged differently – in rows so that everyone is looking in the same direction. The room is dark – it takes a moment for our eyes to adjust.

There's a podium to our left as we cross the room, and a man standing at the podium, waiting for everyone to be seated before he speaks. He adjusts the microphone on the podium – in a way that suggests he has done this many times before.

I wonder how much they are paying him.

We take our seats at a table on the far side of the room, against a wall. It is a brick wall – bare except for a series of framed photographs of unfamiliar stretches of water and shoreline.

Can everyone hear me. The speaker gives the microphone a flick of his finger.

Loud and clear, someone up front shouts.

Where to begin, he mutters. The lights go down still further – except for the one shining on the speaker.

He removes a pair of glasses and looks out at us again. He

fixes us with his stare. Evelyn taps the edge of the table.

Start where it hurts the most and go from there, someone suggests.

That's easy, the man laughs. I'm like most of you I suppose. The thing that really hurts is when you find out that your father is not just mortal but an asshole. I see a couple of you nodding there, so you know what I'm talking about.

A gravely voice answers back, You bet your ass, bud.

Every life story is different, yet there's a common theme. And what is this common theme. Your Father is an asshole. It could be he's just a little bit of an asshole. Or he could be a complete asshole. But he's an asshole.

You can divide life into four stages. Childhood is when you look up to your father, like a god. Adolescence is when you realize that your father is an asshole. Adulthood is when you forgive your father for being an asshole. Old age is when you forgive yourself for being the offspring of an asshole.

This is the wisdom of old age – if we ever get wisdom. Some people, needless to say, remain adolescents all their lives. Your basic criminal, for example. He pauses but no one challenges him. No one questions his basic assumption.

What I'm going to do here tonight is show you a few slides and let you judge for yourself. This is my story but it could be yours. The son has to depose the father. It's an iron-clad rule. Sometimes the father – God bless the son of a bitch – takes it upon himself to depose himself.

Maybe for daughters it's different. I don't know. First slide. He turns to look at the wall behind him. If you will.

A curtain opens to reveal the same sort of brick wall I'm sitting up against. On the wall is a screen, in size somewhere between what you might expect for home viewing and what you might expect at a modest neighborhood theatre.

The first slide shows a young boy dressed up in clothes from a hundred years ago. Here's good old dad all natted up. What is he here, maybe ten, maybe eleven. Already his character is formed. Just look at the expression on that mouth. Upper lip lifted, defiant. Bottom lip pressed tight to the upper.

And look at the way they've dressed him up. Like a little monkey. Heavy wool coat, one size too small. Heavy wool vest below that, buttoned tight. Stiff white collar, with something around the neck that looks like a cross between a bow tie and a hanging noose.

The eyes are blazing – it's clear he's not going to sit still for this much longer. If he were alive today and could speak, we know what his words would be. Fuck this.

There's a clicking sound, then the screen goes blank – white. All eyes turn again to the man at the podium.

He reaches for a glass of water that's been placed there for him on top of the podium. It's his show – he won't be rushed. We wait, as the next slide is loaded.

There's the same clicking sound, and on the screen we see the same face, the same sly look, forty years later.

Exhibit B. Here he is again, many years later. He's all grown up, the father of six, at the very height of his assholeness.

Everything about him is false. White, ruffled shirt, slicked-down hair combed back, soft, round face. Look at the eyes. See how they hide from you. He's not really there. He's already plotting his escape.

But it's no wonder. Take a look at the woman standing next to him. She's as tall as him, and twice the size. Look at the way she's got her elbow out, ready to give it to him in the gut.

And over here to the right, the oldest boy, that's me by the way, already five inches taller than Father – God help us. Do I have a clue what's going on in his pea-brain. Not a chance. I would've killed the bum.

I'm looking at Charlie and Evelyn and wondering what we're doing here. Charlie's sipping his wine, holding his glass in the palm of his hand as if to keep it warm.

He sees me watching him and gives me the thumbs up. That big stupid smile of his. I guess this kind of rant is right up his alley. He seems to be enjoying himself no end.

Evelyn has her head down, turned a little to one side, and she's listening as hard as she can, as if some secret is about to be revealed.

I have a pain in the gut that drives me suddenly forward into the table. I brace myself with both hands and steady myself. What's that all about, I wonder.

I haven't taken a leak in several hours. If I'm diabetic, I almost forgot it. There's a price to pay!

I'm standing by myself at the urinal down the hall – a brand new urinal modeled on a design from the fifties – ultra white, ultra clean, not a crack in it, with a flushing mechanism that is triggered the moment you step near – waiting for the first feeble flow to come – when the memory of a phone call I received late one night last week slowly washes down over me like a warm shower from above.

The caller had a name I didn't recognize, and a voice that could have been a man's or a woman's. He – she – was calling to invite me to speak at a genealogical conference scheduled for this coming weekend.

Would I say a few words about my family history.

Why me, I wondered. I've never been interested in genealogy. Why start now.

But I said yes – just so I could go back to sleep.

A moment of panic hits me now when I realize that what I've stumbled into here, on the second floor of Boomerang's, is an assignment that I had forgot all about. I'm the next scheduled speaker – and I've prepared nothing.

There's no way around it. The piss comes gushing out – in a yellow stream that splashes against the back of the urinal, flows down, and vanishes into the white of an all-absorbing post-ejaculatory ceramic.

I have no idea what I'm going to say. Get a grip on yourself man. It's a genealogical conference, so talk genealogy. Try to remember what you know – the stories you heard growing up.

Just keep talking – nobody will know the difference.

When I walk into the room all eyes are on me. The introduction has been made, and everyone is waiting. There's no backing out.

I look for Evelyn and Charlie in the back but it's too dark. I can see as far back as the table where Angela is sitting with her partner, Guglielmo, the Bogman, and the other singers, along with Ray and his wife.

Angela is laughing and talking to the others – not even looking my way.

Not knowing what else to say, I say what I have said many times before, in class. I talk about the different ways we have of entering into the past – keeping old photographs the way our speaker here tonight has done, handing down stories from generation to generation, doing the hard work of historical research, sometimes simply remembering to remember.

I talk about the different kinds of memory – the way the mind remembers, the way the body remembers, the difference between conscious memory and unconscious memory, the difference between memory as a skill and memory as an art.

People begin getting up and leaving. I'm desperately thinking of something interesting to say, to keep them back.

My name may look French, but it's actually Scottish. We were victims of the Highland Clearances, just as much as anyone else. The fucking English – is there anything they didn't screw up! But we don't hold it against them.

My ancestor was one of the first through the Cumberland Pass. This would be – oh, round about 1760. There's a direct line of descent from Daniel Boone's brother, Ned. Or was Ned his son. I'm sorry if I'm boring the hell out of you.

The meeting breaks up, and everyone heads for the stairs. Because I'm the last one down the stairs I turn off the lights.

Evelyn and Charlie have disappeared out the front door – into the warm April night. They've made the mistake of assuming that I can find my own way. But it is dark out, so dark, and after a certain hour my sense of direction begins to fail me.

Angela is near the coat rack with her boy friend, her Bogman. He's helping her with her coat – a long black wool coat that looks brand new. As I come near she smiles at me.

You fanned you fanny, she says. The way she looks at me I can tell that she is disappointed with my performance.

She's passed up a perfectly fine party at a friend's house to come out and hear me and what does she get.

Someone who obviously came prematurely.

My memory's not what it used to be, I reply.

Cossi fan tutti, she laughs, and together she and her Bogman follow everyone else down the front steps and out onto the street.

Fifty-One

When I wake in the morning, the house seems strange again – empty – and I know she's gone.

It's the same empty feeling I had last summer when we lived apart for two months, and for a moment I wonder if I'm the one who has left and found my own place.

There was another woman in my life – a student – and Evelyn would not tolerate it. Get out, she said, just get out.

The funny thing is, the other woman – Ineke – is gone now, living in Chicago, attending the Art Institute. She's interested in the theory of art. I wonder who the new Art is in her life.

I'm living alone for the first time in a long time. I look around the apartment, and see that Evelyn has taken all her things. I open the door to a walk-in closet that's been stripped bare.

This closet opens into a large room on the other side that I did not know existed. Inside is a complete second bedroom, with a large queen-size bed, and the pink duvet from our old place on Grand Street.

I tidy things up, brush the cat hair off the duvet – clumps of black hair from our cat Shadow who has not been feeling well in recent days. By the side of the bed, on the floor, in a cracked, discarded suitcase that's wide open, is a pile of old dusty books.

Somehow I know before I look that they once belonged to my son Alan. There's an old school Shakespeare, a copy of The Tempest, in faded blue cloth with warped boards.

I open the book and see penciling inside. I can make out the first letter, A, easily enough, but the others all run together. Is it Alan's name. Or notes that he jotted down. It could be anything.

While I'm studying the letters and trying to decipher the word, I remember what I have been trying to forget for such a long time – that Alan died when he was eight, in an automobile accident that was mostly my fault – and I'll never see him again.

It's sad enough when children grow up and leave home, but when they die young it's even sadder. With grown children you can see their progress and if you're lucky they'll still talk to you and remember you in your old age.

Even if that never happens, you can always dream that it will. But such a dream is impossible in my case. Alan is dead. I'll never see him again. There is nothing left for me, but to close my eyes and weep.

Maybe crying will help. I doubt it.

Fifty-Two

It's my second or third trip to the can tonight. I'm still half asleep as I stumble back into the bedroom – thick red socks on my feet, tips of the toes all black and blue.

The clock on the dresser says five minutes after four. Evelyn is sound asleep, and I don't want to disturb her. I lie on my back in the dark and let my dreams wash over me.

The terrible dream about Alan. Could it be true.

A long time ago I stopped writing down my dreams. When I know I'm not going to write them down, they seem to stay with me longer, in more vivid detail.

At five, when it's clear I'm not going to sleep again, I get up and go downstairs. I sit at the kitchen table with a glass of orange juice and the book that Charlie brought with him, on the history of the Monon.

The first thing I discover is that the word Monon derives from a Potawatomi Indian word that sounded to the first settlers like metamonong or monong and meant something like 'swift running.'

The original name was The Chicago, Indianapolis & Louisville Railroad, but in 1882 the company started printing 'The Monon Route' on its maps and later used 'Monon – The Hoosier Line' on timetables, letterheads, and rolling stock.

The Monon opened its route from Lake Michigan south to the Ohio River in 1853. It was one of the few north-south lines at the time, and provided service to Union forces during the Civil War, carrying volunteers to mustering centers free and hurrying sick, wounded, or discharged men home at half-price.

In April, 1865, a Monon engine pulled President Abraham Lincoln's funeral train over the 90 miles from Lafayette to Michigan City – one of twenty railroad lines taking part in the 20-day, 1,666-mile trail of sadness from Washington, D.C. to Springfield, Illinois.

From 1854 on, every new slab of Indiana limestone rode a Monon flatcar first, whatever its destination. Many famous buildings are constructed with Indiana limestone, including the Empire State Building, the Pentagon, the National Cathedral, the Washington Monument, and The Chicago Museum of Fine Arts, as well as countless private buildings, museums, bridges, churches, statues, and gravestones.

Indiana limestone is prized because of its uniformity of color. Repairs or additions can be made with the promise of limestone being identical in color, even years later.

The center of the limestone industry, the town of Bedford, just south of Bloomington, is where my father was born and lived the first few years of his life. For a generation or two – probably longer – Bedford was home to my father's side of the family.

If I know precious little about my father, I know next to nothing about his father, Edward Avon. The family Bible lists a few facts but that's all they are – facts. Borned (sic) Dec. 28, 1883, Bedford, Indiana. Married Nellie Buddhu at Louisville, Kentucky, June 23, 1907. Left his family, November 20, 1927.

Everything else is guesswork – speculation. I've seen the same photographs that Charlie has seen, and when I look into his eyes (Edward Avon's) I see the same thing that Charlie sees – a shiftiness that can only mean that he's always wondering how he got where he is and how he can get out of it.

I like to think I know him a little, but really, when I think about it, I don't know him in the slightest.

They were cold, unyielding men – my father, and his father before him, and the fathers that came to this new land, America. How far back does it go, this coldness that runs in the family. Back to the frontier years in Kentucky, back to the hard days of crossing the Appalachians, back to Scotland and the nightmare of the highland clearances, back to the days of clan warfare.

My father did not have a close relationship with any of his children – continuing an old family tradition. He was a gruff, impatient man who was also capable of tenderness, sensitivity and compassion.

I remember occasions when he tried to talk with me, but futilely. Either I was not listening, or he got twisted up in his words. He would give up and turn away.

Oh, all too easily he would turn away.

And as for me, I would never think of going to him with a concern of mine. Never.

Shortly after the birth of my father the family moved from Bedford to Michigan City. For me, as for Charlie, Bedford is bedrock, where we come up against the mystery of Edward Avon – who were his ancestors, what shaped him, why did he leave his family after twenty years of marriage, where did he disappear to, and what happened to him in the end.

Every time I've tried to dig into these questions, I've come up empty.

Two years ago Evelyn and I spent a weekend exploring Bedford. We went to the house on Lincoln Street where, according to my notes, the family was living the year Father was born.

The present owner, a woman in her sixties, a retired high school teacher, was able to remember the couple she had dealt with when she bought the house, but nothing about any of the owners or occupants previous to that. The woman's name was Darling – not a name that meant anything to me.

We walked downtown, trying to get a feel for the place where my father's side of the family had spent so many years.

What is true about limestone buildings is not true, sadly, about human lives. Repairs can be made, material added on, but it's never the same.

In the lives of human beings everything changes – except a mysterious inner core, where we might be able to say, with or without conviction, that's me.

Towns too change, and cities, and you go looking for what is at the heart of them and what defines them and what stays the same, and sometimes you find what you are looking for and sometimes you do not.

We found where the old train tracks ran through the middle of town. But now it's not called the Monon, it's not even the old Chicago, Indianapolis & Louisville Railroad, it's something called CSX Transportation.

We had lunch at a place downtown – Mel's Diner – that probably hasn't changed much in a hundred years. We ordered the chowder with homemade bread. The chowder was mostly corn and potatoes.

In the booth next to ours four men were talking about farming methods, conservation practices, and corn yields. They argued about the use of chemicals and techniques of crop rotation, but agreed that to support a good crop of corn the soil has to be acidic, not alkaline.

That doesn't mean acid rain is a good thing, the man sitting at my back said. Acid rain kills lakes and rivers, and that ain't the kind of acid we need.

The man who was talking loudest and driving everyone else crazy was a retired real estate agent who was living on two hundred acres just outside town. You want to know why there are fewer family farms. Because the young people won't stay on the farm. There's no money in it, they say. That's the only thing that matters. Money.

Easy for you to talk about money, said the man behind me. You've got it socked away.

I could feel him bouncing against the back of the booth as he talked. You've got it coming out your ass.

A train came by on the tracks across the street from the diner, drowning out the voices. Clickety-clack, on and on, a hundred times, each time seeming louder.

Even shouting across the table at each other was useless. The four men next to us fell silent.

Hop a freight train, the old song says, but that was when trains had a romance about them that no longer exists. Part of that romance was the idea that 'place' might mean something different from being rooted in one spot, in one town, or village, or community – never wanting to leave.

It might mean coming to a place, exploring a place, and moving on. Life is transitory, what's here today is gone tomorrow, and if that's a reason to be sad, it's also a reason to be glad.

The answer to the riddle of life is to keep moving.

Listening to the train rumble by, I ask myself, what am I doing here. What am I expecting to find here. When I think about it, I realize I don't know.

The noise of the train fades into the voice of the waitress at the cash register talking to a customer – a tall heavy-set man I do not recognize at first because he's got his back to me.

They are talking about a movie she's just seen for the first time, and the man keeps shaking his head and saying, No, Billie, I don't agree. It was too violent. Two hours of gore.

As he talks I recognize the voice as one of the four men who were sitting in the booth behind us.

You missed the whole point of the movie, Billie says, in a strident voice. He wasn't asking us to judge this or that person, he was asking us to be there as witnesses to what happened.

What about the way he showed the Jews. That was wrong.

We don't know what happened back then, so many years ago.

Maybe it was, maybe it wasn't. There's no way we'll ever know.

When she sees me looking her way, Billie, the waitress, cuts short her conversation and comes over to our booth. She asks if everything is okay.

The chowder was delicious, Evelyn says.

She gathers up our bowls. Is there anything else she can get us.

I glance at the menu even though I know what I want. I've had my eye on the pecan pie since we came in.

Evelyn is content with a cup of coffee.

You just sit back and relax, folks. I'll be right back.

The booth behind us is empty. There's no one at the cash, no one else in the diner.

The waitress is in and out of the kitchen and does not want to talk anymore.

It's suddenly very quiet.

After coffee, after dessert, when no one else comes in, we get up and leave.

Fifty-Three

His first name was Edward. His middle name was either Aden or Avon. Aden is the name written on a family photo. Avon is the name written in the family tree I was given a long time ago, by an aunt, my mother's youngest sister.

Aden could be Hayden, a common enough name in the family. Or it could be Eden. I prefer Avon.

I like to think that his middle name foretells a life of travel and searching, disappearances and discoveries, high adventures, close scrapes, paradise just up ahead, around the next corner.

The two photographs I have of him as a grown man and father show him to be a short, plump, pleasant-looking man. He has a relaxed expression, a soft gaze, already plotting his get-away no doubt.

The one picture I have of him as a child shows him with an older sister and a still older brother. Edward Avon is about ten, Minni Mae maybe fourteen. Fred Clancy looks to be a mature sixteen. They are dressed in their Sunday best.

The two older siblings look sure of themselves, steely-eyed, hard-nosed. Avon has a lost, scared, defiant look.

His gaze falls across Minni's path of vision. He's keeping his dark thoughts to himself. Later he will act on them and blow a hole in the heart of his family that can never be repaired.

In 1924, three years before he disappeared, Edward Avon brought his son with him to Chicago, to show him where he worked. My father was sixteen years old. It was the first and only time they traveled together, the two of them.

The Monon arrived on line number nine. There was a momentary lull in activity. Another train sat idly on line number two. Maybe this is the famous Santa Fe Express, Father thought.

Edward Avon's office was on the second floor of the station, at the corner of Dearborn and Polk. It was as big as the downstairs of their house in Lafayette – home to two adults and six children.

The view from the window looked toward the lake. Father looked through a pair of binoculars, searching the horizon for the ships that plied the waters between Chicago and Michigan.

Look, look more closely, Edward Avon shouted in his ear.

I can't. He did not like the way his father lived, in luxury, while at home the family struggled.

On the wall next to the window was a painting of a sailing ship on the high seas. This is just between you and me, his father admonished, as if there were something in that scene that should be kept secret.

I don't want anything to do with any of this, the son thought to himself.

The sixteen-year-old boy has one wish – to see the exhibition of airplanes that has opened recently in a new building at the edge of the campus of the University of Chicago.

In a yellow taxi they drive from Dearborn Station to South Lakeshore Drive, then south to the campus, circling in front of the monumental Museum of Science and Industry.

As they past the museum, the driver points out Clarence Darrow's house, on an island in a lagoon. It's called Japanese Island, he tells them, but I'll be dogged if I know how come.

It's five o'clock – only enough time for a short visit before closing. The exhibition is in a large room made from combining three standard sized gymnasiums.

There are fifteen airplanes hanging by wires from the ceiling. They are freshly painted, in bright attractive colors.

Father stands on a wooden folding chair in the middle of the display, to see more closely. Avon is amused and happy to see this enthusiasm.

He asks his son a personal question – one of the few times he ever did. He asks him, What would you like to do when you finish school.

Father has never before considered the question. He answers without thinking. I'd like to be a journalist.

Ah, well, then you can uncover all the dirt, Avon laughs. He knows all about dirt from experience.

Father is afraid of him then, because he seems to be saying that his element is dirt and for that he will make no apologies.

From the museum they drive to Avon's apartment to change before dinner and a night out on the town. The apartment is a two-bedroom walk-up on Harrison, about a mile from Dearborn Station.

Easy walking distance for a man in his early forties, a few pounds overweight but athletic in his build and movements.

In a cherry-wood cabinet in the living room is a stash of expensive whiskeys. Avon prepares himself a vodka martini.

Would you like one. Father declines.

Father is told he will sleep on the sofa in the living room. It's quiet, and I won't bother you if you don't bother me.

The second bedroom is off limits. He receives no explanation. Father does not ask for one, though he burns to know the reason why.

Is this where he keeps the woman. Avon disappears into his own bedroom for a few minutes.

Above the sofa is an oil painting of a sailboat cutting through rough waters. On an end table is a stack of books – mystery novels.

Father glances at the book on top. It's a novel by Edgar Wallace.

Father feels like a stranger here. He has a sense that it's not his body but someone else's that he's inhabiting.

He's glad they do not stay long.

They decide to drive directly to Avon's favorite night spot, for dinner and a drink.

It is still light out …

The night is young …

Fifty-Four

The light in the window is not as faint as it was. I cover my chest and shoulders with the purple shawl that Evelyn left behind when she went up to bed. I'm lying on the sofa in the living room.

I turn over and try to sleep some more. There's a tap tap tapping on the glass above the sofa, and when I look I see a bird wanting to get in.

It's a large bird with a curved beak. Two or three times it comes to the window, makes a tapping noise, then backs off. It's startling to see such a creature close up.

Then it's inside the room. My only explanation is that there must be some opening in the wall under the window allowing it to get in.

I'm on my feet, backing away, as wary as a night janitor when he stumbles upon thieves making off with all the electronic gear from the office he thought he'd locked tight.

Before I know it, the bird is perched on top of my head. It's firmly anchored, and there is no possibility of even thinking about shaking it off.

It goes with me wherever I go.

Evelyn is asleep upstairs – I cannot wake her. This is a bird that could be dangerous, I think to myself.

Eagles eat small mammals. They attack and eat monkeys. The beak of an eagle can break open the skull of a monkey. Therefore, logically, it could break open my skull.

The beak of an eagle is as sharp as a razor. If I try to reach up and brush it away, it might panic the way a cat panics, ripping you open with its claws.

I step outside the room where I was sleeping, and discover that we're living in a large building that turns out to be the dorm on a university campus.

I walk down the hallway, skirting a set of stairs, and peek into a room full of teachers, all women, talking among themselves with great animation. I'm in danger, I say. Can someone help me.

When they see the danger I'm in, they know exactly what to do. They do not hesitate. Call Mr. Travers, they shout, as one.

Apparently, Mr. Travers is a fellow teacher known for his take-charge attitude. His office is just down the hallway.

He teaches chemistry, but his great passion is the outdoors.

He knows his birds backwards and forwards.

I walk back to my room, more relaxed because I know help is on the way in the form of Mr. Travers.

The noise I make coming into the room wakes Evelyn. She gets up and goes by me into the bathroom, half asleep.

Can you do something about this bird. She goes on by without looking.

I'll be right back. She disappears into the bathroom.

I hear her taking a shower. The bird is loosening its tight grip, and its whole body beginning to slump down onto my shoulder.

It must realize that help is on the way and that it had better play dead if it does not want to end up actually dead.

I go to the window. I push back the window and lean down so that the bird can slip through the opening and outside.

It slides down the grassy hill to the water below. When it hits the water it comes to life.

It's not an eagle anymore, but a swan – a dirty white, with ruffled feathers.

I am glad it's alive, even if it's no longer the bird that it was.

Fifty-Five

It feels strange having Charlie here on his own – without Anne. I was surprised when he called and said he was coming down alone. I had been assuming, until that call just a few days before he was due to depart, that Anne would come with him.

They've always traveled together. For ten years they've been inseparable.

Something must have happened between Charlie and Anne. But when I asked Evelyn what she thought, she shrugged her shoulders and looked away.

I was sitting on the bed, watching her and admiring the ease and grace of her movements. She walked from the dresser, where the drawer was still half open, to the bathroom, and the way she moved her shoulders reminded me that she had once wanted to be a dancer.

She began to sing a little song I had never heard her sing before. You're in love with the single life / And you're married to the road / And I'm in bed with loneliness / And I'm broken and I'm blue.

Since then, I've been hearing this song wherever she goes. Is she thinking about Anne when she sings the song. Or about herself. Am I missing something here.

If I try to ask her, she smiles and looks away. It seems she's living something that I have no clue about.

I try to imagine where she's coming from, where she's going.

Is she lonely. Is she broken. Is she blue. And if it's true, then what am I to do.

But now here comes Charlie, pounding down the stairs in his Sunday clothes – black turtleneck, blue jeans, thick black socks.

His hair still wet from the shower.

I've never seen his hair this long, and when he combs it straight back and tight to the skull he looks brainier than he actually is if you ask me.

We sit down together at the kitchen table. Evelyn has prepared the perfect omelet – folded once, still steaming hot on the inside, soft but not runny.

She cuts it into three equal portions, like slices of a pie. On the table is a cutting board with neatly arranged slices of tomato sprinkled with flakes of basil.

The coffee's brewing, the muffins are in the oven, rays of the sun fall across the table, setting the jar of grape jelly on fire.

Charlie says he woke up several times during the night, with dreams so vivid he thought he would not be able to get back to sleep. No, sadly, he can't remember any of them.

I don't feel like talking about mine. I grind the pepper mill some more.

Nobody has much to say until Evelyn asks, How did you meet Anne. I'm surprised, because I thought she knew the story.

He's sitting with his back to the window. In the window there's a flutter of birds at the feeder – red poles and song sparrows.

He's thinking to himself, Does she want to hear the short version or the long. He puts his knife and fork down and takes a sip of coffee. He's lost his appetite.

In general, Charlie finds it hard to do two things at the same time, I've noticed. If he's driving, he just drives. If he's making love, he just makes love – never mind the small talk. If he's telling a story, he just tells the story – no breakfast.

He's told it over and over but he never tires of it. It's his favorite story. He gets better at it all the time.

Evelyn has heard bits and pieces of it – from me – but never the whole story. So I can see why she would like to hear it from Charlie. It's his story, after all, not mine.

For twenty years after coming to Canada Charlie and his wife lived in Halifax, Nova Scotia. They had two children. Everyone said they blossomed as parents.

But as the years went by, they argued about more and more things – money, friends, jobs. They even fought over the children. The marriage fell apart and soon, without knowing really what happened, he was on his own.

He started up a bookstore and struggled to make ends meet. One day he met a woman who happened to come into the store, and they began to go out together.

She was from Ottawa and worked for the government, in foreign affairs. She was in Halifax for a conference.

They corresponded and saw each other every week or two, in Halifax or Ottawa. Twice they met in Florida, arriving on separate planes.

He wanted to get married but she didn't. Then she learned

that she was to be posted to an embassy overseas for two years.

Charlie placed his store up for sale. But as the time drew close the girlfriend, let's call her Kat, began to have serious health problems.

They fought and split up. But it was too late – he had already sold the store.

For a few months he was lost and good for nothing. No girlfriend. No store.

Almost in despair he decided to open another bookstore. It was the only thing he knew how to do – the only thing he wanted to do.

For reasons both practical and ethical he decided that it would have to be in another town. His main consideration was to choose a town close enough so that he could visit his daughter, who was still in high school in Halifax.

He took out an old map and studied the possibilities.

The only fair-sized city that was within driving distance seemed a bad bet at best. The only thing he knew about it was that people in Halifax liked to make jokes about it.

Sitting at the table with the map spread out, he felt that what was happening was like a game of 'Pin the Tail on the Donkey.'

He made a preliminary tour of the city, and concluded that there was room for a good used bookstore. He rented a space a block from the public library.

Four days after his arrival, on a warm July day, he sits down for a coffee at an outdoor café. He's been working hard unpacking the many boxes of books he's brought with him, and building the bookcases to fill the nice space he's found.

A woman sits down at the table with him. Does he mind, she asks him. No, he doesn't mind. All the other tables are full.

Her name is Anne. She speaks perfect English, and it's not until later that he finds out that her first language is French.

Everywhere he turns people are speaking French.

He tells Anne that he's opening a bookstore in town. She's thrilled and says whenever she goes traveling she always seeks out the secondhand bookstores and clothing stores.

She asks him where he's from. He talks about his origins, his reasons for coming to Canada, his years in Halifax. She says she has always admired men who have principles and act on them.

He's not sure he was acting on principle when he came to

Canada but decides it's too complicated to explain.

They part company without any promises to meet again.

When he doesn't see her for the next month he thinks that she's probably traveling somewhere. Or perhaps she lives out of town, by the sea, surrounded by friends and family.

She's probably married.

He doesn't expect to see her again. He's just glad to have the memory of that first meeting and the way she looked at him when they shook hands and said good-bye.

Then one day, just after he's opened his store, he sees her walking by and rushes out to say hello. He invites her in.

She's with a friend and says she will come by another time.

She arrives promptly the next morning. They pick up where they left off. They talk as if they've always known each other.

She comes by the store every day, with one excuse after another. Finally he points out to her that they never seem to have time to finish their conversations.

Don't you think we should do something about that, he asks.

Without a moment's hesitation, she invites him to her house for dinner.

One thing leads to another, and he begins to stay the night. It is not love at first sight – they are both too cautious for that – but when it happens it sweeps them off their feet.

For a week he doesn't eat or sleep, and when he walks on Main Street and looks at himself in the windows he seems to be floating an inch or two off the ground.

The strange things is, he says, when I look in the mirror or glance at myself in a window I don't see just myself, I see everyone in the family – Fred, Charlie, Ellen, Father, Mother, even the grandfather I never knew except from photographs.

But above all it's you I see, he says, meaning me. He reaches across the table to where I'm sitting packed into my chair, backed into my chair, racked up like a sack of old potatoes.

The same facial structure, the same body structure, the same way of walking, with the shoulders hunched a little, the head forward. And the thing is, I'm glad I resemble you. Glad.

For the first time in my life it feels good to know that I'm like you. I'm not different from you. I'm not better than you, or worse than you. I'm you.

I don't feel ashamed the way I did before. Or jealous, or

angry, or whatever it was.

What did you have to be jealous of. He's embarrassing me, and if he doesn't stop soon he'll make me angry too.

I was very jealous. It seemed like you were always just about to knock me off my perch.

You were the one we looked up to. Fred was as clever as you – more clever in fact – but he was terribly shy. You had it all. Brains. Ability. A sense of self.

I had no sense of self. I was just numb most of the time.

Evelyn begins talking now and it takes me a moment to realize where this other voice is coming from. You don't get a sense of self until you begin to separate yourself from everyone around you. Jung's concept of separato. That usually doesn't happen until much later.

Yes, Charlie says, you have to fall in love and really love someone and find out that even then she's not yours. When he talks like this, he gets so intense, so determined to find just exactly what it is he is trying to say, that his face turns red.

The idea that you could ever own someone else I find bizarre, Evelyn says.

Now it is my turn to babble. A good marriage is when each partner is guardian of the other's solitude. To quote Rilke.

Charlie's hands are flying left and right. He says something quite different. What he says is that each partner appoints the other guardian of his solitude. Each appoints the other, get it. That's the difference.

He looks at me dead in the eye, as if he'd like to punch me in the nose.

It's a new game, called I Know My Rilke Better Than You Dear Brother Ass. It's my turn to play.

He also says, even more famously, that love is when two solitudes protect and greet and touch each other.

I don't suppose you'd be talking there from bitter experience.

Love is sweet, never bitter. If it's bitter it's not love.

He sits up, puts his hands behind his head, and takes a breath. He flaps his arms like the wings of a bird. End of game.

I'd love to continue this discussion. But I'm beginning to feel the sweet pull of necessity.

He stands up. I think there's a bathroom downstairs, if I remember correctly.

Try the door in the hallway, I instruct him. The one that looks like a closet.

Charlie disappears into the hallway.

Evelyn helps me clean up and put things away.

She takes the dessert into the living room, on a tray together with three small glass bowls and three spoons.

I remain in the kitchen, loading the dishwasher and drying the more fragile cups and glasses.

Fifty-Six

The television in the living room is on but Evelyn is nowhere to be seen. Two grim-faced senators are telling us that things are not as bad as they seem.

I switch channels, and the four-star general on CNN is saying the same thing. I switch channels again.

A panel of four outdoorsmen is talking about hunting black bears in the mountains of eastern Canada, where the Appalachians cut through New Brunswick into Quebec and stretch the length of the Gaspé Peninsula to the sea.

The bears come out when they hear the bird calling, one man says. They have to eat.

It's a tiny little bird, another says. Very pretty.

They almost look like canaries, a third says.

I leave them there, in their glory, and go to the window.

I can see Evelyn at the end of the driveway talking with a neighbor, Ray Little, who is walking a new dog that I haven't seen before.

Ray and his wife, Belinda, have a house full of cats – sometimes as many as four. This is the first time he's had a dog.

I'm watching this man and this woman talking quietly in the driveway, and they seem so far away – strangers.

I don't know Ray very well, even though he teaches at the same college as I do and we have been bumping up against each other almost every day since God knows when – on campus, at dinner parties, at concerts, at late-night parties, downtown at one bar or the other.

I don't know Evelyn at all, even though I've been living with her for years now. I don't know where she came from. I don't know what it was like growing up in a different culture.

All I know is she's here, and I'm married to her.

I stand in the window, helping myself to the dessert she prepared – red seedless grapes in a concoction of sour cream and brown sugar – and the only thing I know is that I don't know anything.

She looks toward the house but she doesn't see me. The phone rings.

It's probably Anne calling for Charlie but Charlie is upstairs so I answer it.

She speaks so slowly at first that I don't recognize her voice. It could be one of my students, worried that she might be bothering me calling Sunday morning.

She says something I can't hear, and I say, I think there's something wrong with your line.

Hold on, I'll try the other phone. I'm still not sure if it is Anne or the anonymous student. It's a young voice but Anne has a young voice.

Can you hear me now.

Is this Anne.

It's snowing here. And cold!

I wasn't sure if it was you or not.

How are you. How is Evelyn.

We couldn't be better. We're really enjoying Charlie's visit.

Is he there.

The phone is in the hallway, on a desk at the bottom of the stairs. I can hear Charlie close the door to his room. He's just coming down the stairs.

She waits for him to come down. I miss that man.

A brown walking shoe, with black stripes, appears on the step just above my head. He misses you too.

As soon as I say it, I realize I don't know what I am talking about.

She makes a noise that sounds like Huh.

I'll let him speak for himself. Here he is.

I hand the phone to Charlie. It's Anne.

He looks at me a moment before saying anything. It is a moment – a look – that seems to last forever. It is a questioning look. What does she want. What does she know. What does she suspect.

It is a look that says, I'm not as strong as you think I am. It is a look that says, I'm not sure anymore about anything. It is a scared look.

It is a look that says, I've tried, I've tried, but all I want to do now is give up.

It is a haunted look. It is a look of someone who knows he's standing on shaky ground.

It is a hurt look – a look of someone who's been wounded and feels he's about to go down.

It is a look that says, Go away from me, leave me, I'm

sinking, I'm going down, but there's nothing you can do.

It is a tired look. It is a look that says, It could be that I've been wrong all along.

It is a look that says, I've got so much still to learn, and I don't know where to begin.

He is still looking at me when he starts talking. I find this so unbearable that without even knowing what I'm doing I'm walking out of the house and shutting the door and refusing to let any of the words that escape his lips enter into my consciousness.

Outside, on the driveway, someone is calling my name. Dave, someone is calling.

I look around. Dave.

I'm halfway down the driveway before I see who it is. Ray has a big smile on his face, as if he's just won the lottery or chosen early retirement.

Evelyn is looking at me too, and she's the one who keeps saying my name. Dave, I've just heard the nicest story.

Everyone is waiting for me – including the dog, who sits at attention and keeps looking up at me and then back down when I look back at her.

She's a border collie – not young – broad in the shoulders, heavy in the belly, but as bright as she ever was. She has eyes that see everything without being aggressive.

The story that Evelyn wants me to hear begins with Ray's next-door neighbor, a man named Godfrey, and the discovery that Godfrey has lung cancer.

His doctor advises him to get as much rest as possible and avoid all strenuous activities. This immediately means that he can no longer walk his dog as he has for so many years.

When Ray and Belinda hear this news, they volunteer to take over the responsibility of walking the dog. As with all dogs of her kind she's not happy if she doesn't have a long walk every day.

Ray has never liked dogs, and this one is no exception. It's not his thing.

Belinda is the one who gets up every morning at six o'clock and walks the dog around the block. But after a few weeks Ray grows attached to the dog.

What happens is that the dog takes a fancy to Ray and Ray feels flattered. Ray assumes the duties of walking the dog.

He starts getting up earlier and earlier, before dawn. The

walks get longer and longer. Sometimes they're gone for two hours. Ray loves it. He's never felt better.

He loses ten pounds the first month. He's in the best shape in years.

His neighbor is happy because he knows the dog is being looked after.

Ray is happy because he's getting a good work-out, he's making friends, he has something to take his mind off the busy day ahead of him, and the dismal state of the world.

Belinda is happy because she has the house to herself in the morning. She can do her yoga exercises and eat her breakfast in peace and quiet.

She can call her boy friend without worrying that Ray is listening on the phone upstairs.

The dog is happy because she's on the go, and Ray lets her greet everybody and everything along the way.

Sometimes, in the park, he lets her off the leash.

Everyone benefits.

It's Evelyn who's telling the story, while Ray fills in details where Evelyn comes up short.

When they're finished, I ask, What's her name.

Jackie, Ray says.

Jackie thinks that Ray is talking to her, and she scoots closer to his foot, keeping her gaze down, continuing to sit at attention.

I think you've got a friend, Ray.

Friends come and go but true love is hard to find.

I had a dog once, a long time ago. Her name was Laska. One day I thought I would have a little fun and I dug up a bone she had buried and replaced it with a tennis ball.

When she found out what I had done, I don't think she ever forgave me. She would not look me in the eye the way she had before. A few months later she jumped the fence in the backyard, and we never saw her again.

I don't know if I feel more sorry for you or for the dog.

Oh, feel sorry for the dog. I don't think it was easy for her, whatever it was she had taken it upon herself to prove to me and to the world.

The front door opens and Charlie shouts out something from the top of the steps. Ray takes one look and says, We have to be running along. What do you say, Jackie.

Jackie is on her feet, barking in agreement. The two of them go charging off around the corner at the end of the block, Jackie in the lead.

Ray is the image of someone who has found 'the way' and it is not an image that appeals to me. But why not. Perhaps my idea of freedom has to be broadened.

Ray Little is a little like the brother I never had, and the more I know him the more I love him. Even though his ways and his ideas are different from mine we are alike in so many respects.

Charlie worries that the argument they had the day before has got him, Ray, all worked up. I would like to tell Charlie that Ray is not like that.

In his house, when he speaks, his word is final. It's an article of faith, that the wife is obedient. Belinda accepts that.

It's a teaching of the church they belong to.

I have no idea why they fall for it.

Ray is too bright to fall for it.

Nevertheless, he does fall for it.

As I said, all I know is that I know nothing.

But still I love him.

PART THREE

Fifty-Seven

The garden is behind the house, in an open area just out of the shadow of the spruce trees farther back. Already a few plants are up – chives, mint, marjoram, Egyptian onions.

The rain has softened the soil in the rest of the garden but it needs working. It needs peat moss and compost if it's going to be productive. David plans to get at it as soon as I leave.

He doesn't seem to be in the best of health. He's fat. He's diabetic. I've suggested he hire someone to turn the soil.

Tulips and daffodils are in bloom along the south side of the house. The rhubarb is high, with large loping leaves like the ears of elephants obscuring the vent from the dryer in the basement.

Things are advanced here, compared to where I live. It will be another week or two before we see tulips forming.

The clouds are breaking up, revealing patches of blue. We move past the garden, toward the back of the property.

Under the big, low-lying branches of the spruce trees grass gives way to dry, bare ground, sprinkled with needles, bits of bark, and small twisted branches knocked down by one storm or another.

Evelyn is watching in the kitchen window to see where we are going, her face pressed against the glass.

When I stop and look in her direction, she holds up the bread knife in her hand and waves it back and forth, as if to say, Everything's under control in here, take your time, talk it over, he's your brother, who knows when you'll see him again.

She's preparing sandwiches for my trip. When she says 'sandwiches' she means a variety of healthy things in addition to the usual ham on rye – including carrot sticks, celery sticks, raisins, walnuts, apples, and oranges.

I'm wearing my traveling clothes – soft gray turtleneck, well-worn blue jeans, jogging shoes. I'm leaving this afternoon, doubling back the way I came, with the aim of reaching Lafayette by early evening.

I want to walk the streets of my home town again. I want to breathe the air. I want to look up into the sky and see the same shapes and the same colors I saw forty years ago – fifty years ago.

I want to stop at the cemetery where my father and my mother are buried. I want to pay my respects.

Tuesday I've got a plane to catch out of O'Hare. When David asks me if I plan to be on that plane all I can say is, I don't know.

Last night, when we almost came to blows, I was sure I would not be on the plane. Now I don't know.

Make up your mind, stop your dithering, don't be an asshole, I tell myself.

I don't wait for him to ask but begin talking about Anne, about the phone call that I have just come away from and that has left me shaken.

At first I didn't know what she was trying to tell me. She kept talking about Sally and how she and Sally got together yesterday to look at the I Ching. Anne's always been fascinated with the I Ching. Whenever she has a question that's bothering her, she goes to the I Ching.

Obviously the question that's bothering her these days is me because the question she asked was something like, What am I supposed to think about my husband, when he's putting so much distance between himself and me.

It was no great surprise when the hexagram she was presented with was called The Wanderer. It has a bottom trigram that represents the mountain, which means everything that stands still. Above it fire flames up and does not stay in the same place.

The two trigrams do not stay together. They cannot. Strange lands and separation are the wanderer's lot.

I asked her if that's the way she saw me now, as a wanderer, and she said yes. Then what should I be doing to make things come out right. She had the book there with her on her lap and she read out the judgment.

The wanderer has success through staying small. He must be cautious. His home is the road, so he should not put on airs and puff himself up. He associates only with good people, and when he senses danger he does not tarry, but moves on.

Pretty good advice, I'd say.

I'm looking up into the branches of one of the spruce trees, where a squirrel is making high-pitched, angry noises. It's a powerful image, fire on the mountain. The mountain stays still, and the fire flames up and leaps from place to place. It never stays in any one place for very long.

David is looking at me, with his round, watery eyes. The effort of listening, suppressing the urge to talk, to guide my train of thought, causes him visible pain.

I've always lived like that. I've never tried to hide it from Anne.

What else did she say.

The hexagram she was working with, which is number fifty-six by the way, if you want to look it up, was not stable, but opened up into a new hexagram and a new reading and a new outlook.

What makes a hexagram unstable.

It's when one of the lines is unstable. In this case it was line three.

What makes a line unstable.

It unstable when it's so highly charged with energy, either positive or negative, that it cannot stay the same. When a line is charged like this, it has special meaning.

So in this case it was line three that had special meaning.

It warned of danger. It said that if the wanderer meddles in affairs and controversies that do not concern him, he risks losing his resting place. He becomes a stranger in a strange land, with no friends and no one who will take him in. But if he's aware of the danger and stops his meddling, he'll be all right.

The new hexagram, number thirty-five, which is called Progress, holds out hope that the wanderer can continue on his journey. Fire, that is the sun, rises over the earth.

The man who has gone down into darkness and taken on the burden of death and decay has a sense that everything is possible for him now. There are no clear answers, but it no longer seems important to have clear answers.

What does Anne think.

What does Anne think about what.

Your wanderlust, for want of a better word.

In a word, she approves. Go for it, she says. She's always had the ability to see what's bothering me and to find a way to get out in front of the problem.

For example, when we were first getting to know each other, I didn't have the money to get my store up and running, and I thought this meant that we couldn't get married. Anne made an appointment at her bank, borrowed the money, said pay me back when you can. It was like breaking open a log jam, everything could flow again.

She sees that I'm restless and I've got to be on the move. I don't know what it is, I don't know what's behind it, I don't know where it's taking me. Anne says it doesn't matter, the important thing is not to deny it.

The only hitch is, she wants to come with me. Don't shut me out, she says. She's talked with Mary and they've agreed that Mary could run the bookstore just fine all on her own. As for the art gallery Anne's tired of that and wants to shut it down.

The squirrel climbs higher in the tree, all the while continuing to lecture us, so we move away, across the yard, to the northern edge of the property, where there is a row of lilac bushes, growing tall now, in definite need of trimming.

I wonder how many years it's been since he last cut them back. Where has he been all those years. What has he been doing. What has he been thinking.

We come around the garage to the front of the house, closing the circle. The rental car is parked at the top of the driveway.

Inside the car several of my shirts hang from the hook behind the driver's seat.

I do not remember bringing them down.

Fifty-Eight

There are still puddles of water on the asphalt from yesterday's rain though the sun is beating down.

I remove the medal from around my neck and hold it up for David to see, the dark brown string to which it is tied looped over my thumb, the thumb jigging the string, rocking the medal in its cradle of air.

In answer to his question I say, Aunt Betty wanted me to have it.

He might have wanted to have it if she had asked him. The thought flashes through my mind. I didn't know you were still talking to Aunt Betty, he says.

Just in the last couple of years. I wrote to her and she wrote back.

He takes the medal into the palm of his hand. I let go of the string, and it falls down in such a way that two fingers, the index finger and the middle finger, are both inside the loop.

He turns it over to look at the words on the back. They are hard to read, as they are thin and crammed together in a dark brown background.

He removes his glasses and holds the medal close to his eyes. He tilts it away from direct sunlight.

There is mention of two different emergencies, a 'limited emergency' proclaimed on September 8, 1939, and an 'unlimited emergency' proclaimed on May 27, 1941. But there's no mention of Pearl Harbor or the declaration of war that followed Pearl Harbor.

If I'm reading this right, he says, he was still alive when the medal was issued.

I've got my dates down pat. Pearl Harbor was December, 1941. I was born February, 1942. Uncle Charlie wasn't killed until April, 1942.

Do you know how he was killed.

His ship was sunk during the battle for Midway Island.

Something bubbles up in the back of his brain and bursts out like moths banging against a lampshade. You were named after a dead man. That explains everything.

But I'm non-plussed. That's why aunt Betty thought I should

have the medal.

He studies the woman on the front side – the bare breasts, the long almost transparent skirt, the sword in one hand, raised above her head, the shield in the other, wearing a helmet with a crest that curves forward and something that trails behind at the neck.

She stands on what looks like the branch of a tree. Her face is in profile – the expression stern, determined.

The words AMERICAN DEFENSE form an arc above her head. That looks to me like one liberated woman, he says.

I loop the medal over my head again but instead of tucking it inside I let it hang on the outside of the gray turtleneck. I wore it for several years but when Aunt Betty died I put it away. It meant nothing to me. I hadn't thought of America as my country for a long time.

But when I met Anne and told her my story, she said that in her eyes I was quintessentially American and I always would be American. I couldn't figure out why she should be proud that I was American when I wasn't.

She liked to wear the medal because she said it was like a part of me that she could take with her wherever she went.

While I'm talking David is looking around for a place to sit down. The front steps are dry – hard but dry. He rubs one knee then the other, down to the shinbone, to bring back the circulation.

I ask him if he's all right. He assures me that he is. When he stands too long in one place without moving his legs go numb.

I sit down next to him and clear my throat. Anyway, I don't think she's worn it once in the last year. She's just as upset as I am with what's going on. She put it away in a drawer and forgot about it.

But the other day in Chicago when I was unpacking my things there it was, in a little blue box inside a shoe, with a note from Anne, telling me she wants me to wear the medal as charm to protect me from the ghosts I'll inevitably encounter on my trip.

I thought, how silly, until I found myself in some pretty bizarre situations, running into people I thought I knew but discovered I didn't know and people I thought I didn't know but who seemed to know me better than I knew myself.

My mention of the word ghosts gets him going – not that he believes in ghosts. I never did tell you what happened between

Bernie Davis and myself, did I.

No, I don't believe you did.

I know you were crazy about her, and you just about went mad when she didn't want to have anything to do with you.

She spurned you, to use an old-fashioned word. Rhymes with sperm. I'm sure there must be some connection there.

Very funny. Just tell me what happened.

Even when you went away to college you couldn't stop thinking about her. You were sure she'd come around if only she could see how true your love was.

You thought that by staying faithful even after she had told you to get lost you'd show her what real love was made of and the intensity of this love would knock her over.

But love doesn't work that way. You can't make someone love you. In the meantime she was dating other boys, including Mike, who you had always thought of as your best friend in high school.

They were doing more than dating because they had a child together. I bet he never told you that.

When he found out she was pregnant he wanted her to have an abortion. She refused and she gave birth but the child was stillborn.

She blamed herself – she said she hadn't done enough to protect the child from Mike's negative energy. She talked that way. She wouldn't say Mike was angry or hateful or a pigheaded fucking bastard, she'd say he had 'negative energy.'

She'd always find the word that was one step removed from reality, as if she needed that comfort zone to deal with it. For a while after the birth she was very depressed and even made a half-assed attempt at suicide.

I met her at the same clinic where Ellen our sister was going, and we went out together a few times.

I'm sitting next to him on the step, my head turned just slightly his way, my eyes closed, listening very hard. He would like me to look at him but I won't.

We'd go to a movie then sit in the car and talk. Or we'd just drive somewhere and get out and walk. We kissed a few times and I thought she might like me better than you.

I told her how much you still loved her and she got angry

because she thought I was trying to be your advocate. Did he tell you to ask me out, she wanted to know. No, it was my own idea, I assured her.

She didn't believe me. She'd already made up her mind about men. Men were not to be trusted. They always walked out.

Later on she did get married and have children but the marriage didn't last long. The husband met someone else and left her, just like she knew he would.

She was alone, with three young children to look after. She sold real estate and found she had a real talent. She had a few very good years, professionally and personally, but it didn't last long though.

The boys eventually wanted to get to know their father. She couldn't stand to hear them say anything good about the man who had deserted her. The boys went away to school, or found jobs, or drifted away. One of them lived with his father for a while.

She put all her energies into her career, and even started up her own business. She began drinking a lot. The more successful she was, the more she drank.

When he stops to catch his breath, I think he's said all he's going to say. Does she still live around here, I ask.

She's in Lafayette. Last thing I heard she was seeing Mike again. I bet he didn't tell you that.

As a matter of fact, he told me he didn't know where she was living and he hadn't seen her in years.

Mike will tell you what he thinks you want to hear. It might be true, it might not be true. With Mike you never know.

I remove my glasses and lay them on the step next to me, on the side of me away from David. I don't know what to think.

A few houses away we can hear the sound of a lawn mower.

The sun has dried up all the puddles of water in the driveway.

I am sitting next to him, with my eyes closed, my hands folded between my legs, rocking slowly back and forth.

I enjoy the play of sunlight on my face.

Fifty-Nine

She told me that she was engaged to another, but she would not tell me his name. I stood across the street from her house in the rain and watched for her.

She told me to go home. She wanted to be left alone. I made her nervous.

I said I wanted to die.

It's not clear how I came to be obsessed with this particular girl, instead of some other girl.

It could just as easily have been Lana Jo Lane or Susan Fuqua or Judy Swick or Peggy Korschott or Jane Ellsberry or Joy Lynn Gentry or any one of the other girls in my class or in the class below me who had caught my eye.

She was the sister of my best friend at the time. I had a chance to see her at home, when her guard was down, when she was just being herself without pretense.

At home she was playful and took delight in teasing me because I was very shy. I'd blush when she came into the room. I didn't know that just because I felt I might die if she did not love me it didn't mean that she ever would.

So it's not the same as in Joyce's story 'The Dead' where the woman is remembering when she was young and a boy loved her so much he wanted to die. In this case it is about a boy who loved a girl so much that he wanted to die, but she did not love him.

She turned against him when she realized that he had gone a little crazy. Nothing he could ever say or do would change her mind or her heart. He has never felt a love like this again, so strong that he wants to die.

Or if he has felt it, he tells himself that it's a shadow of this first intensity. He does not love with the same intensity. This is the source of his melancholy. This is the ghost that haunts him.

What happens when a ghost haunts us. Some force enters into our body and we feel tired and heavy, depressed. We cannot do anything with ease.

When the ghost leaves we feel light again. We might even have a moment of euphoria. Then we settle down, we are normal, but anxious because we never know when it will return again.

It's a mistake to think that we have no control over when the ghost enters and when it leaves. It is possible to take measures.

The medal that I wear around my neck works if I imagine it to be a shield big enough to hold up in front of my body and block the energy that wants to take over.

This hungry energy is a negative energy that at times seems to have a mind and personality of its own.

A few months ago I was invited to a native ceremony in one of the eastern provinces in Canada where I live, called 'The Feast of the Ancestors.'

In the native tradition, the way it was explained to me, there is an initial ceremony held four days after someone dies, then it's necessary to wait for one year in order to give the spirit of the deceased time to make its way to the other world.

It's important not to call the spirit back too soon. During the first year the deceased has many ghosts, demons, and enemies to encounter.

There is no re-birth in the sense of coming back to this world, but there is re-birth in the sense that after one year the deceased is born again into the spirit world and is at peace.

Once he or she is born again in the spirit world it's all right to call them back and ask their help.

After a year the time is right for the living to gather again and hold a feast in honor of the dead. Food is prepared over a sacred fire and the first portion of each food is offered to the ancestors.

You don't make a direct request to the dead to return. You honor them with an offering of food, and they come back of their own accord.

You do not go in search of them. You welcome them, and they find you.

You give up something, in this case a portion of food, and in so doing you open up a space into which the ancestors can enter and come close.

The central idea is the idea of sacrifice. By giving up something of your own you honor the dead and give them their freedom.

In this way the dead are no longer ghosts that haunt you but ancestors that watch over you. When you stop wanting to possess them they stop possessing you.

They can come and go as they like but they are never too

close and they never want to take over your life.

Sixty

The entrance is poorly indicated and the first time, as you drive along, because you are caught in heavy traffic, you miss it.

Two white posts on either side of the one-lane road mark the spot. You see it now in your mirror as you drive on.

You turn around in the parking lot of a strip mall. You drive even more slowly. You ignore the honking of the cars behind you. You ease your way between the posts.

The road is uneven, with clumps of earth rising up through the broken pavement.

To the left as you enter there is a hill, maybe twenty, twenty-five feet high, topped by a grandiose red marble monument and a mausoleum sheltering the bones of the one of the city's illustrious families.

You see the main office straight ahead and a shed that houses various pieces of equipment needed to maintain the grounds.

You drive past the open door of the shed. You find the parking lot. You are the only car in sight other than the car of the workman inside the shed.

You approach the shed. It's dark inside. There's music playing – Johnny Cash.

Four strong winds.

The workman is on his back on the floor, under a tractor, on a mat. You wave. He waves back.

You have no trouble finding the gravesite, though it's been fifteen years since you last visited.

There's no headstone, but two plaques, one for your mother, one for your father.

You make rubbings from the two plaques using paper and pencil.

Each plaque has a simple design on it – in addition to name, birth date and death date.

Mother's design shows a series of almost prehistoric wheels in an arc that rises from left to right.

Father's design has one of these same primitive wheels, upper right. Lower down, to the left, a couple of whirligigs with five petals each, like the flowers of the phlox plant.

You sit for a long time on a stone bench facing the gravesite.

There's a dirt road, big enough for one car, between the bench and the gravesite.

A single tree on the other side of the road.

It's a mature tree – sturdy, comfortable in its surroundings.

The leaves on the tree are green and fully formed.

Most of the gravesites in this section of the cemetery have headstones. Some of these have been heaved up and tilted sideways after years of freezing and thawing.

You listen for the voice of your mother and for the voice of your father.

You hear blue jays in the trees along one side of the cemetery.

You hear the wind rustling the leaves in the solitary tree across the road from where you are sitting.

You hear cars going by on the busy street just to the east of the cemetery.

None of the cars turn in here.

You are alone.

You are the only one who has come.

Today the dead get a day off – except for your dead.

You hear a voice speaking. It could be your own voice. It could be another's.

You cross the dirt road. You walk toward the gravesite.

You see that though your mother's plaque and your father's plaque are flat in the ground the ground has lifted and split and there is a crack where their spirits can get out – if they haven't already.

You do not come as often as you did in the old days but when you do you bring something – an offering, perhaps the branch of a tree you stumbled across on the way, or a handful of wildflowers you picked by the edge of a field.

You speak to her, but softer now.

You speak to him.

You stay awhile, listening to the sounds – the blue jays calling back and forth, the squirrels chattering, the cars on the road that winds invisibly through the hills.

You hear a rustling in the woods, and a deer steps into the clearing.

You remember the way he held his hands, fingers interlaced,

when he lifted you up to the limb of the tree.
    You remember the way he said to you, Go now, just climb.

Acknowledgements

The Breach House Gang, nine Moncton-area writers, have supported me in many ways during the writing of this novel. I also want to thank Jean Humphreys for her close reading of the manuscript and for her many helpful comments. The book would not have been possible without the presence of my wife, Elaine.

About the Author

Edward Lemond was born in Lafayette, Indiana and came to Canada in 1969. He lived in Halifax, Nova Scotia for 24 years before moving to his present home, in Moncton, New Brunswick. For twenty-one years he owned and operated the Attic Owl Bookshop, a secondhand and antiquarian bookstore. He is one of the founders of the Northrop Frye Literary Festival, held annually in Moncton, Frye's home town.

His novel, *The Baptism of Alden Oaks*, won first prize in the 1986 Writers' Federation of Nova Scotia Competition. He has published poems and stories in various Canadian literary journals. He has published a poetry collection, *Overheard*, a short story collection, *This Close To Me*, and a novella, *Birds of Appetite*, which was short-listed for the 2010 Ken Klonsky Novella Contest.

www.ingramcontent.com/pod-product-compliance
Lightning Source LLC
Chambersburg PA
CBHW050508260626
47157CB00004B/1235